LIEUTENANT COLONEL JOHN CLARK PRATT was born in Vermont in 1932. He received his B.A. from the University of California at Berkeley, his M.A. from Columbia University, and his Ph.D. from Princeton University, and after serving in Southeast Asia, joined the faculty of the United States Air Force Academy as a professor of English. John Clark Pratt is the author of *VIETNAM VOICES*. He is presently a professor of English at Colorado State University.

Avon Books are available at special quantity discounts for bulk purchases for sales promotions, premiums, fund raising or educational use. Special books, or book excerpts, can also be created to fit specific needs.

For details write or telephone the office of the Director of Special Markets, Avon Books, Dept. FP, 1790 Broadway, New York, New York 10019, 212-399-1357. *IN CANADA:* Director of Special Sales, Avon Books of Canada, Suite 210, 2061 McCowan Rd., Scarborough, Ontario M1S 3Y6, 416-293-9404.

THE LAOTIAN FRAGMENTS

John Clark Pratt

AVON
PUBLISHERS OF BARD, CAMELOT, DISCUS AND FLARE BOOKS

AVON BOOKS
A division of
The Hearst Corporation
1790 Broadway
New York, New York 10019

Copyright © 1974 by John C. Pratt
Published by arrangement with the author
Library of Congress Catalog Card Number: 84-91206
ISBN: 0-380-69841-2

All rights reserved, which includes the right to
reproduce this book or portions thereof in any form
whatsoever except as provided by the U. S. Copyright Law.
For information address Avon Books.

First Avon Printing, January, 1985

AVON TRADEMARK REG. U. S. PAT. OFF. AND IN
OTHER COUNTRIES, MARCA REGISTRADA, HECHO EN
U. S. A.

Printed in the U. S. A.

WFH 10 9 8 7 6 5 4 3 2 1

For the Ravens, and for Dory——who have given me so much more than just the opportunity to write this book.

*There are two aspects to the life of every man:
the personal life . . . and the elemental life of the swarm,
in which a man must inevitably follow
the laws laid down for him.*

TOLSTOI

EDITOR'S PREFACE

It was in 1962, I think, that I remember first noticing William Blake, then a captain in the United States Air Force. He was one of twenty-three students in my graduate seminar, Politics 553, "European Renaissance Diplomacy." I recall that he was quite an intense student, did competent work on specific assignments, and was absent from class only during the two-week period which was later called the Cuban Missile Crisis. He had been ordered to "pull alert," that is, to stand by in the cockpit of a military fighter aircraft for a possible air defense mission. He assured me that he would take his textbooks with him and do the assigned reading.

Otherwise I do not recall his being any different from my other students, except in what I think was an obsession with detail and with the personalities of political history. He seemed less interested in the general institutions, the overall interplay of forces which affect the representative actions of governments and nations. Facts themselves, as every political scientist knows, are properly the province of the historian; it is how events relate to each other that should concern the student and practitioner of politics.

Captain Blake received the Master of Arts degree in June 1964, and because I neither had him in class again nor sat on his examining committee, I was understandably quite surprised to receive the letter from him which constitutes document 136 of this collection. I have not heard from him since.

As for the documents themselves, I have called them *The Laotian Fragments* in what amounts almost to surrender. If I were a writer of fiction, I might have taken the clue from one of the entries, calling this book *The Muffled Drum, The Bamboo Drum, The Darkling Plain,* or some such literary title. I have not, for this group of notes, memos, letters, tape-recording transcripts, articles, book excerpts, poems, and official United States Government studies stands as it is—a collection of comments on one of the most significant conflicts of our time.

In editing the documents, I have incurred many debts, some of which are acknowledged by appropriate notes. Without specific assistance in identifying unfamiliar—to an academician like me—terminology, abbreviations, and place names, I would have foundered more than I actually did. I offer thanks to those men, military and civilian alike, without whose advice and counsel I could never have established chronology or properly classified these papers. Even though they have asked not to be identified by name, they know who they are—and I am deeply grateful.

To Major Blake, I extend my gratitude and my apologies. I did not know, almost ten years ago, precisely what kind of a student of politics he would eventually become.

York Harding, Ph.D.
Professor of Political Science

A NOTE ON THE TEXT

As in any editorial task, my job has been to make these documents available in as accurate a form as possible. Consequently, I have conformed to standard practices, emending as little as possible and commenting only when absolutely necessary for the sake of clarity. Editorial additions within the text are enclosed with brackets, and the documents themselves are first described, then presented precisely as they were written, arranged in divisions corresponding to the calendar months in which they were composed, copied, or read by Major Blake. Some messages and letters have been placed by reference to internal events, as have some tape-recording transcripts. Occasionally, as with the Senate *Hearings,* I have taken the liberty of exercising my option as editor, for a document so clearly pertinent for the reader's background information should not be relegated to the end of a work, as this publication in actuality was for Major Blake.

Although certain readers of this manuscript have seen the need for a glossary of terms and military acronyms, I believe that the comprehensive appendix of any edition of *The Pentagon Papers* should provide sufficient identifications, if needed.

That the *Fragments* do not cohere is obvious, and even though tempted, I have not yielded to the desire to fill in gaps or excise irrelevant material. This collection represents a part, and only a part, of what probably happened.

DECEMBER

1

Manuscript journal of William Blake, Major, United States Air Force, hereafter referred to as Blake, *Journal*. It is written in a standard 8½×11" spiral notebook, blue cover, with a white outline of a bulldog and the superimposition of a block letter "Y." The inside front cover is dated in inked script "1954," which has been lined through, with "Southeast Asia—War" added below. The first thirty-four pages contain miscellaneous notes from an undergraduate course apparently entitled Philosophy 375, "Asian Thought." The margins are covered with penciled and inked circles, stars, hatched lines, and other marks. Mixed in with the class notes are girls' names, telephone numbers, addresses, and a list of military fighter aircraft such as F-100, F-94, and F-84. The latter aircraft is always followed by a question mark, and the name "Mary" is often underlined and once surrounded by the words "Yes," written three or four times in what resembles Gothic script. This section ends halfway through page 34 with an entry in heavy pencil, underlined and apparently retraced many times (the first letter of the first word has worn through to the leaf ahead). Approximately two inches in height, spanning five or six lines, and followed by eleven exclamation points, this two-word entry reads, "FUCK IT!!!!!!!!!!!!" The pertinent portion of the *Journal* begins on page 34.

26 Dec.: Somewhere (hah) in northern Thailand— No one told me about Christmas here. As a matter of fact, no one really told me anything. Six months of FACing in RVN [flying as a Forward Air Controller in O-1 and O-2 observation planes in the Republic of Vietnam], where there was a war, a real war, and now this. Like World War I all over again. Here, the fighter jocks get up, eat good food at a good club, brief, fly, go drop bombs, get shot at a little, land, debrief, change clothes, get drunk, go downtown, find an LBFM [Little Brown Fucking Machine], come home (hah!!!), sleep, and then do it all over again the next day. It's like meeting the Boche—except there's no front. It's all a no-man's-land.

Last night was too much (I'm writing this at 3:00 PM in a hell of a nice hotel, even if you can't drink the water and the shower sprays all over the bathroom)—I suppose the Thais deserve *some* credit, but nobody's told them the difference between Christmas and New Year's. *Remember:* the Golden Palace LBFMs in their spangled padded bras saying "Melly Clistmas, GI," and the horns, rattles, noisemakers, paper hats, and a pseudo rock band trying to play Christmas Carols. And at midnight, the lights blinking and the band playing "Auld Lang Syne." And the balloons—Jesus, the balloons—hundreds of them up on the ceiling with strings hanging down until someone found out they were filled with hydrogen and started setting them off with cigarettes. Sounded like Da Nang Airbase during a rocket attack. Someone screamed "incoming" and somebody else yelled "Dead Bug," and suddenly everyone was on the deck, tables and chairs flying everywhere. All the customers were American, and when the balloons were gone, the Thai band tried to get something going, but everyone just sort of sat there—quietly—and I saw one big blond guy crying—and then we all left and went back to our rooms. It was starting to get light when I got to sleep. And to all a good night (hah)—humbug.

This is, I suppose, as good a place as any to begin. Tomorrow Vientiane and whatever the hell is up there. [Written in margin are the numbers "404-404-404."] They say the flying will be similar to what I've been doing—FACing fighters with a few Lao T-28s as well—but that I may be living anywhere. No uniforms. Feels funny going off to "war" in a sports shirt. Not that I'll miss RVN—not after seeing Thailand. *Remember:* first impressions six months ago of Vietnam: thunderstorms over the coast—not being able to tell sea from shore (it's all blue-green)—and having a Lt. Col. going back for a second tour point out the landmarks (he sat next to me for eighteen hours—asked once what book I was reading—told him it was a novel about World War II (hah! *Catch-22*). "That was a real war," he said, "not like this one." Then our airplane coming over the shoreline, like Florida with wide breakers on shallow reefs—houses not in clusters but in strings along the few roads. Tin-roofed squalor of shanties, glistening. Pockmarks of bomb craters, on crossroads, in clearings, along canals, in brown rice paddies—and then the B-52 droppings, straight lines of round holes in the dark green trees for what looked like miles.

Don't forget: (Maybe I should make a tape to my wife—nuts—she doesn't care and I can't tell her what I'm going to do anyway—time for another bloody Mary). [After "Mary," a line is drawn across the page.]

Don't forget: difference between Vietnam and Thailand (and the people back in the world don't have the slightest idea what's really going on. I don't either. Maybe I'll find out)—*Vietnam:* initial briefing in what looked like a Toonerville railroad station (the Tan Son Nhut Airport)—Army MP with loudspeaker (no one could understand anything he said)—some kind of instructions given by the numbers to all the people standing around—everyone looking at everyone else to see who would make the first move—dark-ribbed wooden baggage platforms and old bus station seats which nobody used (everybody stands). A few Vietnamese clustered quietly, watching the Americans who were pretending not to watch them (there were, I think, over 200 on our Pan Am 707, and the stewardess—obviously second-string—saying perfunctorily, "Hope you enjoyed your trip on Pan Am—see you in a year"). And the *heat.* Ceiling fans in the terminal straight out of a grade B Bogart movie. And the noise—airplanes, Honda traffic like a constant Indy 500, the go-go music at the Officers' Club (God, will I ever forget the perpetual boom-boom), the Army choppers blatting overhead all day and night, sirens, and in the background (like in another world), the crunch and thump of artillery and bombs, like thunder on the horizon (but far off—far off that first day). Don't forget the first rocket attack later at Da Nang—the really lovely sparkling arch of the 122mm—and through it all, George riding his bicycle from bunker to bunker looking for the flight surgeon because he thought he had the clap—and the sharp cracks as the rockets hit—God they're ugly—I wonder if the bad guys use them in Laos—). *Just don't forget!* [This last sentence is underlined twice.]

But *here:* it's a party, except when you're getting shot at. No wonder it's the best kept secret of the war. Ran into an old buddy from pilot training last night (in SEA [Southeast Asia] you see everybody you've ever known). Hank's in F-4s now—said "Welcome to wonderland, babes." Claims he'll write the real story some day and call it "Phallus in Wonderland" *(Idea:* possible sex story for pulp circles, re the massage parlor racket, sex in Southeast Asia, etc.). Hank says flying in northern Laos is a piece of cake, except on the eastern end of Route 7 and around Sam Neua. The Trail in southern Laos, though—something else again. It must be as bad as downtown [Hanoi]. Hank asked me what I was doing here and I said I couldn't tell him—smiled and said "Shit, another spook job, eh. The woods are full of them." Seemed cold afterward. The BOQs here are OK, but a lot of the officers live in town. New hotels, all built during the last three years—white concrete—like Holiday Inns, but with teak furniture—and hot and cold running chambermaids. Thailand is so much nicer than Vietnam (then again, we haven't been here as long)—there's a different air—even though it still smells as bad. The Thais seem to be building, while the Vietnamese just let things rot. Remember all the construction in Bangkok and here: hotels, stores, gas stations—but mainly hotels—and none of those goddamn Viet minicabs, no motor scooters without mufflers. The Thais still seem to like us (I wonder how the Lao will be). All smiles, not the sullen hatred and distance of the Vietnamese. The Thais seem to have an innocence about them that the Vietnamese lack (maybe it's the French influence in Vietnam). I used to think all Orientals were alike—still can't really tell them apart either—interesting study in contrasts—guess it depends on which side of the neocanthal [sic] fold you're looking from—or does it?). Remember Christmas Eve at the Officers' Club—all the guys in their unbelievable blue, yellow, and green party suits—everybody waiting for the stripper before going downtown because she was a Caucasian—turned out to be an English act, a girl with a Venus bod and a real Soho face—took off all her clothes—shaved twat—and Dang, the head barmaid, they call her Super-Thai (good phrase), saying "No pussy. She no hab pussy," and all the little Thai waitresses giggling and pointing, and Dang saying "Me hab number one pussy, you bet your sweet ass." Unbelievable—the whole damn thing.

More latter. Maybe this time I can keep some kind of a journal going—after how many false starts, and I don't know quite what for. Sure as hell can't write about this to my wife, poor wife. (Remember—here you can get real tomato juice, not the cadaverous (sp?) reconstituted stuff of Vietnam.)

2

Teletype message addressed to Horowitz: Vientiane, Laos, from Bryan: Washington, D.C., dated 24 December. This message, on yellow standard teleprinter paper, was clipped to page 37 of Major Blake's journal.

SUBJECT: New Raven

Your new boy is Blake, William, FR$@#&%42375 [sic]. Grade: Major. Good record. Tiger in RVN. No derog. info. Slightly more than usual problems with wife (she's playing around at home)—so watch that he doesn't go native with the others. Ivy League seems not to have hurt him too much. Word here is that he's supposed to whip the Ravens into shape, make them more military and more responsive to Bangkok, USAF, and the attache. See if you can't soothe some feelings—say, schedule another inspection trip for somebody. Don't fprget [sic]. It's mainly their money. Also, our friend from Arkansas is rasing [sic] his annual stink about opium in Air America birds. Take care of this problem, now. Don't let Vang Pao get dejected again—how's the White Horse supply? Last item: Senate hearings may get to DOD [Department of Defense] badly, but I don't think they're going to hurt us much. Barnes was good. Will advise. PS: Where's Martha's four seasons bracelet? Her birthday's next month. Regards, WJB.

3

Hearings before the Subcommittee on United States Security Agreements and Commitments Abroad of the Committee on Foreign Relations, United States Senate, Ninety-first Congress, First Session, Part 2, October 20, 21, 22, and 28 (U.S. Government Printing Office, Washington). Excerpts from this 606-page report represent passages underlined in or marked in the margin of Major Blake's copy. The report has been declassified and officially released in a limited edition. Major Blake's copy is stamped "Office of the U.S. Air Attache, Vientiane, Laos." The editor has transcribed marginal notes made in Major Blake's handwriting. This publication is hereafter referred to as Senate *Hearings*. This selection is headed "Testimony of [the] . . . U.S. Air Attache, Vientiane, Laos" and begins on page 457.

PROJECT 404

Project 404 was approved by DOD in 1966 to provide augmentees and logistic support for the Army and Air Attaches to Laos. Prior to 1966, augmentation was provided on a TDY [Temporary Duty] basis from units in Southeast Asia and the United States. A total of 117 military and five civilian personnel were approved in the initial 404 package. There are currently 106 personnel in the project. Project 404 personnel are assigned administratively to Deputy Chief, JUSMAG [Joint United States Military Assistance Group], Thailand. Duty stations are in Laos under the operational control of the Army and Air Attaches. U.S. Air Force Project 404 personnel (42) fill operational, intelligence, and administrative support functions on the Air Attache staff in support of the total air effort in Laos.

Senator SYMINGTON: If I may interrupt in context, would you define what is operation 404?

Air ATTACHE: Yes, sir. It provides augmentee personnel specifically for the Air and the Army Attache officers in Laos, and also logistical support for the operations within Laos.

Senator SYMINGTON: Who heads it?

Air ATTACHE: Who heads it?

Senator SYMINGTON: Yes.

Air ATTACHE: It was approved by the JCS [Joint Chiefs of Staff] in early 1966 and funded by CINCPAC [Commander in Chief, Pacific], and the Deputy Chief JUSMAG, Thailand, is responsive directly to CINCPAC, who administers the project. [Marginal comment: "Yes, but who runs the goddamn thing? Why didn't he answer the question?"]

Senator SYMINGTON: What is the project?

Air ATTACHE: The project is to provide people and support to the operation in Laos under the Army and Air Attaches.

Senator SYMINGTON: To do what?

Air ATTACHE: To provide in the case of the Air Attache, for instance, the operational aspects of our functions.

Senator SYMINGTON: That means what? Give me, say, two illustrations of that. We ought to understand what the project means, because you use it throughout the statement.

Air ATTACHE: Well, we provide the necessary coordination that the USAF commands outside of Laos. We provide operational support to the local Lao Air Force, and we also assist them in their targeting effort.

Senator SYMINGTON: Let me see if I understand. Say the Ambassador decides a strike is to be made at a certain place in Laos. He gives these instructions to you and you, in turn, through project 404, give these instructions to the people in Thailand and/or Vietnam, including the fleet at Yankee Station. They will execute the strike; correct?

Air ATTACHE: Essentially that is correct. Normally, if an operation in the field requires support, the request is made, and this is coordinated with all concerned, and if the Ambassador approves or disapproves the requirement, if he approves the requirement, then we do go in with an official request for the support required.

Senator SYMINGTON: I understand, it can work both ways.

THE DECISION TO STRIKE

Mr. SULLIVAN [former U.S. Ambassador to Laos]: Could I comment on that, Mr. Senator?

Senator SYMINGTON: Sure.

Mr. SULLIVAN: Because I think there has been some misunderstanding.

Senator SYMINGTON: Yes.

Mr. SULLIVAN: Particularly the phrase that the Ambassador decides a strike should be made, and then instructions are given through the Air Attache. This is not the Ambassador's role. The Ambassador approves or disapproves whether a strike can be made, but the direction to make a strike comes from the U.S. military, 7th Air Force [the main Air Force Headquarters of Southeast Asia, located in Saigon] or, if it needs to go higher, CINCPAC. In other words, a proposal is made to the Air Attache.

Senator SYMINGTON: By whom?

Mr. SULLIVAN: Either by the Royal Lao Air Force or by a general of the Royal Lao Army or through various intelligence antenna (deleted) [Although this testimony was released in an unclassified version, certain portions were deleted at the request of the Administration. These are so noted as they appear in the transcript.] which bring the suggestion to him that a strike be made. He and his staff take a look at it, and then bring it to me or to one of my representatives. We apply, in effect, political criteria. Are there people, villagers, are there areas [which] the Prime Minister or someone has indicated should not be involved; is there a risk, for example, of being too close to China or is there anything which, in my judgment or my representative's judgment, goes beyond what is prudent to do and, if so, it is disapproved. If not, it is approved. But then what he makes is a request to higher military authority, and higher military authority decides whether or not it will execute.

At this point Major Blake stopped marking this section with a marginal comment: "Pity the poor soul who reads this for the first time."

On page 465 of the report the following entries are heavily underlined, with the comment: "They've just blown our cover—and the irony is that, because nobody's read the report, they still keep secrets."

ORGANIZATION OF THE U.S. AIR ATTACHE OFFICE

At present, there are 125 USAF officers and airmen assigned to the U.S. Air Attache Office in Laos. Our administration includes an air operations division, a targets division, an administration division, and an intelligence division. Under the air operations division we operate (deleted) 24-hour command posts, one at Vientiane (deleted). Approximately 60 of our total authorized personnel are assigned to five air operations centers (AOC's) located at Vientaine (deleted). Twenty-one USAF forward air controllers are included in the total personnel figure. They are assigned to the five air operations centers noted above.[. . .]

The 21 FACs (forward air controllers) are designated "Ravens." Raven FACs are USAF volunteers provided from the 504th Tactical Air Support Group, stationed at Bien Hoa AB, Vietnam. All are seasoned FACs with combat experience in Vietnam. The personnel are reassigned from the 504th to (deleted) and then assigned TDY to Laos. Tenure in Laos is dependent on the time remaining on the individual's tour in Southeast Asia. Normal tours average about 6 months in Laos. All Raven FACs are assigned to military region II (MR II). The remainder are assigned to the other four military regions.

Senator SYMINGTON: I want to understand. You say these men are volunteers. Do they receive any extra remuneration?

Air ATTACHE: No, sir. The reason they are in a volunteer status is because they are on a regular 1-year tour in Vietnam, and it means a transfer to another area of operation.

(Deleted.)

Senator SYMINGTON: I see. It is important we understand. You have lost some of these men, have you not?
Air ATTACHE: Yes, sir; we have lost about (deleted).
Senator SYMINGTON: (Deleted.)
Air ATTACHE: Yes, sir.
Senator SYMINGTON: Thank you.

Marginal note: "You're welcome. And here, for now, I stop. Tomorrow will be quite a day—hell—it *is* tomorrow. Tomorrow and tomorrow is today and today."

4

Article from the Bangkok *Star* (English-language edition), December 23, p. 4. Bylined "Jonathan Price," the article is headed "Main Laotian Base in Plain of Jars Hit by Sappers." Accompanying is a photograph captioned "Phou Nok Kok—Another Laotion Outpost Besieged by North Vietnamese." The picture shows a scarred hilltop, covered with craters and splintered trees. A few sandbagged bunkers are barely visible. No soldiers can be seen. Jonathan Price is not listed among accredited correspondents in Southeast Asia; hence there is a possibility that this is a fictitious name, used perhaps by one of the many British, French, or American correspondents who covered the war in Indochina. In order to maintain their standing with Thai, Vietnamese, and American authorities, these reporters were required to use only the official dispatches from the daily briefings held in the Headquarters, Military Assistance Command, Saigon. Nevertheless, some of these journalists also submitted pseudonymous reports to Thai, Indian, and Japanese newspapers.

With yesterday's carefully planned attack on the Xieng Khouang airstrip, the North Vietnamese are apparently signaling their long awaited dry-season offensive. Only the outpost atop Phou Nok Kok, overlooking the main enemy supply route, stands between Hanoi's forces and the strategic Plain of Jars, an area which the Prime Minister of Laos has said "will be held at all costs." Despite massive air support by U.S. bombers and aerial resupply by the U.S. civilian contracts airline, Air America, the small band of Laotian guerrillas is not expected to withstand the numerically superior enemy forces.

At Xieng Khouang, the major logistics and supply base for the government troops, there is much confusion today. Although the newly resurfaced runway, capable of handling large cargo aircraft, is undamaged, most of the oil storage and ammunition dumps are in flames. Six of the fifteen captured Russian PT-76 tanks were destroyed, and ten of the defenders were killed. Many are still missing. Twenty-seven dead enemy soldiers were reported found, clad in nothing but loincloths, their bodies blackened. Royal Laotian pilots, flying American T-28 converted trainers from the Military Region II base at Long Tieng, this morning refused to refuel at Xieng Khouang. "It is too dangerous now," one is quoted as having said.

With the attack on Xieng Khouang, it appears that the tide may once again turn in favor of the North Vietnamese/Pathet Lao alliance, as it has done at this time every year since the war began. Now, however, a government spokesman in Vientiane privately expresses more concern than in previous dry seasons. He said, "If they (the North Vietnamese) take the PDJ (Plain of Jars) again, this time they won't stop. They want Long Tieng this year, and they want Vang Pao." Long Tieng, a twenty-minute flight north of Vientiane, is the United States' and Royal Lao Government's main base in northern Laos. It is also the home and headquarters of Laotian Major General Vang Pao, the charismatic guerrilla leader. Although not an ethnic Lao (he is a Meo tribesman), Vang Pao recently led the most successful government offensive ever accomplished during a wet season, penetrating deeply into territory the enemy has always considered secure. But with the sapper attack on Xieng Khouang airfield, as well as the mounting pressure on Phou Nok Kok, the Royal Lao Government's exuberance of just last week seems to have considerably paled.

Booklet *Welcome to Laos: A Practical Guide,* published for the American Women's Club of Laos, undated. This 5×7" light blue paperback of eighty pages was apparently given to all personnel, civilian and military, upon their arrival in Vientiane. It is a useful guide to shopping and customs in Laos, and while almost no mention is made of the war, occasional warnings appear, such as this one on page 6: "There are roads into southern Laos from Saigon and Phnom Penh, but for obvious reasons they are not well traveled. Unless you wish to end up as a statistic, we don't advise you to try them until the security improves." The following section, outlined with an orange felt pen in Major Blake's copy, begins on page 13:

Legend of the Seven Dragons

Hundreds and hundreds of years ago, a very wise holy man lived on an island in the Mekong. He was loved and obeyed by all the animals on the island, including seven dragons. As the years passed, the holy man grew tired of his island and decided to move to the lovely green bank across the river. So he gathered his people and all moved to what is now Vientiane. They settled down peaceably and happily. All the animals were happy too. The people were so happy that the neighboring towns grew jealous and attacked them. But every attack was foiled by the seven dragons.

There came a time when the holy man approached death. He gathered his people around him for his farewell, and bequeathed to them his large drum. This drum was to be used to summon the dragons from their cave whenever the town was threatened by attack.

Years later a man came to live among the townspeople; he lived in disguise, for he was a spy come to destroy their defenses. For fifty years he lived among them undetected, and gradually he convinced them that their drum was a symbol of distrust and should be given away. So, in trust, they gave their drum to this stranger who lived among them for fifty years.

Soon after, the Thais attacked Vientiane. With no drum, the people could not summon the dragons to defend them, and they were conquered. The victorious Thais then built a stupa [shrine] over the cave's entrance, the stupa of That Dam, so that the dragons could never escape. People say that occasionally at night rumblings can be heard from under the stupa as the dragons try to escape. The ancient drum, incidentally, can now be seen in a Wat [temple] in Nongkhai.

At the bottom of page 13 appears this comment in Major Blake's hand: "Distant drummer? Who's the dragon—who's the spy? The Dragon or the Drum. Novel? Title—*remember*—'The Muffled Drum'?"

6

Excerpt (Xerox copy) from the memorandum *Revolution in Laos: The North Vietnamese and the Pathet Lao,* published by the Rand Corporation. A copy of the complete study, actually a book (233 pages, printed on stapled multilith), was also among the documents; but apparently Major Blake first saw this excerpt (pp. 198-200) on the recommendation of Major Thomas Jerrold, assigned to the Laos desk, Internal Security Agency, Department of Defense, Washington, whose attached letter, dated 24 December, reads: "Dear Bill: Ran across your name on some reports the other day and thought you might be interested in this. It's unclassified. If you want the whole report, let me know and I'll spring a copy loose for you. Just thought you might like to see what RAND says the other side is doing. Sound familiar? Best, Tom." This excerpt also has as an attachment a DD Form 95,

Copy of Memorandum, addressed to "All Ravens from Blake," dated 19 February. The memorandum reads, "How about this, guys? Love, Yossarian."

Our interviews are rich in detail about the measures taken by the North Vietnamese to conceal their military presence in Laos, or at least to make it unobtrusive. Many units were required to bivouac outside of populated areas, often in the jungle, so as to reduce their contact with the local population to a minimum. Vietnamese soldiers often wore uniforms resembling those of the LPLA [Lao People's Liberation Army]. We had a number of statements similar to the following:

> Before coming to Laos, we were issued uniforms which were made of Vietnamese material but in the style of Pathet Lao soldiers. The shirts had epaulets as the Lao uniforms have, the hats were Lao hats.

Both military and civilian Vietnamese advisers took Lao names, and those who worked in a civilian capacity, even if they were military officers, wore civilian clothes similar to those of their Lao counterparts.

At the time of their departure from North Vietnam, most of the enlisted men in combat or support units were not informed that they were going to Laos, and though some guessed their destination, many claimed that they had not realized it until they found themselves on Lao soil. Only a few of our informants said they were permitted to receive mail, and a small number said that they could write home but pointed out that they were prohibited from mentioning that they were in Laos. One soldier . . . explained it this way:

> We received explanations that we had to keep our activities in Laos secret . . . word of casualities might discourage families at home and word would get back to the troops and hurt their morale.

Vietnamese personnel in Laos are severely cautioned against discussing Vietnamese plans, troop movements—or, indeed, any activities—with unauthorized persons. In short, just as in South Vietnam, the NVA's internal security in Laos, in contrast to that of its opponents, is very good.

The North Vietnamese involvement in Laos is further protected from discovery by the fact that most outside personnel is [sic] prohibited from entering the Communist-controlled zone. In the past, ICC [International Control Commission] observers occasionally gained admission to limited areas under careful scrutiny, but it has been years since the ICC was last able to go anywhere in NLHS [Neo Lao Hak Sat, the official name for the Communist Party of Laos] territory, and the Commission has effectively been paralyzed. Furthermore, unfriendly newsmen are unwelcome in the Communist zone of Laos. Foreigners who do gain access, such as a Japanese film crew and, in 1968, a French visitor, usually are known to be well disposed to the Communist cause and are always carefully guarded. The few foreign residents in NLHS territory are Communists. The few other foreigners who come as visitors are given little opportunity to assess the extent of the Vietnamese presence in Laos.

7

Teletype message from AOC (Air Operations Center) 20A to OUSAIRA (Office of the U.S. Air Attache), Vientiane, dated 27 December. Long Tieng, General Vang Pao's headquarters, was often referred to as 20A, 20 Alternate, or just "Alternate" by the Americans. In the Laotian Department of Transportation publication entitled *Guide to Airfields and Approach Facilities, Laos,* these landing strips, often nothing more than rough dirt runways, are designated Lima Sites, each being assigned a number. Long Tieng was numbered 20A. Although all airfields in Laos appear in this publication, those in enemy hands are designated UFN (unfriendly) after the place name and number. Because of the fluid nature of the war, there is a note on the inside front cover which warns pilots that the UFN category is not to be considered reliable.

SUBJECT: Weekly Operations Report

1. This week's activities were highlighted by the unfortunately successful NVA sapper attack on Xieng Khouang (Lima 22). On 22 Dec. at 0230 local, a team of about eighteen (18) highly trained North Vietnamese regulars infiltrated the outer perimeter and inner defenses and succeeded in placing satchel charges on both ammunition dumps, the POL [Petroleum, Oil, Lubricants] storage area, and all but one of the five (5) operable tanks. They were not detected until one of them apparently tripped over some empty gasoline drums. At this point, shooting started and the base came under a heavy mortar attack. At daybreak, two (2) enemy bodies were found, along with those of thirty-six (36) friendlies, many of whom had been killed by their own troops in the extreme confusion which developed. Apparently the Neutralist battalion attempted to desert, but ran into the Meo guerrilla company posted on the perimeter. Col. Bounlouth, the overall Lao commander at Xieng Khouang, says that if Major Ma, the Neutralist commander, ever shows up again he will be severely reprimanded. No American casualties.

2. Weekly sorties and munitions expenditures were reported in yesterday's special message, which requested more ordnance. If we are to keep up this pace, the little guys need more stuff.

3. Important item: understand from Company grapevine that new Chief Raven is due in shortly. Suggest he be thoroughly briefed on this operation as compared to Vietnam and be exposed to all other military regions before coming to Alternate. As you know, we've had a smooth show for some time, and we all believe that to be forced back into a "military" structure would preclude us from doing our job. What's next—haircuts? [Marginal comment in Major Blake's handwriting: "Oh for Christ's sake."]

4. Otherwise, nothing new. A few of the natives are getting jittery, but generally their morale is good. So is ours, thanks to the new generator which keeps the beer

palatably cool. Hamilton [The name "Hamilton" is circled in ink, with the word "Dante????" added].

8

Senate *Hearings,* pp. 542, 543.

WHY PRETEND GENEVA AGREEMENTS ARE OF VALUE?

Senator FULBRIGHT: If both sides are not living up to ere Geneva Agreements, what is the use of pretending it is of any value?

Mr. SULLIVAN: I think our consideration is that the value would be in the future when negotiations are started. Our effort is to try to get negotiations resumed on this and reestablish it. I think our chances of doing this depend, as you said the other day, to some great extent on the outcome of the situation in Vietnam, and if there is a situation which would permit the reestablishment of the 1962 Agreements, and permit a neutral regime to obtain in Laos, that we hope would lead to a situation in which we could quietly disengage from the military activities that are currently there. . . . The question I was addressing was would the United States have a greater obligation then, and in theory I think we would. As I have said constantly here, currently we believe we have no commitment in Laos. Our actions could be reversible today. They could, perhaps, be reversible more because they are not matters of the public record than they could if they were. That is another consideration. But our primary concern is to try to preserve the possibility of returning to what we had hoped in 1962 was going to be a settlement that would arrange to get everybody out of Laos and leave the Lao to their own devices. [Marginal comment: "Amen."] . . .

PREVIOUS TESTIMONY TO COMMITTEE

Senator FULBRIGHT: When did our operation begin? Has it been going on just a few weeks or when did the sup-

The Laotian Fragments

port of the Air Force and the bombing become significant?

Mr. SULLIVAN: I think the testimony we have had over the past few days, sir, has traced that from 1964, the incidence of the first air action over Laos.

Senator FULBRIGHT: 1964. Well, you have just said that your reports to this committee are evidence of our open society. I was under the impression that we did not have an advisory or military training organization in Laos, much less that we were carrying on bombing raids.

Mr. SULLIVAN: Well, I have testified before this committee in the past, I believe, on that same subject.

Senator FULBRIGHT: I thought your testimony before was to the effect that we did not have advisory organizations in Laos or military training.

Mr. SULLIVAN: We have not had advisory organizations in Laos, and the training that we are talking about is being undertaken in Thailand.

Senator FULBRIGHT: Or military action by our Air Force there. I thought that was the testimony.

Mr. SULLIVAN: I do not recall ever having given any testimony to that effect. I have given testimony concerning—

Senator FULBRIGHT: I misunderstood it, I guess. In your own testimony in 1968 before this committee, Senator Cooper was questioning, and I quote from page 19:

> According to newspaper accounts, three or four thousand troops advised and trained by the U.S. advisers, equipped with howitzers and Wessons, and ammunition, according to the newspaper reports, these troops just fled and abandoned the howitzers and abandoned the ammunition and no fight at all after five or six years of our training.

Then he said:

> You said a while ago that Souvanna Phouma [the Prime Minister of Laos] was considered as a nationalist and fighting for that country. How do you explain the fact that these people flee again after they are trained?

Your answer then was this:

> Ambassador SULLIVAN: I would like just to correct the record, we do not have a military training and advisory organization in Laos. And we, therefore, do not have advisers with these troops. We don't have advisers with them. However, some of these units probably had been trained in Thailand under American supervision, but we don't have people with them. We don't have a military advisory group there.

I learned yesterday that we do have a very substantial group of military people there.

Mr. SULLIVAN: No, sir. I think if you will read what I said, we do not have advisers with the units, and they do not go out into combat action with the units.

Senator FULBRIGHT: I did not have any idea that we were doing anything like we are. What is a better way to describe what we are doing? We are just fighting our own war?

Mr. SULLIVAN: No, sir. There are—the Americans who fly in aircraft certainly on many occasions engage in combat.

AMERICAN ARMY PERSONNEL IN LAOS

Senator FULBRIGHT: How many people? I thought it was the other day, wasn't it, when it was mentioned that over 700 American personnel and more than 100 Army people [were] in Laos? . . . What do they do there, do they just spend the time in the officers' club? Don't they do something? Don't they advise and train and do something? What do they do? . . .

Army ATTACHE: I would like to testify on that. The personnel at the military regional headquarters do provide advice insofar as key personnel can at the individual level. But these are sizable areas in Laos, and this is—the only people involved in this role are those people at the regional level. I have also a sizable communications facility that is provided. It provides work in Vientiane and through operations and intelligence.

Senator FULBRIGHT: But they do not ever give them advice?

Army ATTACHE: I did not say that.

Senator FULBRIGHT: I am asking you, do they or don't they?

Army ATTACHE: My personnel at regional level do provide advice, yes.

Senator FULBRIGHT: Then what is an advisory group?

Army ATTACHE: An advisory group, sir, is an organization that is constituted for the sole mission to provide advice to include it down to lower unit levels.

Senator FULBRIGHT: So if they do anything else they are not advisory. We are getting so technical with your semantics it is impossible for us to understand. If they give advice it does not matter whether they are an organized group, solely and exclusively in such an organization, does it? What I think this testimony tends to do is to mislead the committee when you rely upon these finespun theories as to how you describe them. You are there in force, aren't you, and you are working with the Lao. You are bombing for them, protecting their troops whenever they are attacked; is that not true?

Army ATTACHE: I said there is an air campaign which is conducted in Laos.

Marginal comment in Major Blake's hand: "Irony—it was during the third week in October (same-same these hearings) that I first heard of the Raven program."

9

Blake, *Journal*, pp. 37–38.

28 December: Laos. I'm "across the fence," as they say. *Remember:* Smack in the middle of Vientiane, the vertical runway—a four-sided Oriental Arc de Triomph [*sic*] (I may even get to use my rusty old French). The vertical run-

way— made from concrete they say was supposed to be used for a new airfield. Monuments instead of airplane pads. The sight of it, sticking straight up in the air behind the morning market with the hundreds of samlars (sp?) [a three-wheeled, chain-driven pedicab]—the sammlar drivers squatting beside their cabs and those great domes in the background. Isn't finished, either. If Thailand was like World War I, God knows what this is up here. The last of the truly colonial cities? Red tiled roofs and wide boulevards and large villas—seems like Saigon right after the war—and the shanties begin a block from the main street. Reminds me, for no good reason, of New Canaan, Conn. Feel as if I'm going backward in time. At least they drive on our side of the road up here, as opposed to the Thais. (Don't forget the U.S. vehicles in Thailand (left-side traffic) all have standard American drive, while up here the American jeeps all have their steering wheels on the right side for right-hand traffic. Seems like someone should switch cars. Crazy.)

Quarters are palatial (how can I write home about this?) —I'm sitting at a lovely teak desk in my own room—with bath—have two housemates I haven't met yet (flying today) who have the other two bedrooms. A *private* house with garden, terrace, concrete fence (can't see over it), and an armed guard (Lao?) who salutes. Cook, named Nguyen Van something (Vietnamese?), and maid, who Van sleeps with but says is neither sister nor wife. Fantastic dinner with wine. Jesus.

Remember: sight of the Mekong between Laos and Thailand. Unlike Vietnam, you can see it move here. Now that dry season's starting, it's due to recede, but right now it's a shit-colored frothy brown—a mile wide—many floating logs, leaves, palm branches, and an occasional dauntless sampan. It really looks angry. Saw it first from the Air America C-123 shuttle flight from Thailand. Jungle on both sides right down to the river, then wet rice paddies, blue-green trees (like Vietnam, but no craters), and then suddenly Vientiane, peeking through a low, broken cloud deck. Tiny city. The airport deserted—grass growing through cracks in the concrete and what looked like old hulks of airplanes sagging off to the sides—C-46s and C-45s, some without wings—in the weeds. No people in sight. Stopped in front of large quonset hut, all the other round-eyes got off. Me too. They all had civilian clothes, crew cuts, and combat boots. Rode to AOC in a white jeep with a Lao driver, who said, "Mr. Blake?" as I walked by (don't forget the right-hand drive in left-hand traffic). Seems Col. Barnes had a hurry-up meeting.

This is turning into more of a saga than I had planned—but so far there's time and even the inclination to write. Plus the fact that it's lonely as hell. Cool evening (I borrowed a sweater from one of the other closets—nobody told me to bring one—it's a *jungle* war—hah!) and there's a breeze. Don't need the overhead fan. It's been almost two weeks since I've flown—must remember to keep rudder pedals tight after touchdown, the 0-1 is no F-4. Wonder what it will be like to fly the T-28 again? —car coming—gate opening—I wonder if [Entry ends here without punctuation.]

10

Memorandum, handwritten on 6½×9" yellow engraved bond with the printed heading in blue: "From the Desk of A. Horowitz."

Delighted to have you aboard. Do plan to come to dinner at 7:00 PM on Tuesday next for an early evening. Mrs. H. and I look forward to meeting you.

Horowitz

11

Excerpt from the book *To Move a Nation: The Politics of Foreign Policy in the Administration of John F. Kennedy,* by Roger Hilsman (New York: Doubleday, 1967). The copy with Major Blake's pa-

pers bears the stamp "USIS [United States Information Service] Library, Vientiane." The charge slip on the inside of the back cover shows only two due dates: one 22 October and the other (presumably Major Blake's) 12 January. Assuming the standard two-week charge period, Major Blake probably checked the book out on December 29. Two underlined passages, from pages 116 and 94-96, follow.

Interagency Rivalry

Each of the American agencies concerned with Laos—the State Department, the Pentagon, the Agency for International Development (AID), and the CIA—sent people there to carry out their agency's programs, people with money to spend and influence and leverage to exert. Each had different interests and views on how to handle Laos as a foreign policy problem for the United States and each had its own private channels of communication to Washington, where the battles were carried on just as vigorously in the large arena. In time, the differences between the agencies and departments became more marked and the exchanges sharper, with the CIA and the Pentagon generally on one side and the State Department and AID on the other. Each agency came to pursue its own programs and policies with less and less regard for the others, and with little relationship to an overall American policy. The Ambassador, certainly, was not always right. One ambassador, a man who sided more often with the Pentagon, for example, became so blindly wedded to the policy of rigid anit-Communism that in congressional hearings much later he was still ascribing the rampant inflation of the time—so obviously caused by the mismanagement of the United States aid program—to Souvanna's negotiations with the Pathet Lao about a government of national union! Another ambassador became so thoroughly anti-CIA that he repeatedly informed the press not only of their actual gaffes but of his wildest suspicions. But the tragedy was that neither the Lao nor our allies could tell who really spoke for the United States—whether it was the CIA, the military, the AID officials, or the Ambassador. In the end there was open quarreling among the representatives of the different

Amercan agencies, and, to the shame of all Americans, the United States became the butt of jokes among both friend and foe.

Marginal comment in Major Blake's hand, penciled and erased: "And this was 1957!"

The Terrain

And the problem for the United States was compounded by the terrain of Laos, by the primitive state of its economy, and by the people and their politics. Laos is shaped like a caveman's club [Marginal comment: Great metaphor!"], with a knobby head in the north and a handle extending southward. The very butt of the handle is the border with Cambodia. In the east, the border is the crest of the Annamite chain, shared for only the bottom half of the club with South Vietnam and for all the rest of both handle and head with the Communist North. On the west, the border is the Mekong River, shared for most of the whole length of Laos with Thailand. . . . One knob at the very top of the head marks a part of the border shared with Burma, and the next knob over to the east, still at the very top, is the border shared with Communist China.

The royal capital of Laos is at Luang Prabang in the north, where the valley is narrow as the Mekong makes its way through the mountains. But most of the Lao people live on the lowlands of the river farther south. One concentration is in the terrain compartment at Vientiane, located about midway between the point where the river makes a great bend to flow east for 150 miles and a second bend where it turns south again. Most of the rest of the people of Lao descent live in these southern lowlands—in villages grouped around the old market towns of Pak Sane, Thakhek, Savannakhet, and Pakse. There are also in the mountains a few scattered valleys and plateaus—of which the largest and richest is the Plain of Jars, with its market town of Xieng Khouang, not far from the center of the head of the club.* But except for these, Laos is a jumble of hills and mountains. [Marginal comment in Major Blake's hand: "And here's where I'm flying tomorrow," thus probably dating his reading of this passage to December 29.]

The climate of Laos is dominated by the monsoon. In November, December, and January the weather is delightful, with cool, clear nights and bright, comfortable, sunny days. Then, slowly, day by day the weather gets hotter and hotter until the mighty Mekong is a trickle wending its way through cracked mud. Then suddenly in May or June the rains come. And when the rains do come, they come in torrents, coursing down the steep-sided mountains in raging floods, turning the dirt roads and trails into quagmires and washing out bridges, culverts, and fills—gullying even the very best of modern roads, which, no matter how well engineered, require constant upkeep. A measure of the rains is what happens to the Mekong. For six months of the year it is fordable at many points in its long journey through Laos. But when the monsoon comes it begins to swell, until in September it is 30 to 40 feet deep and frequently over a mile wide.

12

Letter (Xerox copy), Office of the United States Air Attache, Vientiane, undated. Typewritten on 8×10½" bond, with strikeovers and other errors corrected in ink.

Dear Walter:

I'm writing you personally and asking our new man, Blake, to handcarry this down to you in Bangkok. I don't want to transmit what I have to say on the wire, for reasons which should be obvious. Please give Blake a good

---

*The Jars on the Plain of Jars are, literally, jars. Two sites on the plain are littered with several hundred each. The jars themselves stand about four feet tall and are carved from solid rock, many with well-fitted lids. Their origin is a prehistoric mystery, but the most likely explanation is that they were the burial urns of some ancient people. Souphanouvong, the Communist leader, told me that legend relates that the jars were already there when the Lao people first arrived. [Hilsman's footnote.]

briefing on your end of the show, and don't pull any punches. It may be time.

I suppose this letter is by way of an apology. I tried, but there is still no way to program more visits up here by your people. It's a shame, especially with the Xieng Khouang mess and the rather tense situation which is developing. I'd hoped the problem might be solved by the hearings, but the politicos may be pretending they don't know what is going on so that they can be suitably shocked. The hearings were rough, by the way—you should be grateful you're a new guy and didn't have to go back to Washington. Anyway, without a major miracle our civilian friends won't bend. They have been here too long, I'm afraid, and their methods are too well established. Boat rockers are definitely not welcome. Additionally, I don't really work for USAF on this job—I report directly to the Ambassador, have no contact at all with your boss at CINCPAC, and my only association with the military chain of command is through intelligence reports to DIA [Defense Intelligence Agency, Washington]. The Army Attache has the same problem, but his seems to be compounded because he isn't speaking to me this month.

What I think we can't do at this time is raise a stink through channels and embarrass the Ambassador from above. He's a bit touchy now, being new himself, and none of us has him really figured out yet. Perhaps the short tours for our military here account for the continuing power of the Company—after all, they've been around for more than a decade. Ironically, they're intelligence people, not operational combatants, yet they've been forced into a direct role because of the nature of the beast. And as you will understand, I'm sure, the Ambassador does write my ER [Effectiveness Report].

Consequently, even though most of the official funding (God knows how much *they* spend) comes through your office of Deputy Chief, you just can't get up here to check on things the way you could if this were a normal situation. The Company exists on secrecy—and I must confess to more than a little sympathy for their position. Last year one of your well-meaning Army boys came up for an inspection—in uniform. We got him some clothes in a hurry, and he set out to inspect the Lao ordnance storage (his specialty—his *only* specialty, I might add). If you'll pardon the language, he damn near shit when he saw Savannakhet. I suppose he had been thinking in terms of normal Army depots, and he took a rather dim view of bombs and fuel drums piled together, all the spilled oil, the lack of supply records, and the like. I don't have to tell you how he reacted when one of the Lao officers lit a cigarette while sitting on a pile of 250 pounders. The angrier he got—the more "military" he became—and the more the Lao turned off. Buddha, not precautions, keeps that ammo dump from blowing up—or so the Lao believe. Anyway, he asked me what I intended to do about the deplorable situation (him a major—me a colonel), and I told him to talk to the USAID people, his own augmentees, and when they told him that they had no command authority, that they worked for him but the Company set the policies, I'm afraid he went away muttering. There was some kind of a report made to CINCPAC which went to Washington—DOD to State and back down to the Ambassador—but he won't let me have a copy. Don't you have one?

So—the upshot of the whole mess is that despite my hopes of a few weeks back when you arrived, nothing's really changed. It's delicate at best, and believe me, if I thought there were any other way to conduct this war, I'd jump at it. As I mentioned to you last month, I'm still amazed at how little this operation evolves from year to year—and since my first tour five years ago when you were protecting our country in your B-52, the whole thing has just gotten much bigger. More airplanes, more people, more money, and more problems. Does it help to tell you that I'm sorry?

I'm impressed with Blake, however, and I would like to reiterate my request for support to him. Let him read your old correspondence files, for instance. He's a cut above the usual Terry-and-the-Pirates type we get here, and I suspect he's been given some very specific instructions from Seventh Air Force to get the show on the road. He hasn't said anything to me yet, but I noticed his raised eyebrows when I introduced him to the "colleagues" he'll be living with—Lt. Jenkins who wears the long scarves and the captain whom they call Weird (I've even succumbed—see?). I think I told you about having to put the kibosh on their bell-bottom flying suits. I'm certain that if the tour here were any longer, some of our incognito soldiers of fortune would have hair down to their waists. I'm going to try and use Blake for more than just a FAC, though, and I'll definitely let him act as a safehands courier between us. Don't—and I must stress this—don't correspond personally with me over the teletype. It's secure for classified material, of course, but the Army communications people run it, and wires marked "Air Force Eyes Only" come through Army channels. And their attache thinks we get all the gravy while they do all the work. Over it all hovers the Company.

Nothing else at this time. Again, I'm so sorry, but that's the way it is in Laos. Let me know if you want me to buy anything for you, and if worst comes to worst, think back to our plebe days at the Academy. Even *this* is better than that. And let me know if you hear anything about the BG list [promotion list for Brigadier General]. We're rather cut off from the main stream up here.

I'm sure that Catherine would ask to be remembered.

My very best,
[signed] Jake

13

Bureau of Engraving and Printing certificate: "The United States of America/ To All Who Shall See These Presents, Greeting:/ This is to Certify that/ the President of the United States of America/ Authorized by Executive Order, August 24, 1962/ has awarded/ THE SILVER STAR MEDAL/ to Major William Blake/ for/ Gallantry/ 22 September/ Given Under My Hand in the City of Washington/ this 1st Day of December/ [signed] George S. Brown, General, USAF, Robert C. Seamans, Secretary of the Air Force." Accompanying this certificate in a blue 8½×11" plastic folder is the following citation.

Citation to Accompany the Award
of the Silver Star Medal
to Major William Blake:

Major William Blake distinguished himself by **extreme** gallantry as a Forward Air Controller, 20th Tactical **Air** Support Group, Republic of Vietnam, while engaged in air operations against an opposing armed force on 22 September. On this date, Major Blake controlled and directed thirteen different flights of fighter bombers against heavily defended enemy positions which were supporting an attack against a Special Forces Camp. Disregarding his own personal safety on numerous occasions, Major Blake directed repeated strikes against enemy gun positions which effectively silenced them and prevented the friendly camp from being overrun. When another Forward Air Controller was shot down, Major Blake successfully directed the rescue effort, resulting in the retrieving of the other pilot. During this effort, Major Blake's light, unarmed observation aircraft received twenty-three hits from small-arms fire, and the right window of his aircraft was shot out. Despite these difficulties, and despite oncoming darkness and growing fatigue, Major Blake substantially contributed to the saving of many allied lives. The exemplary leadership, personal endeavor and devotion to duty displayed by Major Blake reflect great credit upon himself and the United States Air Force.

14

Holograph letter from Major Blake to his wife, on standard airmail stationery, 7×9½″, undated. The first page is neatly written, but the following three pages become increasingly messy. All pages appear to have been crumpled up, then smoothed out. It is reasonable to assume that this copy of the letter was never mailed.

The Laotian Fragments

My dearest Mary:

It is some time since I have written you, and I apologize. It's been hectic. I thought, though, that you might want to tell the boys I've just received notice of a Silver Star for a job I did a few months ago. Since then, I've changed to another location, and it's great not to be sleeping in a tent anymore. The work is much the same, however, and I'm still flying regularly. Please note the new APO number on the envelope.

It's hard to believe that the year is half gone, and I wonder if we can work something out for a few days in Hawaii when my R&R comes up. What do you think? I've had a lot of time these past few months to think about us, and perhaps another "honeymoon" might help. Please let me know what you think.

I do wonder often how you are and how you feel, and I don't know if it would help to say again that I did *not* "want" (your phrase) to come to Vietnam, and I did not want to get away from you and the children. Since being here, I'm more certain than ever, but I'm also certain that I am doing the right thing. Eight months ago, neither of us really knew anything about Southeast Asia. Regardless of *why* we're here, I am a military officer and I'm doing my job.

It's funny, but being at war gives one a chance to think —about his family, his home, his ideals, his values (no, my love, I'm not going to engage in what you call my "big-word generalizing")—but why not, you bitch, you'll never try and understand anyway about my sense of duty, regardless of the apparent idiocy of the cause. I did not *have* to volunteer to come to this war—you're right there—but neither could I in all conscience *not* volunteer. I love my country and I'm good at my job. It's like Yossarian finds out (and you wouldn't understand *that* either)—you're wrong no matter what. And furthermore, if I hadn't come here I wouldn't get promoted and you wouldn't have all that extra dough——but I'm no Yossarian and I loved you all the time, regardless, even though you don't think I'm capable of love. And I did a fucking good job in that fucking republic of Vietnam (fucking and Vietnam, your two favorite subjects) and I volunteered for this fucking new job and I still don't have a fuck of an idea what's going on. I've got two comrades in arms who look like rejects from a commune who came in smashed tonight with three of the ugliest, fattest white Caucasian females I've ever seen. Secretaries, or something. One was supposedly for me. Honestly, dear wife, I'd rather fuck you. And they all left after about a hundred martinis and I have to fly my first Laotian mission tomorrow, so I'm going to jerk off and go to sleep—and I guarantee I won't be thinking of you, whoever you are. So good night, sweet princess, and flights of Ravens sing thee to thy rest.

15

Teletype message, AOC 20A to AOC Vientiane, 292330ZDec (11:30 p.m., December 29; "Z" is an indicator that the accompanying figures represent the date and the time in the twenty-four-hour system according to Greenwich mean time).

SUBJECT: Recurring Problems

Will you please tell those idiots over in RO/USAID to get us a heater? I've exhausted all the normal channels. It's the dry season (supposedly). It gets cold at night. This wonderful new concrete blockhouse you all built for us is great, and it will be nice and cool in the summer. Unfortunately, it's winter. I know most people don't think of Southeast Asia as having winter—but we do up here. These mountains are eight thousand (8000) feet tall in places, and I'm sorry your supply list or whatever you go by does not normally include heaters for a jungle war. Nevertheless, repeat, nevertheless, this part of the war is definitely not normal and we are freezing our a---- off. Extra blankets don't work. Burning charcoal on the floor as the natives do only smokes up the place because you didn't build enough windows. It's a hell of a note to have to fly six hours of combat a day and come back to what we have now named the Ice House. Do something, we beg you, or we'll have to ask Vang Pao to loose some of his bad Phi [Laotian spirits who, according to the animists, inhabited the high hilltops] on you. Beware, and reply ASAP. Hamilton.

16

Letter (original copy) from Mr. Dante Hamilton, Commander, AOC 20A, to Col. Barnes, U.S. Air Attache, Vientiane, dated 29 December. Typed on white 8×10½" bond paper. No envelope. Attached is a letter which follows as item 17.

SUBJECT: New Chief Raven
TO: OUSAIRA

Dear Colonel Barnes:

My schedule here precludes my coming down in person, therefore I am writing you about this and sending it via courier. It concerns something I have just found out, namely, the identity of the new Chief Raven FAC, William Blake. While I have every respect for Mr. Blake's abilities as an officer and a gentleman, there are a few points I feel I should make in hopes that something can be done to alleveate [sic] a potentially unfortunate situation.

First: although I have not seen him for years, I have known Mr. Blake since we were in pilot training together. He was in ROTC and I was in the Aviation Cadet Program, similar to West Point. After graduation, we both became IPs [Instructor Pilots] in the Air Training Command, flying T-33s in Texas. I stayed in fighters all the way until my first assignment here in 1966, and as you know, have been back and forth to Laos ever since. Mr. Blake, on the other hand, went to staff jobs and had an AFIT [Air Force Institute of Technology] sponsored graduate school assignment, after which he taught at the Air Force Academy. Except for his O-1 training before coming to SEA, he has had no real operational experience. I have heard his combat record in Vietnam is good, but he only flew there for six months, and as you know, it's a different war over there.

My concern is not, sir, primarily that I will be outranked

on the job (his ROTC commission was six months ahead of mine from Aviation Cadets) but that the mission will suffer. Being on my third tour here, I feel that I have no little understanding and appreciation of the complexity of our situation. Your last ER on me showed, I think, that you agree.

We have a fine show going here now. The little guys trust us; they know we'll die for them and they will for us, too. Of course, we don't act all that military, but neither do they, and we aren't supposed to. But I'm very concerned that Mr. Blake, with his desire for organization and to please his superiors during his very first combat tour, will cause animosity between the Ravens, the other Americans, the Company, and the Meo. I don't think, for instance, that Mr. Blake will be able to comprehend the difference between the Lao in Vientiane and the Meo who work for Vang Pao. Each of us here are dedicated to helping these men win the war. We don't consider our job just a tour to get experience and medals. We have been accepted by the native populace and we love them—and they us. If a big new round-eye comes in and starts making waves, there is no telling what may happen. Remember please what happened last year when that Army guy from Bangkok came up.

I do not have anything personal against Mr. Blake—far from it. We are both USAF officers, regardless, and we are both here for basically the same reason—to fight the Communists and keep them from taking over a free country. But I do suggest that you might give Mr. Blake a job on one of your staffs in Vientiane, not the Chief Raven job which will place him in command of all twenty-one FACs in Laos at all the bases, thus running the entire war. I am sure that the other Ravens and AOC commanders would agree that this war is better fought by letting the men in the different military regions handle things their own way. You just can't change Asians overnight.

Please forgive the length and personal nature of this letter. As you know, my communications are usually shorter. But I repeat, regardless of *who* he is, a new man, especially an inexperienced (combatwise) officer, cannot do the job we are charged to do here. Only those of us from Special Forces who have been trained to work in counterinsurgency and guerrilla operations can successfully fight this war to a conclusion.

> Respectfully,
> [signed] Dante Hamilton
> Commander, AOC 20A

17

Letter, handwritten on official stationery headed "Office of the United States Air Attache, Vientiane, Laos," undated.

SUBJECT: [no entry]
TO: Mr. Blake

Bill:

Please read my letter before you look at the attached. I'll be in effect incommunicado for about three days, so please plan to see me with your comments right after New Year's. It seems that the RLG [Royal Lao Government] has quite a celebration for their non-oriental friends over the holidays, and it's a command performance. Do stop by my office early next week.

The attached letter is from Mr. Dante Hamilton, the Long Tieng AOC commander, who I gather is rather an old acquaintance of yours. Never, please, let on that I have shown this correspondence or the other messages to you. Our command situation is tenuous enough as it is. But because you are "officially" a civilian, I'm going to take a chance and create a channels breach that well may backfire if it gets out. I want you to become much more acquainted than your predecessors have been with some of the unique problems we have here, mainly because I sense the climate may be changing, hopefully for the better. The senators are beginning to take an official look (even though they've known what's been going on all the time), and our job may be unclassified soon. Until then, we have to play the game—no matter who is making the rules.

What we do internally, however, is our business, and I'd

like to begin with Mr. Hamilton and what he has done since his assignment to Laos. Without reservations, he's the best man we have. He has previous tours as a FAC and an AOC commander, and even though he's committed to the bescarved, cowboy-hatted SOF [Special Operations Forces] thinking, he has managed to establish quite a rapport with the natives. He's the only one I know of, for instance, who can eat Lao food regularly, and he even has a "wife" who has been given him by Vang Pao (I'm not supposed to know about this, by the way). He knows his maintenance and supply needs, can get the Lao to follow him, and he's a fine pilot (although a bit foolhardy at times).

He also gets along extremely well with the Company—perhaps because he gives them the impression that he won't tell me what they're doing. I've worked with him long enough, however, to be able to read between the lines (and when you look at his messages, you'll see that he's rather blunt). Regardless, he can take a small group of Lao and Americans and create quite an efficient little force—in his own unorthodox manner, of course.

There are two problems now: first, "little forces" are passé—it's a great big war, and the enemy is readying for a large, conventional push against Long Tieng. If it goes, so does the whole Lao government, and the resulting mess will probably lead to a right-wing coup, a request *formally* for U.S. military aid, and then the lid blows off. Secondly, we do not have many like Hamilton. In effect, what he is able to do is adapt himself to a centuries-old tradition of feudal warfare, and it is because of his abilities and those of the very few like him that Vang Pao, for instance, has become the effective little warlord that he is. Five years ago—fine—but when you're talking about the USAF strike commitment of today and the very large North Vietnamese force now poised in Laos, there's got to be a change. That's where you come in. In effect, you and your Ravens will run the war—it will be your selection of targets, your command and control, your knowledge of the situation which will determine how and where the billions of dollars of U.S. equipment, men, and supplies will be applied to hurt the enemy most. I haven't been officially informed of exactly what your instructions are or who issued them, but I want you to feel that you have my complete confidence and support. Call it intuition if you wish, but I somehow think that if you're going to succeed where others have failed, you have to begin by bridging that gap between the myriad number of small empires which have sprung up here because of the mission's classification—and somehow get all of them working in the same direction. If you don't, we're going to continue working at cross purposes to an extent (as we are now) never before seen here. For one, I'm tired of wasting much of our effort and allowing the enemy more opportunities than he deserves.

How does it feel to be a major (pardon me, almost a Lt. Col.) who's just been charged with conducting a war? I'll see you Monday or so, and after we get through with a discussion of Hamilton, we'll tackle Horowitz and Company. And if you feel a bit snowed, please try and think of me tomorrow as I raise a friendly glass or two with the Soviet and Polish attaches. Happy New Year.

[signed] Barnes

18

Tape recording, Sony cassette. On the first side is the inked notation: "Dollar ride in Laos, 30 December—me and Weird." It was common practice for pilots to take along portable tape recorders on combat missions, plugging into the aircraft radio and interphone system by means of a single adaptor. Major Blake retained many such tapes. Although both sides of this cassette are recorded, there are frequent periods of silence and static, and occasionally the transmissions are incomprehensible because many voices are talking at once. The editor has attempted to indicate comments made over the O-1's interphone by the symbol "I"; otherwise the comments were transmitted or received by radio. The map reproduced on pages 50–51 was no doubt the one used by Major Blake on this flight. The original was cut to approximately 5"×7" in order to fit on his standard pilot's kneeboard.

Weird (I): So welcome to Laos. Let's go win the war. Do you want to use my callsign or yours?

Blake (I): Let's use yours. You're in the front seat.

Weird (I): OK. I'll try and give you the full rundown on what we do. Want to go anywhere in particular?

Blake (I): Let's go as briefed.

Weird (I): Rog [USAF slang, short for "Roger (I understand)"]. But if you want to change, let me know. Once we're airborne we run our own show.

Weird: Brickbat, this is Raven 22.

Brickbat [callsign of the Airborne Command Post, a USAF C-130 which coordinated airstrikes]: Go ahead, Raven 22.

Weird: Raven 22 airborne at forty past the hour, heading north. Orientation mission. If you need us, give us a call.

Brickbat: Understand. PDJ [Plain of Jars] altimeter 29.99 [the pressure setting for the aircraft's altimeter].

Weird: Roger. 29.99. (I) OK. We'll head up a little bit east of Alternate to the PDJ and I'll show you Xieng Khouangville, then Ban Ban, over to Site 32, down to Muong Soui and then maybe into Alternate for fuel. Want to put in any strikes if we can get some?

Blake (I): Sure, if there's time. Is Xieng Khouangville the place that was hit by the sappers?

Weird (I): No—that was Xieng Khouang, right in the middle of the Plain. Xieng Khouangville's to the east of the PDJ. It's pretty well destroyed.

Blake (I): Oh. Sounds the same.

Weird (I): Confusing, isn't it. Wait until you sit in on a Lao briefing when they try and give you an intelligence report in English. They used to do it in French, but this Ambassador doesn't speak French, so now they try it in English. [One-minute pause.] About the strikes—there's usually somebody available. We always check in with Brickbat after takeoff and give him the general area we'll be in. That way, if he gets a call from one of the ground FAGs [Forward Air Guides, usually Lao officers who controlled airstrikes from the ground], he can send us over in a hurry. Old Brickbat does a pretty shit hot job, too. [Indeterminate time lapse.] We're crossing the ridgeline south of Xieng Khouangville now—the PDJ is at about nine o'clock. Note the valley running west up that way. Where the low clouds are is the plain. The good guys have got artillery positions on both of the ridgelines north and south of that valley all down to Xieng Khouangville. When the bad guys come back in, they'll want to get those big guns out of the way first. Intell says they'll come down from the north on Route Seven, but I don't believe it. Not at first, anyway. They've already sent out probes down here, and you can expect to be working pretty close to the ridgelines. Nobody stays in the towns anymore—not for long, anyway.

Blake (I): Is that Xieng Khouangville underneath us?

Weird (I): Yeah. Those five burned-out structures along the creek bed are Xieng Khouangville. I think it's changed hands three times now. VP [General Vang Pao] owns it this week, at least during the day.

Blake (I): Where are the bad guys?

Weird (I): All over, but mainly about ten clicks [kilometers] down the valley to the east. This is one of the main routes into the PDJ.

Blake (I): I don't see a damn soul down there.

Weird (I): You won't. It's not like Vietnam. Most of the time you won't even see our guys, either. [Time break.] Hey, what did you think of our lovelies last night? How's that for a welcome? I'll take the blame. Jenkins didn't want to. He's really pretty straight.

Blake (I): No comment. Where'd you guys go?

Weird (I): We took all three of 'em down to the White Rose to watch the cigarette tricks. They love it. You been there yet?

Blake (I): Not yet.

Weird (I): You won't believe it. One of the White Rose girls can keep six butts puffing at once, and she's pretty great in bed, too—or so everybody says. Claims she's half Vietnamese, half Thai, half French. That's why she's a fuck and a half.

Blake (I): Is that Phou Nok Kok at about ten o'clock?

Weird (I): Rog. Look, a couple of Thuds [F-105s] are going in.

Blake (I): Where?

Weird (I): Twelve o'clock going eleven. Lead's just released. There. Just north of that scarred peak with the brown bald spot. See the brown smoke coming up through the trees? There's Two's bomb. Same place. See?

Blake (I): Got them.

Weird (I): Shit, not a secondary [a secondary explosion, caused by a bomb hitting an enemy storage or ammunition target] in sight. Look how goddamned close to the summit they're bombing. [Transmission]: Brickbat, Brickbat, Raven 22.

Brickbat: Go ahead, Raven 22.

Weird: What's the status of Phou Nok Kok?

Brickbat: Still friendly, but they're reporting incoming DK-82 mortar rounds.

Weird: Need some help?

Brickbat: Negative. Raven 26 is working there.

Weird: OK. Give us a call.

Brickbat: Rog.

Weird (I): You'll like working the Thuds better than Fours [USAF F-4]. They usually carry bigger bombs. Me, I like to work the A-1s [propeller-driven fighter-bomber]. Those guys really get down there and scrape them off. Big balls, too. Shit, here comes a flight of F-4s. Let's get out of here. You'll find it gets right congested at times.

Blake (I): Especially during a firefight, I'll bet.

Weird (I): Hell no—not for us—there aren't any firefights when we work, during the day. The bad guys only attack at night. They're duly respectful of all the air we've got. During the day we put in most of our strikes on coordinates given us from the ground. You'll fly with a Lao observer who'll talk to the ground and tell you where to put your smoke [target marking rockets]. We don't have any Americans on the ground who'll talk to us.

Blake (I): What if you don't like the target?

Weird (I): It's tough shit. Anyway, you don't know what the FAG's saying to your GIB [Guy In the Backseat]. For all you know it might be a good target. Sometimes something even goes off under all those trees.

Blake (I): Oh.

Weird (I): Get Hamilton to tell you what it was like in the old days. They'd take a whole crew up in a U-17, some-

The Laotian Fragments

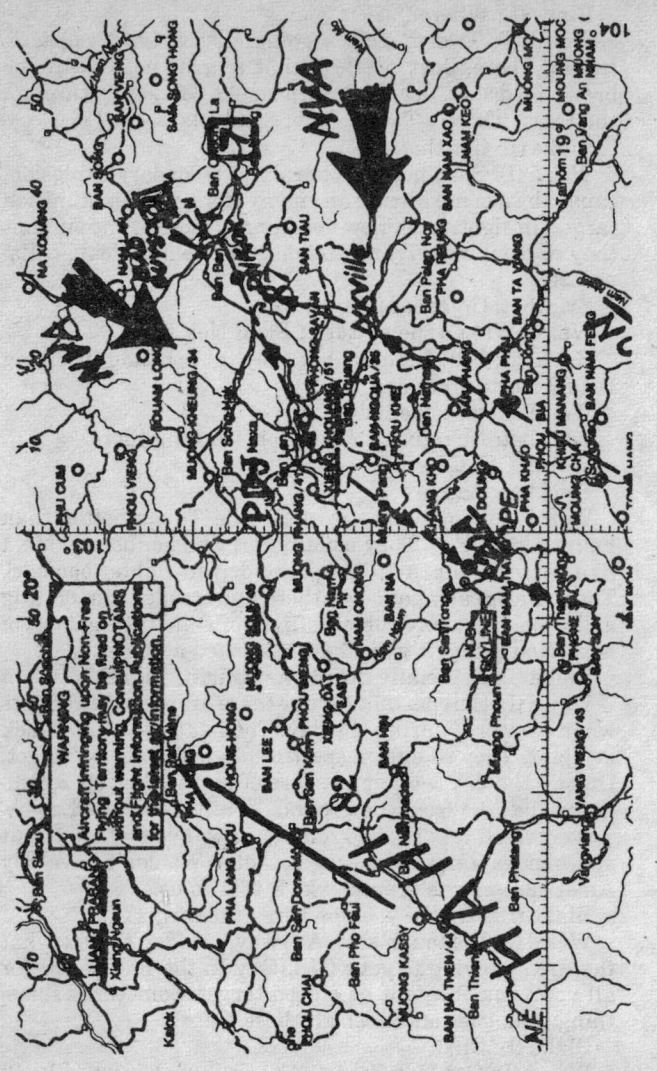

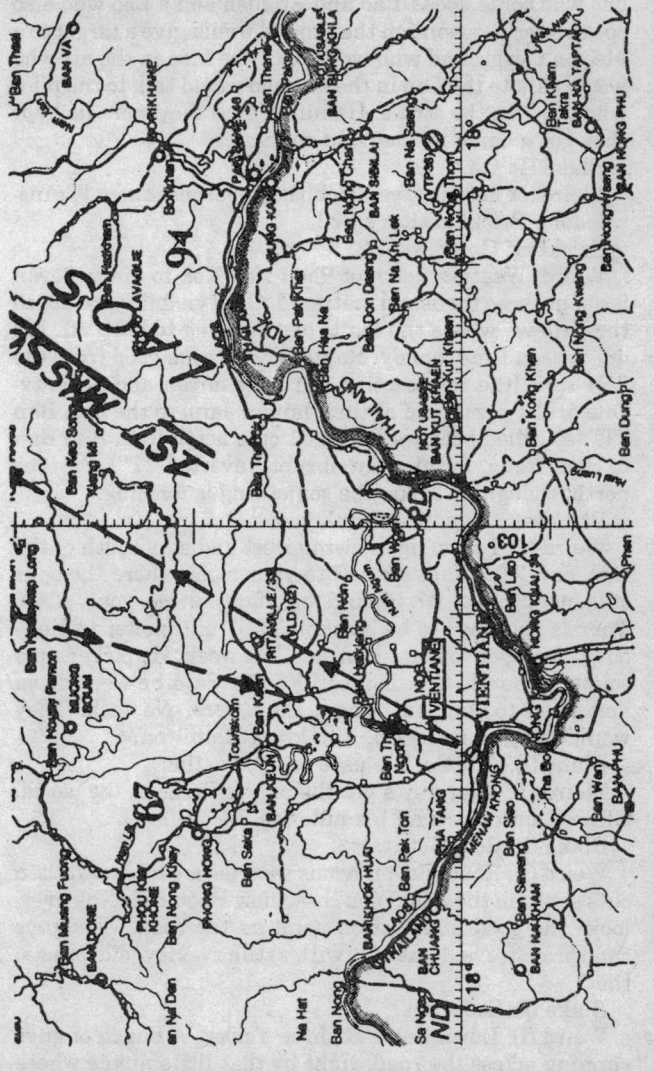

one who could speak Lao and English and a Lao who also spoke Meo. Someone on the ground would give a target to a Meo on the ground who would call the Meo in the air who would talk to the Lao in the air who would talk to the pilot who'd call in the strike. Hamilton says they were lucky if they got a bomb in the right country.

Blake (I): Oh.

Weird (I): Let me give Brickbat a weather report. [Transmission]: Brickbat, Raven 22.

Brickbat: Go ahead, 22.

Weird: Weather north of Phou Nok Kok to Route Seven is about three thousand scattered. Good visibility except in the valleys, where the fog is just starting to burn off. It's dry season time, buddy. Route Seven looks good from the 7/71 split [the intersection of routes Seven and Seventy-One at the north end of the Plain of Jars] to the Ban Ban "T" [so called because Route 61 cuts north from Ban Ban to Sam Neua, forming an abrupt, inverted "T"]. Farther north, though, it looks like something is forming.

Brickbat: Copy, 22—thank you.

Weird (I): I'm going to swing west and stay south of the Ban Ban "T." That's it, off to your right where the spur cuts north. See it? Should be right under your strut. There's supposed to be a couple of 37 millimeter triple-A down there, or so Hamilton said last week. He picked up a couple of bursts that looked like 37s. Said he went down and tried to find out where they were. No luck. They wouldn't come up again. You know Hamilton?

Blake (I): A little. We used to fly together.

Weird (I): That guy's got the biggest balls in the world. Either that or he's off his nut. See the "T"?

Blake (I): Rog. Got it.

Weird (I): Route Seven heads west for a while now, then cuts south to the PDJ. You'll see how Phou Nok Kok overlooks the good interdiction point on the road. VP's guys can spray the hell out of it with artillery. Hey, did you see that?

Blake (I): See what?

Weird (I): Down there at three o'clock. A bunch of guys running across the road, right by that little nipple where the road bends.

Blake (I): I don't see anything. Where? That place where the little trail comes in?

Weird (I): Just west about a click. See? They came from where that little nipple points into that couple of acre clearing. Shit, there must have been thirty of them. They were dragging something across the road.

Blake (I): I still don't see them.

Weird: Brickbat, Brickbat, Raven 22.

Brickbat: Go ahead, Raven 22.

Weird: Brickbat, we got any friendlies about five clicks west of the Ban Ban T? No villages in the area.

Brickbat [a different voice]: Negative, Raven. It's a free strike zone.

Weird: What you got available, Brickbat? I got a bunch of troops in the open along the road.

Brickbat [original voice]: I got Dombey flight of four F-4s. What's your position?

Weird: Just south of the "T."

Brickbat: Can you use them in five minutes?

Weird: Shit hot. Give 'em to me.

Brickbat: Say again, Raven 22.

Weird: Affirmative, affirmative. Have them come up my frequency.

Blake (I): The road looks perfectly clear now.

Weird (I): I know it. They're all back in the trees wondering if we saw them. OK to put in a strike?

Blake (I): If you say so. Want me to watch for groundfire?

Weird (I): Shit hot.

Dombey Lead: Raven 22, this is Dombey Lead, over.

Weird: Dombey, Raven 22. Rendezvous 050 at 52 [a point bearing fifty degrees from a radio navigational facility fifty-two miles away]. Your target will be troops and possible storage. Target elevation 3100 feet—weather three thousand scattered with a light haze. Negative observed surface winds. Negative reported groundfire. What's your lineup? ["What ordnance are you carrying?"]

Dombey Lead: Mark 82s and pistols. Got the numbers. ["500 pound bombs and a gun pod. Understand your instructions."]

Weird: No CBUs [Cluster Bomb Units (anti-personnel bombs)]? No nape [napalm]?

Dombey Lead: Negative. Just the little old iron bombs.

The Laotian Fragments

Weird (I): Shit. That's what I mean. 500 pounders just can't hack it, and that's what they usually send. If the bad guys are listening in, there's a big cheer going up. Damn it all, anyway. What the hell, let's see if we can't disturb them a little anyway.

Blake (I): Fighters at three o'clock, high.

Weird (I): Got 'em.

Dombey Lead: Got you, Raven, my nine o'clock just south of the road. Green 'em up, Dombey ["Select armament position"].

Weird: Tally Ho, Dombey [slang for "I have you in sight"]. Going in to mark. (I) I'm going to put my smoke just north of the road beside that small clearing. OK?

Blake (I): Whatever you say.

Dombey Lead: Got your smoke, Raven. Want us to hit it?

Weird: Lead, aim fifty meters east. I want Two, Three, and Four to each bomb fifty meters from your bombs west down the road. Make your passes from north to south and bomb north of the road. You're cleared in hot.

Dombey Lead: Roger. Lead's in hot. FAC in sight.

Dombey Two: Two's in hot.

Weird: Good bomb, Lead.

Dombey Three: Three's in hot. FAC in sight.

Weird: Keep your spacing, Dombey Two.

[The next few minutes of the tape are almost entirely incomprehensible. Apparently Dombey Four experienced radio failure, and the transmissions overlap too much for accurate transcription. Occasionally phrases such as "hold high and dry," which means "leave the bombing pattern and orbit above us," and "how's that, Raven?" are intelligible, but there is generally nothing but five minutes and thirty seconds of garbled speech.]

Dombey Two: They're shooting at us, Lead.

Weird: Negative, Dombey. That's just impacts from HE [high explosive] (I) Fucking new guy. See anything at all, Bill?

Blake (I): A lot of smoke. Nothing else. Those were impacts from Lead's strafing. Two's pressing too close.

Dombey Lead: Lead's in hot with the gun, last pass.

Dombey Two: Two's in hot.

Dombey Three: Three's in hot, last pass.

Dombey Lead: Dombey flight, join up on Four. He's orbiting south at fifteen thousand.

Dombey Two: Two.

Dombey Three: Three.

Weird: Good shooting, Dombey. Stand by for BDA [Bomb Damage Assessment]. I'll go down and take a look. (I) Watch out for those goddamn 37s, OK?

Blake (I): Rog.

Dombey Lead: OK, Dombey, let's go home.

Weird: Dombey flight, ready to copy BDA?

Dombey Lead: Go ahead, Raven.

Weird: Sorry, have to give you NVR [No Visual Results] due to smoke and haze. 75 percent target coverage—Two was long most of the time. Shook them up a bit, anyway.

Dombey Lead: Copy, NVR and 75 percent. How about some trucks next time, Raven?

Weird (I): Shit, an F-4 couldn't hit a truck standing still on a gunnery range.

Dombey Lead: Hey Weird, how about some trucks?

Weird: Roger, Dombey, I'll try.

Dombey Lead: See you, Weird.

Weird: *Sa-waa-dee, kop* [pidgin Thai/Lao for "Goodbye, sir"].

Blake (I): Who was that? Friend of yours?

Weird (I): Damned if I know. There are so few Ravens that the fighter jocks get to know us, somehow, by our callsigns. Some of the guys talk at the bar when they go south for a party, or something. It's kind of nice, though, not like in-country [South Vietnam] where the whole thing's run by the computer and when they give you a number they really mean it. Tell you what, let's go straight back to Alternate. I'll show you the PDJ and Xieng Khouang, if we still own it after the other night. Watch for the jars. They're neat.

Blake (I): Are those the stone jars?

Weird (I): Rog. The Lao think they're sacred, and even the bad guys won't touch them. I think they were once full of beer, myself. What a frappin' party *that* old king must have had. You want to fly it for a while?

Blake (I): Sure. What's the heading?

Weird (I): Hold one-niner-zero at about eleven thousand.

Better jink a little [climb and descend, with turns, to avoid groundfire] just in case.

Blake (I): Rog.

Weird (I): Well, boss, how'd you like your first Laotian turkey shoot?

Blake (I): Fine—but where were the turkeys?

Weird (I): They were there—somewhere. Where they are now is anybody's guess.

Blake (I): What about giving them some KBA [Killed By Air]? Those guys did cover the area pretty well.

Weird (I): No offense, sir, but I won't do it that way. I won't pass on KBA unless I can count the bodies and they aren't moving. I don't care what headquarters wants, and I don't care what some of the other guys do. There are probably a couple dozen dead guys down there right now, but if you believe the figures that come out of this war, the bad guys are all Chinese by now—we've killed all the Vietnamese, good and bad, in Southeast Asia. Unfortunately, they must be able to fuck faster than we can kill them.

Blake (I): Yeah, and they've shot down all our airplanes, by their figures, so we couldn't have done what we just did.

Weird (I): Right on, *kop*—I see you're getting the idea. That's the way it is. That's the fucking way it is. I think you're going to do all right up here.

Blake (I): It's sort of like . . .

Side 1 of the tape ends here. If side 2 was recorded at this time, it was erased and rerecorded later. Side 2 will be presented below as item 28.

19

Letter from Mrs. Mary Blake to Major William Blake, dated December 20. It is written on light blue, slightly scented Hallmark stationery with the name "Mary," engraved in script, centered near the top of the page. On the accompanying envelope appears the following notation in Major Blake's hand: "Received this on 30 December, a real day of reckoning."

Dear Bill:

I've been trying for weeks not to think about another Christmas, and I've told the boys that the reason we're not able to send you any presents this year is because you won't be able to keep them in your tent. They want to make you some cards anyway, and I'll try to find time to help them. [Marginal comment in Major Blake's hand: "Not received by 21 March. Shit."] I'm sorry, but I just couldn't bring myself to fake another Christmas, and as I tried to decide what would be best, I thought of the many times you used to insist that only the truth would do—so here it is, and I'm sorry—but I think it's best for all of us.

I'm filing for divorce, as soon as I can find out what to do and how to do it.

I know how it looks—husband away at war and all that—but I can't really bring myself to believe that you are at war, just on another one of your trips. It certainly doesn't seem like a war here. I've had a lot of time to think, and honestly, I believe that it will be better for everyone, especially the children, if we call the whole thing off formally. We can't continue pretending that we have a marriage while all the time we're fighting in private, and I know it's only a matter of time until the children begin to notice if we start up where we left off. When things go this bad, sometimes it's best to admit a mistake and just get out.

I don't think I have to go over any of the reasons—maybe it's just that we shouldn't have gotten married in the first place (as you've said so often—remember?)—but we did, and it's time to do something about it. And in case you're wondering, there isn't "someone else," really. I'm just tired of pretending. I don't know when I'm going to tell the boys, but I think I'd better do it myself, so please don't write them anything about it.

I'll write more when I've had a chance to settle down, but I did want to get this off today. It's only fair to all of us that you know the whole story.

I'm sorry, Bill, really.

Love,
Mary

20

Three letters, typewritten on 8× 10½" bond, dated 31 December. Identical texts, addressed to the Wabash Life Insurance Company, the Equitable Life Assurance Society, and the Military Benefit Association. A stamped, addressed envelope is attached to each letter, and it is certain that they were never mailed.

Dear Sir:
Although I do not have my policy in my possession, I would like to amend my beneficiaries as follows: please delete the name of my wife, Mrs. Mary Joseph Blake, and make my children, as listed, my sole beneficiaries, share and share alike.

> Thank you very much,
> [signed] William Blake, Major, USAF

21

Transcript of a tape recording, with title entry, "Blake, 30 Dec. For Mr. Horowitz. Sheila." This transcript is typed in duplicate by an IBM electric on 8½×11" bond with pink copy sheets. It was contained in a standard U.S. Government manila filing folder with a notation on the center tab which reads: "Blake, W./ 404 Augmentee/Sheila."

Mr. Horowitz: Well, how do you do, Mr. Blake. Come in, come in. Come meet my wife. Mary, this is Mr. Blake. Mr. Blake, my wife. And my daughter, Valerie. Val, this is the new Mr. Blake I've been telling you about.

Valerie: Hello, Mr. Blake. And what do you do?

(Note to Mr. H: Here's Val's opening #3. I think she likes him. Sheila.)

Mr. H: Valerie. Come on, dear.

Valerie: I'm sorry, Daddy. It's the first necktie I've seen in three years, and I thought he was someone different. Are you different, Mr. Blake?

Mr. H: Come on, Blake, let me take your jacket. And put your tie in your pocket. Everything's informal up here, even the war.

Blake: Thank you, sir.

Mr. H: *Dawk-mie, ahw coat pie* [Laotian, literally "Flower, take the coat," apparently addressed to a servant]. Let's go out on the terrace for cocktails, shall we? *Dawk-mie, eat bet mong* ["Dinner at eight o'clock"].

Blake: This is certainly a lovely house you have, sir.

Mr. H: Yes, isn't it. One of the rigors of the assignment.

Valerie: It's owned by a Lao Major General who built it with a USAID grant and rents it to Daddy at an exorbitant price to finance his dope smuggling.

Mrs. H: Valerie.

Valeri: Well, it's true, isn't it? Everybody knows it, so why keep quiet about it?

Mr. H: Will a martini suffice, Mr. Blake?

Blake: Thank you, sir. And what do you do, Miss Horowitz?

Valerie: As much as I feel like.

Mr. H: Here's your drink, Mr. Blake. And Valerie, don't monopolize our guest. He's a married man.

Valerie: Are you, Mr. Blake? How married are you?

Mrs. H: Come on, Valerie. Let's see how the kitchen staff is doing.

Mr. H: Don't mind her, Mr. Blake. She's just back from Singapore. She's in graduate school at the University.

Blake: You have a lovely daughter, Mr. Horowitz.

Mr. H: Thank you. I'm afraid there's not much here for a girl of twenty-four to do, especially with the war on.

Blake: Yes, sir.

(Note to Mr. H: Re our telecon on 2 January, I'm deleting at your request all dinner commentary. Mrs. H didn't say much anyway, as usual. I'll file the tape as you asked. Sheila.)

Mr. H: I'm sorry the pool isn't in yet. It's going to be where that big mound of earth is, at the back of the lawn.

It just takes these Lao forever to get anything done. Have you seen that ugly monument in the center of town?

Blake: Yes, sir.

Mr. H: That's a good example. But when they finally do it, it lasts. Take this jar, for instance. No one knows how old it is. Damn, Valerie's been putting her cigarettes out in it.

Blake: Is that from the Plain of Jars?

Mr. H: Right. It's one of the smaller ones. I had a chopper bring it back for me. We never entertain the locals here, so there won't be any flap.

Blake: Then you expect to be here for some time?

Mr. H: I think so. In my position we usually stay for a while, unless the situation or our policy changes drastically. The Congo was a good example of a change. We got out pretty fast there, and most of that team is here now. We've still got a couple of Bay of Pigs people, though, but they're due to leave soon.

Blake: It must be fascinating work.

Mr. H: Oh it is, it is. Why don't you consider working for us, some day, after you retire. Lots of your people do. I wish I could tell you exactly how fascinating our job is, but there are things I can't discuss. Company rules, you know.

Blake: Yes, sir.

Mr. H: But I do want to give you as much background as I can, to make your job easier. We all like to work as a team here. The Country Team, as I'm sure you know. Like in Moore's book [probably *The Country Team*, by Robin Moore].

Blake: I don't think I know that book.

Mr. H: Oh you should, you should. I don't know how they let that one go through. The agency raised hell with us. Luckily, I wasn't in the book. I had another assignment at the time.

Blake: I'll have to get a copy.

Mr. H: Mine's loaned out right now, but check back with me. I require all my new people to read it. No point in making the same mistakes over and over again. So, what do you think of our little war, anyway?

Blake: I really haven't had time to see very much yet.

Mr. H: Hear you got some action today, anyway.

Blake: A little, I suppose. We put in a couple of strikes.

Mr. H: Every little bit helps. I often wish I could get back into the real action. I was a crew chief during World War II, before I got into OSS. But here we're facing a determined enemy with unlimited manpower and supplies, and we've got to keep him off balance while we try and shore up the Royal Lao Government.

Blake: Shore up?

Mr. H: Assist them in maintaining a neutral posture. Without U.S. support at all levels they'd collapse. Same relationship the North Vietnamese and Chinese have with the bad guys. We've come a long way in the past ten years.

Blake: Ten years?

Mr. H: Sure, when we first started training the Meo for guerrilla action. We weren't here before that. You should have seen them then—a bunch of rag-tag tribesmen who believed in spirits and nature gods, with only bows and arrows and some primitive flintlocks. I've got one of their rifles inside, by the way. I swear you'd have to stick it in your target's . . . ear before firing. I'll show it to you. Now they've got modern weapons and know how to call in airpower. That's quite a change, I'd say.

Blake: It certainly is.

Mr. H: Well, tell me about yourself. How did you get into this business?

Blake: I'm a career officer. I volunteered for the job.

Mr. H: Good boy, good boy. Do you mind if I call you Bill?

Blake: Not at all, sir.

Mr. H: Call me Abe. After all, we're both sort of in command around here.

Blake: Yes, sir.

Mr. H: Well, Bill, other than to get acquainted tonight, I did want to find out how I could help you do your job here, so please let me know.

Blake: I certainly will, and believe me, I think I'm going to need a lot of help. I'm doing some background reading now, Dommen, Hilsman, and some others. [For Hilsman, see item 11, above. For Dommen, see item 23, below.]

Mr. H: Oh yes, Dommen and Hilsman. Well, it won't be easy reorganizing things here. Everyone's been doing it his own way for a long time.

Blake: Reorganizing things?

Mr. H: Well, Bill, you know—a new man, change of command, new policies, orders from on high to clean out the rat's nest—you know. You're going to have quite a job, I'd say.

Blake: Frankly, sir, I think it will take my full six months here just to find out what's going on.

Mr. H: You're so right. I've been here or down south a total of five years and I still don't know what's going on all the time. Another martini? It's House of Lords gin, you know. We get it for two dollars a quart here.

(Note to Mr. H: Next hour or so is mainly pre-dinner and dinner chit-chat. If I may say so, I think Major Blake handled Valerie extremely well, which may account for her directness later. He seems like quite a gentleman. Can't wait to meet him—now don't worry—he reminds me of that agent Valerie met just before the Biafran thing. *He* didn't do so good, though, did he, eh? Sheila.)

(The scene: Much later, in the drawing room, with Blake leaning on the piano looking at the beauteous daughter of the chief. At least I think that's where and what. Right? Sometimes, Mr. H, when I do one of these for you I think I'm writing a play. I could do a lot better if you'd invite me over sometime.)

Valerie: That's not all I do beautifully—the piano, I mean.

Blake: I can see that.

Valerie: No you don't. Watch. Time me. I can do the minute waltz in fifty-five seconds.

(Note to Mr. H: According to my timing of the tape, it took her one minute and twenty-one seconds. Sheila.)

Valerie: How did I do?

Blake: Fifty-eight seconds. You must be slipping.

Valerie: Your watch is slow. I hope you aren't. I never slip. I'm the only Dragon Lady around here, didn't you know?

Blake: Oh. I didn't know.

Valerie: Well now you do. Are you really the new Chief Raven? You look so young.

Blake: I work with your father, yes.

Valerie: I see. You're going to play the game. Let me have a sip of your drink. I left mine upstairs when I helped mother with her dress. The big game, except that everybody knows what everybody else is doing, from Mr. Heung at Villay Phone's—he's the best jeweler in town—to the dumbest slope who works in the kitchen. Big game. Honestly, sometimes I think that all you big men are a bunch of comic-book characters. I've got a radio in my room that picks up everything you say when you're flying. So does the other side, I'll bet, but I use mine to decide who's still alive to take me to dinner.

Blake: If it's all so dumb, why do you put up with it? Why don't you just get out?

Valerie: Because I really love it all, you big dummy. What girl wouldn't? Here's poor little me, the daughter of the Big Chief—and I'm not so bad, am I?—and there's a constant flow of neat young men coming every day—the best America has to offer—except they all look alike. Steely blue-eyed and dedicated. The faces never change— only their cock size. *That* got to you, didn't it? But someday there'll be one who's not really married and I'll just woo the shit out of him and he'll take me away from all this and there won't be any bad memories because nobody will ever be able to talk about it. How's that for openers, Mister Chief Raven FAC who has a wife named Mary, the same as my mother's name. Would you like to be my father, too?

Blake: You *are* a bit different, Valerie. Do you tell this to all the boys?

Valerie: Only the FACs. I'm Valerie the FAC fucker, in case you hadn't heard. I haven't missed one yet. No sweat, GI. Me mach-mach mama-san. Me number one [slang for "very great woman—the best"].

Blake: Thanks for the welcome, anyway. Who knows what evil lurks in the hearts of men?

Valerie: Who knows anything around here.

Mrs. H: Here you are. Valerie, please see to the servants. Mr. Black, Mr. Horowitz is on the terrace. Was that Chopin, dear?

Valerie: No, Mother, Dvorak.

Mrs. H: Oh. It sounded like Chopin from upstairs.

Valerie: I thought you were asleep, Mother.

Mrs. H: Well, I couldn't retire without saying good night to our guest, could I? Good night, Mr. Black. Do come again.

Valerie: It's Blake, Mother. And your housecoat is open.

Blake: She seems very nice.

Valerie: She's my mother. Go see Daddy. The Big Chief calls.

Blake: Will I see you later?

Valerie: Probably . . .

Mr. H: Well, Bill, how did you like potluck at the Horowitz Hacienda?

Blake: Fantastic. What was the fish course?

Mr. H: They call it plakaphong. It's a river fish. Don't ask any closer than that. They'll all tell you it's a different kind—sole, snapper, catfish, you name it. Soong, the chief cook, does all our buying at the morning market, except for the steaks, which I have flown up from Saigon on the courier flight. You can't get good beef here, but they've got it at the Saigon commissaries. I've always been afraid to find out what Soon buys. But it's delicious, isn't it?

Blake: Yes, sir.

Mr. H: And cheap, too. Everything's cheap up here, by U.S. standards. And with the Courvoisier you're drinking at three bucks a bottle, it's a good life. A good life.

Blake: I'm beginning to see that.

Mr. H: Good. Well—let me fill up that gaboon you're holding—then we'll get to some business. (Note to Mr. H: I hate to intrude, but I think you got a bit schnocked. Love, Sheila.) What can I do to be of help?

Blake: I don't know. I guess be a little patient for a while.

Mr. H: No problem. I'm used to breaking in new people. Except where my daughter is concerned, ha, ha. You know what I mean, Bill. You're a father too. Our job is to keep all the young men from doing to our daughters what we tried to do to their mothers. Eh? Hah, hah. But she's all we've got, and she's a nice girl.

Blake: Yes, sir. I understand. As far as the job goes, I'm afraid I don't even have the right questions yet.

Mr. H: Well, begin by reading all the pertinent directives. The Attache has them, and do come to next week's Country Team meeting as my guest. The Ambassador will be there, as will the USAID Director, both military attaches, and myself and my staff. You'll see how we play the game.

Blake: How is the war going? I mean, how are we doing.

Mr. H: Not bad, not bad at all. Of course, we could never

do it without airpower. USAF airpower. Never let your Air Force guys forget that, no matter what some of my men say. Just keep 'em coming. It's your support to that valiant little guy on the ground with the rifle which makes all the difference.

Blake: I know, sir. I worked with the ARVN [Army of the Republic of Vietnam].

Mr. H: Not with anything like this army, you didn't. This group reminds me of the early days in Saigon, right after the French left. What a mess. Thank God we've still got people around who've had that kind of experience. Otherwise we'd be in a real mess. But the Lao are coming along a lot faster than the Viets did—I think it's because of our know-how, and here we can start from scratch, right off the water buffalo, as they say. We don't have to make them unlearn all those French tactics which lost them the first war—at the lower levels, at least. And the high-ranking Lao officers who worked for the French aren't really very influential. Do you realize, for instance, that only two officers who were French-trained are still flying combat for the all-powerful, hah-hah, Lao Air Force? The rest are either in staff jobs, exiled, or dead.

Blake: How do they fight? I mean, how are they as soldiers?

Mr. H: Not worth a shit. The lowland Lao aren't worth a shit. They'll run at the sound of a drum. The bad guys, the Pathet Lao, aren't any better, but there aren't many of them left. No, it's boiled down to a confrontation between the guerrilla forces and the North Vietnamese. Now those Meo, our guys, they're something else again. They're not trained by the Army—they're trained by us. All the mountain tribesmen are. They're the Yankees in this war. You're not from the South, I hope. They're damn good, what there are left of them. But the enemy, the North Vietnamese, are really coming on strong this year with conventional tactics—frontal assaults, heavy artillery, tanks, and the like. Our little guys on the mountaintops are in for rough going.

Blake: I saw Phou Nok Kok today.

Mr. H: That's the key position to end all key positions. We call it the "cork in the bottle" leading down to the PDJ. We're going to hold it as long as we can—it's completely surrounded, you know, supplied only by air—and then we're going to fight our way back to the plain, from mountaintop to mountaintop. Head to head, we know we're unable to stop the North Vietnamese if they're willing to pay the price—look at Phou Nok Kok. The bad guys have lost over a thousand men, front-line troops, already. We're going to hold the Plain of Jars for the first time in years. That's what Souvanna wants—he's the Prime Minister. Do you play tennis, by the way? Souvanna does. I'll see about an introduction. You just watch. For the first time in five years.

Blake: It should be quite a dry season.

Mr. H: And you'll be one of the very key men—you and all your FACs. But never forget the guy on the ground. He's the one who counts, and your Lao backseater will be getting his word directly from the man who's doing the real fighting, who's carrying out carefully planned operational orders. Don't go staging any big aerial campaigns to win the war. It can't be done, and it only pisses off the North Vietnamese. Don't do anything you know doesn't come from us. I don't care what Seventh Air Force wants. OK? They don't have the big picture down there, and their war is a different war, and they aren't running the show up here. We take our orders directly from the President. Are you beginning to see what's going on?

Blake: It's an interesting situation.

Mr. H: Call it a bucket of worms, my boy, a bucket of worms. It's the biggest bucket of worms since we helped the Chinese before World War II—that's when I was a good old groundpounding crew chief with Chennault. And this time we don't even have any bubblegum wrappers to help us out. [In the late 1930s, as covert U.S. aid to Chiang Kai-shek became acknowledged, an anti-Japanese propaganda campaign was initiated in the United States, including slogans printed on bubblegum wrappers.] Why, I can remember the planes taking off from Laos to bomb the Japs in Thailand. It's the same thing, almost, but backwards.

Blake: You know, sir, it's getting late, and I'm afraid I'm rather tired.

Mr. H: You'd better call it a bucket of worms, my boy. You'd damn well better, or you won't survive. Let's have one for the road, shall we. I've got an early flight to

Bangkok tomorrow, but I can sleep on the way. Old DEPCHIEF's pissed off about something again—and I've been babbling on a bit too much. Don't quote me on anything I've said. I'll deny it all, and your slender little ass will be so much grass. Savvy?

Blake: Yes, sir. If you don't mind, I'll pass on the brandy. I think I'd better hit the sack.

Mr. H: Fine. My driver will take you back. Valerie can't. If I don't see you before, which I won't, Happy New Year.

Blake: The same to you, sir.

Mr. H: I'll thank Mrs. Horowitz for you. She always takes a nap after dinner. Good night.

Blake: Good night.

(Note to Mr. H: I couldn't resist including this last bit. Honestly, Valerie needs a strong hand—especially from a mother [and I'm not suggesting anything.])

Valerie: Was that our new Mr. Blake leaving? I wanted to show him all those pretty jewels you bought Mother and me.

Mr. H: Yes, that was Mr. Blake leaving, Straight, my dear, to the White Rose, no doubt. And all those lovely ladies.

Valerie: Shit, Daddy, you're too much. You're too goddamn much.

22

Draft copy of teletype message, Horowitz, Vientiane, to Bryan, Washington, 31 December. This message was contained in the same manila folder as item 21 above.

SUBJECT: Blake

Dinner with new Raven last night. Foresee no real problems. Briefed him on as much of our operation as necessary and secured his promise of full cooperation. He has also been briefed by Barnes, who seems to be griping a bit more, and he flew his first mission [here the word "today" appears on the draft but has been lined through in pencil] yesterday. Blake did call Ambassador's secretary today and wants to see him. Don't know whay [*sic*], but suspect he just wants to get to know everybody. Seems to be sincerely aware of the complexities of our operation. A fine young man. Too bad he's married. [The previous sentence is lined through and was probably not transmitted.] New item: Your bracelet mailed yesterday, insured, declared value fifty bucks. OK? Happey [*sic*] New Year. Horowitz.

JANUARY

23

Blake, *Journal*, pp. 38–40.

Saturday, 3 January: Vientiane, Laos. Has it only been a week? God. Took a walk around Vientiane today. Hot. Sun scorching the sidewalks. It's a fascinating city—with gold-engraved temples ("Wats"—in Vietnam they were *nhà thờ*) which are very old and the new sports stadium with its modernistic concrete shelter for the royal family. Looks like a press box. Very calm and peaceful, and at two o'clock in the afternoon almost no one on the streets. Siesta time, they tell me. Strange affinity between Spanish and Oriental cultures.

Ran into dear old dirty-mouthed Valerie at Villay Phone's—now *there's* a jewelry shop. She gave me a reference and I opened a charge account. Mr. Heung (Chinese?) said it was good for either five months or thirty days before I left. Smiling and bowing. How did he know? He's probably a spy too. Different side of Valerie, though. We visited a Wat and went throuth the whole nine yards: shoes off, the incense, the gold leaves on Buddha's belly, even slithering across the floor to a venerable old monk sitting on a raised platform who said, "I shall be delighted to discuss the way with you at any time. Please return soon." Perfect English. Perfect composure. Perfectly bald head. The customs remind me of the Roman Catholic service. Wonder if dear old Mary would ever condescend to enter a Wat. But the priest or monk or whatever looked resplendent in his saffron robes (just like the big panels the ground troops use to mark targets). Weird says the robes are made of seven pieces of cloth—told me the story about the flight surgeon at Udorn who had a housegirl whose brother was a monk. She got him a real outfit, but couldn't tell him how to put it on. A secret. He tried to figure it out but no luck. Called himself the only flight guru in the Air Force, until someone gave him a can of gasoline labeled "Do-It-Yourself Martyr Kit." Very bad joke. Valerie went back home for dinner, or something. She spoke to the cab driver in Lao and we were charged half as much returning as I was coming downtown.

Saturday night in the big city, and here I am all dressed up with no place to go. Some of the guys are at the movie in the big house—the films come to the office and they show them on their living-room wall. Sure beats that stockyards of a movie house at Tan Son Nhut. John Wayne in *Green Berets*. Should draw quite a crowd.

One week gone. 23 to go. How long is 23 weeks in the whole span? Not a hell of a lot. On Monday we'll get to work. Fly one day, desk and staff work the next (Col. Barnes says I can't fly every day like the other Ravens—such is life). But there's a lot to be done, not a little of which will be finding out who works for whom. There's an organizational chart of a few years back, but I don't understand it. Still haven't met any Lao—they seem to be hiding—but Barnes says there are some good ones, along with a few crooks. Gave Barnes my copy of Hilsman (whom he hadn't read); he gave me Dommen, *Conflict in Laos*. Just started.

Reflective time—I suppose the key will be in finding out who's really running the show. Everybody tells me that *I* am, but I don't see how I'm supposed to make any decisions unless I know what the policies are—and nothing's written down. All the chiefs seem to be sincere (in their own way, of course), but sincerity never won a war—if that's what we're supposed to be doing here. I'm used to taking orders from somebody who knows the score. Had a few minutes with the Ambassador yesterday. He seems like a real person, although he's not a military type. Reminds me of a congressman from Iowa—a farm boy who's made it to the big leagues and is determined to stay there for what he firmly believes are the right reasons. He probably wore his wide ties in college and now they're back in style. Redfaced, chubby, cheery. Rumor (Hamilton says) is that he was a Company man in the Congo. Got a bit expansive—fatherly-like—and warned me about trusting military intelligence: "They're too interested in their own image—too PR oriented. The Company is just the opposite. They want to minimize themselves and report only the facts." But I have no reason to fault AF Intell. They do good work. The Company certainly is minimized—then again, with everyone walking around in civilian clothes, you never know who's working for whom. Nobody says "sir," and everyone is on a first-name basis. Ambassador calls us "his" Ravens. Reconstruct his speech: "So your [sic] joining my Ravens, are you? Good. Good. It's men like you who make a nation strong—who will sacrifice anything for their country—who will live in circumstances of danger and privation, unknown, unrecognized, unsung, etc, etc (the etc's are mine). God bless you." I can't say he's wrong. Then he looked at his watch. "Come up and see me anytime." Said I was the first Chief Raven who had ever asked to see him. Interesting guy, much different, Barnes says, from his predecessor, whom everyone called the diplomat's diplomat who suddenly found out he was a commander-in-chief.

I don't want to be hard on anyone—and must, I suppose, learn to tread a line between all. The Ambassador's just one man, but he wields aweful power. Then there's Horowitz—as thin as the Ambassador is round. I wonder where he has his clothes made. Beautiful striped shirts. Seems affable, personable, and entirely dedicated to the Company. I feel sorry for his wife, who just lurks in the background and watches her husband do whatever it is she thinks he does. I'm not entirely sure he likes girls (maybe for Valerie they tried it once and didn't like it), but this may be a hasty impression. His people seem to swear by him, though, and he doesn't take any guff. Barnes says Horowitz has a direct line to Washington, and sometimes he plays one-upmanship on the Ambassador at the Country Team meetings (*Remember:* put Wednesday at nine on calendar). Weird says Valerie's a lousy piece of ass—plays with herself while you're screwing her. Poor girl.

And then there's Barnes. God he's a nice guy, but seems sort of sterile. Hamilton says (hah—the connection is unplanned) that he hasn't got any balls—won't fly, for instance, except in the courier. No combat. What the hell, he's not *that* kind of an operational commander—should he be? At least he'll talk with you, and seems to have a good handle about what's going on. Apparently reads a lot. Collects coins. I wonder what's between him and Horowitz. They just don't seem to hit it off.

Enough. I'm at the point in Dommen where he describes the Russian aid to Laos in '61—there's a switch. Soviet pilots, who only speak Russian, trying to train the Lao, who speak French, and the U.S. pays for the gasoline. I'd love to talk to some of the Lao who got "trained." Think I'll read for a while. Tomorrow, believe it or not, is a full day off. I wonder what the bad guys are doing—and who Valerie is screwing—tonight.

24

Teletype message, 7AF (Seventh Air Force), Saigon to OUSAIRA, Vientiane, 3 January.

REF: Your msg [message] 24 Dec.
SUBJECT: Air Support

1. Reference your request of 241645ZDec, know that this headquarters will support all your requests for CAS [Close Air Support] as resources permit. No change, repeat, no change is expected in our policy to provide maximum protection for friendly forces on an as-needed basis,

subject to proper requests and justification. Due to our many other commitments, however, we cannot guarantee unlimited resources.

2. As you know, we support the overall war in Southeast Asia, of which the Laos effort is but a small part. Our activities along the Trail and in the Republic of South Vietnam require particular coordination and advance planning for successful targeting and mission accomplishment. Therefore, to insure proper flexibility of response we must allocate according to our OPLAN [Operations Plan]. Of course, if a major and decisive engagement ensues, we will offer all available air directed from our resources to yours.

3. You should make maximum effort to utilize present forces—with proper targeting provided for the gunships at night. We are particularly pleased with the large gunship KBA figures in conjunction with the latest operations, and are convinced that the enemy was badly hurt as a result of the teamwork which we have utilized. If you can keep this up, it should be a good dry season.

Attached to this message is a note from Colonel Barnes to Major Blake: "This means we don't get the additional sorties we asked for. And remind me to show you where all those Spooky [AC-47 gunship] KBA figures came from. Plan accordingly."

25

Teletype message, AOC 20A to OUSAIRA, Vientiane, 5 January.

SUBJECT: Weekly Operations Report

1. Highlights of this week included the preparations for the Prime Minister's visit and a general slackening of enemy activity following the sapper attack on Xieng Khouang. The troups are ready—for Souvanna, at least. There was a minor hassle over who would be the primary

honor guard, the Meo, the FAR [*Forces Armées Régulières*, Lao regular forces], or the Neutralists. No one knew whether the Neuts would arrive in time to provide a show, but they did, looking green from the flight and thoroughly unhappy to be so near the front lines. The Meo lounged on the perimeter of the airstrip trying to keep their hair out of their eyes, while the FAR stood in ranks polishing their belt buckles. Souvanna's public relations officer solved the problem by stating that the Prime Minister was a Neutralist, therefore the Neuts would welcome him first. So done. We will expect the group on Tuesday, and request that all MRII Ravens be airborne by 0700 and that Brickbat be instructed to divert all sorties if anything develops.

2. Phou Nok Kok has been strangely quiet, except for the almost constant DK-82 shelling at night. To date 482 NVA bodies have been counted at the wire, and yesterday Lt. Vangsana ordered two patrols out past the defenses. They returned after thirty minutes and reported that they saw no one and that the stench from the dead NVA was very bad. Aerial supply working well with Company choppers able to utilize landing pads two and three without coming under fire.

3. However, repeat, however . . . the boys are getting tired. Apparently Company has been unsuccessful in getting FAR troops to replace the SGUs [Special Guerrilla Units—Meo tribesmen]. Lt. Vangsana is twenty-one years old, an ancient compared to his troops, and he has been on the line for two weeks without a break. Request all assistance in obtaining replacements. You might even send them the heater you keep promising us. It gets colder up there.

4. Also, the weather is unusual. Much more haze, much more smoke. Rumor is that the enemy is setting fires, which adds to the usual smoke as the farmers burn off fields this time of year. Ask the weather boys for a climatic forecast. Sometimes visibility is near zero over target, or so the FACs tell me. [Marginal note in black ink: "Bullshit, Hamilton, you were up there yourself."]

5. Finally, a matter of protocol. There's a bauci [farewell party] being given next week by the little guys for one of the Company men. Who pays for the scotch? Us or the

Company? Reply soonest. It's a matter of supply as well as principle. Hamilton.

26

Article from the Bangkok *Herald* (English-language edition), January 5, p. 3. The headline reads: "Laotian PM Cancels Visit to Plaine."

Despite advance assurances, Prince Souvanna Phouma today canceled his projected visit to Xieng Khouang and Muong Soui, situated in the Plain of Jars. No reason was given, and spokesmen in Vientiane quoted the Prime Minister as saying that the programme for defense was unchanged. "According to the 1962 Geneva accords," said Souvanna, "the Plaine des Jarres belongs to the Royal Lao Government. We have simply taken back what belongs to us, and we are going to hold it."

Privately, government officials expressed concern about the Prime Minister's safety on such a trip. According to some sources, the flow of wounded from Phou Nok Kok, a government outpost to the north of the Plain, is increasing as the rebels exert more pressure. A rumor that General Vang Pao, the overall Lao commander, had visited key officials in Thailand was denied. From the war zone, an official Laotian release confirmed that two government T-28 fighter bombers failed to return from a mission yesterday. A search effort is continuing.

27

Letter in feminine handwriting, white airmail stationery, no envelope attached, no date. In the upper right-hand corner is written "Sunday PM."

My dear, dear William:

I knew you'd be back, but God I'm sorry. And after all these years. You always were a silly ass. Do you remember the time you asked me to marry you and I said no, and then a few months later I asked you? Do you remember what you said?

No matter. We're a lot older now (were we only 21?). I'm fatter (three children)—so is Mike, probably from all that good food he gets on his trips (he's away tonight, and I've had a steamy bath and I'm in a neat negligee and I'm writing you for the first time in sixteen years). That night I got drunk and called you up and your wife answered doesn't count.

Anyway—what can I say? That I sympathize? That I agree? You know I don't—not about a divorce for you. It's wrong, and don't ask me why. You know I'll meet you anywhere, anytime, but there is still something sacred about the vows. When I told Mike "I do"—I meant it. Silly me, but that's it. Once you make a commitment like that, you stick to it. So please don't ask anything of me (not that I think you would).

This may not be making too much sense. Forgive me, but your letter came as a great surprise—like out of the past, so to speak, and neither of us can forget the past. There were just too many good times (and I'll confess to still having the tape we made one night. Remember?). I wish Thailand weren't so far away (I called a friend at the Air Base and he told me where the APO number was—see how smart I've become?). I didn't think anyone was really flying out of Thailand.

But I do want to hear from you—and write you—and when you come back through California I want to see you. Keep using Mother's address (she still likes you best), and don't worry about Mike. We get along—that's about all—but we go our own ways. I hope he's got a wench somewhere—I really do.

I won't bore you with details about my children—they're girls, 8, 6, and 4—and one of them looks just like you (I know it's impossible). But they're darlings—spoiled rotten (and they haven't *ever* been spanked. So *there!*). If you remember, they'd love a trinket or two

The Laotian Fragments

from the Orient. I'll tell them you're a long lost uncle—which you really are.

In the meantime, please don't let that witch divorce you, and I'm not speaking only as a Catholic. Perhaps from your point of view, God might understand, but *I* wouldn't.

Hope you had a happy New Year, and I'll always love you. More soon.

Me

28

Tape recording, Sony cassette, dated 7 January. This is the other side of the tape transcribed as item 18.

Hamilton (I): . . . Jackson getting his ass shot down. That queered it then, and the word came out that OAC commanders would refrain from further aerial combat.

Blake (I): You're waxing poetic, old buddy.

Hamilton (I): You were the poet. You did the classbook.

Blake (I): I wouldn't call that much of a poem.

Hamilton (I): How many missions you got now?

Blake (I): About two hundred.

Hamilton (I): I mean up here.

Blake (I): This is my fourth.

Hamilton (I): Getting to know the area?

Blake (I): Sort of.

Hamilton (I): There's no substitute for experience. Now, about today. I want to show you something. Just treat me like any old backseater, OK? But I'll find you a target that won't quit.

Blake (I): By the way, how'd you get on this mission anyway? Not that I mind.

Hamilton (I): It's a long story. Like years. I just saw your name on the frag [fragmentation order—the daily flying schedule] and asked VP to let me go instead of the regular GIB. Our rendezvous is 030 at 30 miles. VP gave me a special target. It's near his cousin's farm.

Blake (I): That's between Phou Nok Kok and the PDJ.

Hamilton (I): Roger that.

Blake (I): I thought the bad guys were north and east.

Hamilton (I): Shit, they're everywhere. Let me tell you something. This war looks different on paper than it really is. You can draw all the arrows and write all the numbers you want, but you never really know. It makes Vietnam look like child's play, and personally, I don't believe there are any more NVA here this year than there were last, or the year before that, or before that.

Blake (I): Then how come everybody else thinks so?

Hamilton (I): It's the nature of the beast. If we kill three thousand, say, by the numbers, then in order for the bad guys to keep fighting as well as they do, they have to replace them, right? And in order to do that, they'd have to bring in new guys, at least on paper. Right? If it happened to us, we'd be pissed off and double our forces. Right? So we think they do, and the whole thing goes from there. The more enemy we say we kill, the more we have to believe they're bringing in. It's really just a nice little war, no matter what anybody says.

Blake (I): Oh. But what about the new division that's been spotted.

Hamilton (I): Damned if I know about that. Maybe they just want us to think they're replacing people. Maybe the best thing here is just to do your job as you see it, let someone else put together the big picture, and hope you don't get caught.

Blake (I): You've got a point, Dante.

Hamilton (I): Yeah. We're coming up on the PDJ now. How are you fixed on the Lima 22 defensive positions?

Blake (I): I've got a general idea.

Hamilton (I): Let's go down and take a look. You'd better know them by heart. You'll be putting in strikes within fifty meters.

Blake (I): You think they'll hit in force?

Hamilton (I): They'll make a lot of noise. VP knows this, and he's planning for it.

Blake (I): Can he hold?

Hamilton (I): Hell no, and he doesn't want to, either. He'll run like hell back to Long Tieng. To save his troops. He hasn't got that many left. He'll make his Custer's last stand there.

Blake (I): What about the Prime Minister's statement about holding the PDJ?

Hamilton (I): That's what the Prime Minister *says* he wants. What he'll take is something else again.

Blake (I): But Horowitz says VP told him he was going to hold.

Hamilton (I): Maybe he did, or maybe that's what the Ambassador told Horowitz he thought VP meant.

Blake (I): Yeah, but Barnes requested additional sorties for a static defense.

Hamilton (I): Barnes. Shit. He used to get good information from me, but he wouldn't believe it. He goes on what his intell people in Vientiane tell him, and they get a lot of their stuff from Seventh Air Force, who gets it from somewhere else, I guess. No, you've got to know the people here to understand what's what.

Blake (I): I understand the Company has a withdrawal plan.

Hamilton (I): Sure they do, but VP won't buy it, not if it costs him some men. But he won't tell Horowitz that. And, anyway, Horowitz won't show it to Barnes until it's too late, because of Company policy. A year or so ago they planned a joint maneuver with about a hundred USAF sorties. Blew the hell out of the place—and when the SGUs went in, there hadn't been any bad guys there for a week. Horowitz blames USAF for compromising security somewhere down the line; USAF said it must have been the locals; and I don't know where the problem was. The little guys talk to each other, that much I know, and neither side likes a really big fight. It's like the Lao commander at Savannakhet said the other day to that newspaperman from Bangkok: "We had a nice friendly little war going here until the Americans and the North Vietnamese came in and showed us how to kill lots of people."

Blake (I): So where do you stand?

Hamilton (I): I'm just doing my job. My job is to work with the little guys—the good little guys as opposed to the bad little guys—in guerrilla operations. You handle the fast birds with the big bombs—me, I like the T-28s. You'll see.

Blake (I): I'm not fragged for T-28s today.

Hamilton (I): No sweat. You will be. Just watch. It'll be

kind of informal, but you'll see. Now, let me have the bird for a minute, OK? That's Lima 22, otherwise known as Xieng Khouang. See the runway going north and south? The bomb dump's at the south end—those are new bombs, brought in after the sapper attack. Those four tin-roofed buildings are messing and storage. Nobody lives in them. All the soldiers are in bunkers beside the gun emplacements. See the guns? The 105s?

Blake (I): Rog. They're spaced about what, a hundred meters apart?

Hamilton (I): Right. And between them is the inner perimeter. See the trench snaking around?

Blake (I): Right.

Hamilton (I): Now look outside the perimeter about three hundred meters. That's the outer wire and trenches. Everything beyond that is booby-trapped—there are mine fields—and those howitzers can be brought to bear in almost a three sixty degree arc. Note how flat it is for two or three miles around. About the only bad place is that little ridge to the northeast, about a mile out, but there's a couple of companies up there to keep watch. See any airplanes?

Blake (I): Negative.

Hamilton (I): Let's go down and see what's what.

Blake (I): I don't see anyone down there.

Hamilton (I): You will. Here we go. We'll make this run from south to north. Notice how the runway has been lengthened. PSP [Pierced Steel Planking] and some packed dirt for overruns. See the little guys come out of their holes?

Blake (I): They're like spiders. Look at them wave.

Hamilton (I): They love American airplanes. They feel safe when we're around. God help them if we ever go home.

Blake (I): That guy with the big floppy hat's shooting, Dante.

Hamilton (I): Sure, straight up. It's their way of saying hello.

Blake (I): Christ, there are hundreds of them.

Hamilton (I): Right. Watch them wave when I rock my wings.

Blake (I): Shit hot.

Hamilton (I): See the tanks—or what's left of them?

The Laotian Fragments

Blake (I): Roger.

Hamilton (I): Sorry, I touched the runway. Do I get to log a landing? It's like being back in Florida, checking guys out from the back seat.

Blake (I): We better get to work. I'll take the airplane.

Hamilton (I): Your bird. It's trimmed nose up. By the way, when are you going for your T-28 checkout?

Blake (I): Thursday, I think. It'll take a few days.

Hamilton (I): Let me know if you want me to help. I'm current as an IP. For test hops, you know.

Blake (I): Thanks. Where to now?

Hamilton (I): Head about 020, level at nine thousand. We'll be going up Route Seven just north of the 7/71 split, where the valley starts to narrow. VP says his cousin told him there's a storage area nearby and "many many bad guys." It's south of the big interdiction point on Route Seven where the Thuds have been blowing up all those trees.

Blake (I): I'd better check in with Brickbat.

Hamilton (I): Rog. Suggest you tell them you don't want any U.S. fighters until after ten o'clock. It's nine now, and it'll take us about half an hour to get there.

Blake (I): OK.

[Apparently Blake turned off his recorder at this point.]

Hamilton (I): . . . Lao T-28s. Those guys are Meo, Bill, not American. That's why they didn't call us. We're on their freq now—you can hear them talking [the transmissions in Meo are garbled and untranslatable]. There may be a ground patrol out. They don't call Brickbat at all. Their targets are usually given to them before they take off, like today.

Blake (I): Then what are we doing here?

Hamilton (I): You'll see. The Lao don't have any FACs. They had one, once. We trained him and then his daddy, General Somebody, said he couldn't fly combat. Word is that he busted his ass on a night opium run. When VP told me about this target, I had a hunch. That's why I asked him if I could bring you up here. I told him all about you. He said OK. Now watch. See that karst outcropping beside the stream, just to the west of the road? See the cave mouth?

Blake (I): Yeah. That karst looks about a hundred feet

tall. Might be fun to do some rock-climbing. It's sheer enough.

Hamilton (I): Sure would, after the war. See the tire tracks going across the stream bed? VP's cousin said someone reported that the stream was muddy the night before last, so they must have been driving across it into the cave.

Blake (I): I don't think I would have spotted that if I was just VRing [slang for Visual Reconnaissance].

Hamilton (I): Roger that. That's one of the problems up here. Most of the time you won't see anything until they start shooting at you, and they don't do that unless they think you've spotted them. That's why you've got to stay down in the weeds so much. To get any action, you've usually got to go trolling for it. Now, watch. There goes Lead in. He'll try to put his bomb in the cave mouth.

Blake (I): Christ he's low.

Hamilton (I): They'll get lower. You just watch. Damn, he's a hundred meters off. It's Vongsaly. He owes me a beer, at least. There goes Two.

Blake (I): They look like little toys, compared to the USAF birds.

Hamilton (I): They sure do, but they do good work. Some of them, that is. Vongsaly's got over two thousand combat missions. He wears six Buddhas around his neck, plus a Saint Christopher I gave him. I told him it was a super-round-eye good luck Buddha. There he goes. See? Three laid it right on the cave mouth.

Blake (I): Sure did, but he'd better watch for blast damage. He was right on the deck. Hey, Dante? Look up there across the stream, where Lead's bomb hit. What do you see? There, in the trees beside the stream. Something's shining.

Hamilton (I): I see what you mean. Let's take a look.

Blake (I): What about the T-28s.

Hamilton (I): No sweat. I'll call them. [Transmission]: Eagle Blue Lead, Eagle Blue Lead, this Mr. Dante. Hold high-dry one minute.

Eagle Blue Lead: OK. OK [followed by speech in Meo dialect].

Hamilton (I): You're right, Bill. See the tracks going along the stream, under the trees. Oh shit, we got a live one, babes. Look at the camouflage netting.

Blake (I): Yeah. And there are a couple of huts, or something.

Hamilton (I): There's more than a couple. Jink like hell, babes, they're shooting. That's ZPU, too [approximately .50 caliber antiaircraft fire].

Blake (I): Rog. Shit, here comes Eagle Blue in.

Hamilton (I): Rog. His minute's up. Look out for the others.

Blake (I): Tell them to wait until we get out of here.

Hamilton (I): Too late Ziggy a little bit to the right of the road, there, and cob this old mother. They'll start shooting at the T-28s.

Blake (I): They're dropping in salvo. Lead just dropped three bombs.

Hamilton (I): They'll do that when they're getting shot at. Look. Look. There must be ten vehicles down there. I count six trucks and . . .

Blake (I): Is that a tank?

Hamilton (I): You bet your sweet ass it is. Look at those guys run around. Four is off. Good bombing, guys. Good bombing. Look, he got one. There goes the gas tank. Come on, trucks, blow. Shit, they're not catching. And that goddamn tank's just sitting there.

Blake: Brickbat, Brickbat, Raven 01, over.

Brickbat: Roger, 01, go ahead.

Blake (I): Give me the coordinates, Dante.

Hamilton (I): Shit hot, Bill. TG870105.

Hamilton (I): Rendezvous 020 at 35.

Blake: Brickbat, Rendezvous 020 at 35.

Brickbat: Roger, Raven 01. What's your target? I've got two Thuds fragged for the IDP [Interdiction Point].

Hamilton: They got 2000 pounders?

Blake (I): Better let me talk, Dante.

Hamilton (I): Sorry.

Brickbat: That's affirm, Raven. 2000 pounders. Say your target.

Blake: Looks like a big storage complex, Brickbat. And a tank.

Brickbat: Understand. Storage complex and tank. I'll see if I can get authority to divert. And there's a flight of F-4s due your area in fifteen minutes. Stand by.

Blake: Raven 01, standing by.

Hamilton (I): Stand by, shit. We may have to get approval all the way from Saigon to get those Thuds off that interdiction point. Keep jinking, babes. They may have some bigger guns down there—with all those trucks. Look at that mother burn, will you. And there's almost no wind.

Blake (I): Yeah. The black smoke is coming straight up.

Hamilton (I): Rog. They'll be trying to put out the fire. Can you see them?

Blake (I): Negative. We're too high now. I'm going to stay this side of the ridgeline.

Hamilton (I): Let's go back down, babes. They may move that tank.

Blake (I): Nope. Not this time.

Hamilton (I): Well shit. Let's cross to the south, anyway, about a mile south.

Blake (I): OK.

Brickbat: Raven 01, Brickbat. Two Thuds, Gordo flight, channel 12. Good luck.

Hamilton (I): Shit hot.

Blake: Roger, Brickbat. Channel 12. Gordo Lead, Raven 01.

Gordo Lead: Go ahead, Raven. Is that you just south of that column of smoke?

Blake: Affirmative, Gordo. Your target's right on that smoke. Want me to put in a mark?

Gordo: Negative, Raven. Give me the numbers.

Hamilton (I): Want me to do it? I know the area.

Blake (I): Go ahead, Dante.

Hamilton: Roger, Gordo, your target elevation is 3850 feet, negative wind, altimeter 30.01. Make your passes from south to north about a hundred meters left of the north-south road. Aim for the base of the smoke. Drop singles. We saw some ZPU and small arms fire a few minutes ago, so watch your ass. And get that tank.

Gordo: Shit hot, Raven. All set, Two?

Gordo Two: Sure am, George. Sure beats making matchsticks. Want to put some money on this one?

Gordo Lead: You're on, babes. Lead's in hot, FAC in sight.

Hamilton (I): Come on, Gordo. Down the chute. There he goes, he's released. Look at that beautiful big bomb. Shit hot. Shit hot. Boom. Christ, look at those secondaries.

The Laotian Fragments

Blake: Gordo Two, bomb a little north—about fifty meters.

Gordo Two: Rog. Two's in hot.

Gordo Lead: Raven, you want me to go after that cave? They're shooting at us from it.

Blake: Negative, Gordo, not this pass. You can strafe it next. Just cover the area where all the fires are.

Gordo: Roger, Raven. Lead's in hot.

Blake (I): Shit, Dante, they're really hosing the Thuds down.

Hamilton (I): Ain't like in-country, is it? If they've got a 37 millimeter in that cave, we'll have some fun.

Blake (I): It looks like there's somebody shooting from every tree.

Hamilton (I): They probably are. VP's cousin was right. This is a big one. The little guys started something here, didn't they? Look at that! Two, three, four secondaries from Two's bomb. Look at that big beauty peel back the trees. I wish we had more of them.

Gordo Lead: Lead's in hot for strafe. How about that cave, Raven?

Blake: OK, Gordo. Go get it.

Gordo Two: I'll work up and down the stream. They were shooting from there.

Blake: Roger, Gordo. Spray it around.

Hamilton (I): Look at that shooting. He's walked that twenty mike mike [20 millimeter cannon] right in the cave mouth.

Gordo Two: Shit, Lead, I can't see anything with all this smoke.

Gordo Lead: No sweat, Two. Just cover the area. I got the guys in the cave. Lead's off, going high and dry. Hey, Two, you really hit something. There goes another secondary.

Gordo Two: Two's off for joinup. Check me over, Lead, I felt something go thump on that last pass. Systems are all good.

Gordo Lead: Roger, Two. I'm at your ten o'clock high, left orbit.

Gordo Two: Gotcha. Be right there.

Hamilton (I): Did you see Two get hit?

Blake (I): Negative. He was right in the smoke as he pulled off.

Hamilton (I): Let's go down for a BDA check.

Blake (I): Negative. There's too much smoke and haze right now. I'll give him some secondaries and NVR.

Hamilton (I): Don't do that, Bill. They got the trucks and maybe the tank, too. Come on, let's go down and see. Maybe they won't shoot at us. They don't know who else we've got up here.

Blake (I): I'm not worried about getting shot at, Dante, if that's what you mean.

Hamilton (I): Sorry. I suppose you're right. We'll have the next Raven check it out. We're getting a bit skosh [low] on fuel, anyway.

Gordo Lead: Hey, Two, guess what? You got a couple of three-inch holes in your slab [horizontal stabilizer]. Any control problems?

Gordo Two: Negative.

Gordo Lead: OK. Let's go home. I'll fly your wing and keep an eye out. Hey, Raven, how about some BDA?

Blake: Roger, Gordo, I'll give you 100 percent of target coverage, unknown KBA, at least four trucks destroyed and one tank probably damaged. We'll get a follow-up ASAP and forward it through Brickbat.

Gordo Lead: Copy BDA. Who won the bet?

Blake: You both did. Good shooting.

Gordo Lead: Thanks for the target, babes. See you again, I hope. Good day, sir. And you too, Dante.

Blake: Good day.

Hamilton (I): See? Now there's a target for you. It's too bad they aren't all like that. We might even win the war.

Blake (I): That's for sure. Look, there must be at least seven different fires down there, and that black smoke is up to at least ten thousand feet.

Hamilton (I): Welcome to the war in Laos, buddy.

Raven 53: Raven 01, this is 53, over.

Blake: Roger 53, go ahead. What are you doing up here?

Raven 53: Raven 53 is just leaving the PDJ heading north. Brickbat says you got something going. My area was quiet.

Blake: OK, 53. Head for the big smoke north of the 7/71 split. It's all yours. And don't drag your scarf on the karst, David.

Raven 53: Rog, Bill. What's the target?

Blake: It's a VP special. There's a cave and . . . [tape ends].

29

Blake, *Journal*, pp. 40–41.

7 Jan. Got down from the big show today, reported to Barnes, and while waiting, read a ten-day-old *New York Times*. Peace talks still stalled. President Thieu quoted as saying that the enemy would not negotiate seriously in Paris so long as he was in a weak position on the battlefield. Then he said that the "Communists have decided to continue the war and to launch another general offensive in the near future." Wonder if he's talking about there or here—or both? Wonder how much he knows about what happens in Laos? Or how much he cares?

30

Article from *Time*, no date, with heavy annotation in Major Blake's hand. The article, headed "Laos/The Tiger in the Pagoda," was cut out and pasted to page 41 of the *Journal*. Major Blake has underlined in green felt pen and written marginalia in black ink. In the excerpt reproduced below, the editor has indicated Major Blake's running commentary in parentheses.

The seldom reported war in Laos (Bullshit. Read your competitors and a couple of good books) ebbs and flows with the seasons (like the Mekong). In dry weather (which we're supposed to have now), the Communist Pathet Lao and their North Vietnamese allies go on the offensive. (I wonder if our delegation to the Peace talks has a meteorologist assigned to it?) During the monsoon rains, the more mobile Royal Laotian Army is trucked (Bullshit—the trucks can't move in all that mud) or helicoptered (that's better) into battle and usually regains what has been previously lost.

The scenario was rewritten last spring (Note the passive voice here. The implication is that no one wrote it beforehand but that it was recorded as it occurred) when the Communists mounted an unprecedented monsoon offensive, captured the town of Muong Soui and threatened to drive all the way to the Mekong River. (Threatened—no. They said that all they wanted then was Muong Soui itself.) Now the scenario has been modified further (more passive voice). In an operation launched amidst extraordinary secrecy (I'll say. It was so secret we didn't know what was going to happen either), Royal Laotian troops mounted a two-pronged attack against the Plain of Jars in the northeast, and against Communist units guarding the Ho Chi Minh trail in central Laos. ("two-pronged attack"? Oh come on now, *Time*. That's like saying the trail is a superhighway.) Last week, for the first time in five years, government forces were in control of part of the broad Plain of Jars (Bullshit! If the RLG troops didn't control part of it last year, how could they have lost it to the NVA?), so called because of the many funeral jars on the area's tombs. (Here's a good example: the jars exist, true, but where are the "tombs"? To some *Time* stringer, the presence of "funeral" jars means that there just have to be tombs somewhere around—ergo, they appear in the article, just like the other "facts.") Preceding the offensive was an intensive (note the rhyme) rain of bombs from Thai-based U.S. planes, which have turned the whole region into a "free-fire zone," where anything that moves is considered fair game. (Boy do I ever wish this were true, from a strictly military sense, that is. *Time* is a master at the qualifying adjective—"unprecedented . . . intensive," etc. They're way off base.) A woman refugee (Aha! The source of information surfaces) from Mahaxay said the town had emptied so completely because of the bombing (nuts—it's because of the *war*) that a tiger had taken up residence in the ruins of the main pagoda. (Beautiful symbol—also the controlling metaphor—and a *beautiful* innuendo: the implication is that the U.S. bombing destroyed the pagoda. Absolute, utter bullshit. I've seen that pagoda, and it was considered "ruins" a hundred years ago. *Time* marches on.)

The government advance met only light opposition, suggesting (not proving, mind you) either that the offensive surprised the Communists or that they had pulled back to avoid the lethal air attack. (Now what does *this* mean? How can you pull back to avoid a lethal air attack if you don't know it's coming because of the "extraordinary secrecy"? Here's where I stop reading. This is as bad as some of our "official" reports. Sheer poetry. Either . . . or. Black—white. Damn it, *Time,* what if—just what *if* the NVA fucked up and sent a lot of troops home for their promised R&R, not thinking we'd "attack," just as we didn't think *they'd* attack last spring. And what *if* there were so few real fighting bad guys (the Pathet Lao don't count, Horowitz says) that the good guys just walked in, as Hamilton thinks. Eh what? This is what I get, I suppose, for picking up an old magazine while sitting on the crapper. I don't want to be unkind—these guys are trying, I suppose—but they seem as if they're writing in the blind—one eye covered for them by the secrecy, the other one blocked by their own preconceptions. You've got to read between the lines, no matter who's telling the story, to understand what's going on in Southeast Asia.)

The article continues with a brief résumé of the traditional political instability of Laos and ends with this statement: "With Washington making every effort to extricate itself from Vietnam, the U.S. is not very likely to make a heavy commitment of ground troops in Laos or Thailand." Major Blake made no other annotations than those given above.

31

Letter from Mr. Dante Hamilton to Col. Barnes, OUSAIRA, Vientiane, dated 8 January.

Dear Colonel Barnes:

I am sorry to have missed you today (Thursday), but you were TDY. I came down on the courier to see you about a matter that I consider to be most important. I hope this letter will express my views.

In my estimation, my earlier comments to you about Mr. Blake were right. I flew with him yesterday on an orientation mission, as an observer, of course, and I think that he is not the man for this job. He is a skilled pilot, I know, but there is something about him that I think will be detrimental in the long run.

For example, after a fairly routine flight where we put in strikes on a very important target (on which Mr. Blake did not want to get low enough for proper BDA assessment), we landed back at Alternate for fuel and to let me off. While we were having some coffee, Mr. Blake said suddenly that he wanted to see Mr. Al Morrinello, the Company Chief here, and if possible, VP himself. He seemed upset when I told him that seeing VP was very hard, that proper channels must be observed. He actually seemed to think that he could walk right down the hill and knock on the General's door.

As for Mr. Morrinello, you know how much he resists interference from Vientiane, or what he calls the "city folks," especially when they are military, and certainly when there's an operation being planned. Nobody likes to have someone he doesn't know just burst in. It's like having her father knocking on your car door when you're parked at the drive-in.

Actually, VP and Mr. Morrinello had gone somewhere in a Porter [short-take-off-and-land utility aircraft], and wouldn't be back until the next day (today). I don't know if Mr. Blake believed me, but it was the truth. And when he asked me if I would show him around the Company compound, I felt called upon to tell him how things really were up here. If you want him to get the full rundown on Company operations, please let me know, and I'll try. It would help, I think, to get him some official Company authorization as well, similar to the handwriting checks and other security measures they require of me. As you remember, it takes about three weeks to get me cleared on each tour.

Already some of my people are asking me "who this guy Blake is and what does he think he's trying to do," and I think it should be made perfectly clear to him that he works for you and I work for you, but that I do not work for him. The men up here, both the Lao and Americans, don't take very well to orders given by people who just fly in for the day and go back to their clean beds every night. For example, Mr. Blake "suggested" to me that I tell the Lao to stop dropping bombs in salvo on a hot target, stating that better accuracy could be obtained if singles were dropped. *I'd* drop singles, if you would let me fly combat missions, but the Lao won't, and I can't order them to. Look at their loss rate. You know their saying, "T-28 pilots fly until they die; C-47 pilots smuggle and get rich." It's all I can do to keep these guys in the cockpit under these conditions, and a lot of times they fly in this lousy weather only because VP says he'll personally shoot them if they don't.

Once again, I think Mr. Blake is going to cause more trouble than he's worth, especially if he keeps concerning himself with matters that are really none of his business. May I please suggest that you send him down to southern Laos for a while and let us get this important job we have to do, done?

                                  Respectfully,
                                  [signed] Dante Hamilton
                                  Commander, AOC 20A

Letter (carbon copy) from OUSAIRA, Vientiane, to Mr. Dante Hamilton, AOC 20A, dated 11 January.

Dear Mr. Hamilton:

This letter is in answer to yours of the 8th. Please forgive my not answering it sooner, but I was in Saigon for a meeting.

First, please know that I have every confidence in Mr. Blake's ability and judgment, and I will ask for your support as well.

Second, please also give Mr. Blake all the assistance you can in finding out as much as possible about all aspects of our operations. I fully realize the standard Company clearance procedures which are in effect, but I also know that with your experience and reputation, you can open many doors. You know (as well as I do) that out here channels are often used to keep from happening something you don't want to happen at all.

Third, please let me know immediately about matters such as salvo dropping, refusals to fly, and the like. I understand that you cannot command our allies, but if you will let me know your problems, I will take them to the Country Team meeting or if necessary, to the Royal Lao Air Force Commander himself. And I, too, regret the losses we necessarily experience in combat, but our first order of importance is to get the job done, as safely and expeditiously as possible, especially with the mounting enemy threat.

Finally, you may not fly combat missions. Your job as a provisional Base Commander, with all its headaches, is just too important, and you've got enough medals anyway. Also, please let me know ASAP what the "operations" are that you refer to as being "planned." Is there something special that I don't know about?

Please do drop in any time you're here, and a call in advance might be in order. I may be up there myself before too long anyway; there's a high-level inspection trip in the wind. More about this later.

[signed] J. Barnes, Col. USAF

33

Intelligence report, "Defense Intelligence Agency Summary" (hereafter referred to as DIA Summary), from OUSAIRA, Vientiane, to DIA, Washington, dated 13 January. Xerox reproduction of carbon copy, typewritten on legal-size paper.

SUBJECT: Analysis of Phou Nok Kok

1. The situation at Phou Nok Kok is, according to all estimates, worsening gradually. Despite relentless shelling, the two companies of irregular troops are doing a good job, although severely limited by supply problems. As of today, 137 men are in defensive positions within the wire; versus an estimated 1000–3000 NVA regulars, most of which are apparently from the 432nd NVA Division, newly introduced into Laos. Two 105mm howitzers remain operable with complete crews, and these are being used for harassing fire against Route Seven, which remains closed to enemy traffic.

2. With Phou Nok Kok representing the "cork in the bottle" to the Plain of Jars, the enemy is prevented from massive resupply until this post is taken. Consequently, AIRA [Air Attache] feels that there will soon be another all-out attack against this position, similar to the unsuccessful frontal assault of 28 December. Company has denied ARMA [Army Attache] request to transport more 105mm howitzers to site, and AIRA still feels that placing 155mm weapons would be a mistake (ref AIRA msg 070045ZJan).

3. However, we believe that Phou Nok Kok can be held for a much longer time period if additional sorties could be allocated for its defense (ref msg AIRA to 7AF 241327ZDec and 7AF to AIRA 031845ZJan). 7AF feels it cannot release these resources from interdiction missions on the trail, citing lack of targets and minimal BDA. We believe the targets are now there. (Note body count figures in DIA

Summary 864 699). All sources point toward the effectiveness of airpower in static defense situations, and the effect on the morale of the defenders is also documented.

4. Consequently, we believe that unless sufficient sorties are released for our use, Phou Nok Kok should be abandoned by the end of the month. With the dry season upon us, all enemy supply routes are now passable, and only interdiction efforts by USAF aircraft are slowing the enemy down. As an example (ref msg AIRA to 7AF 081430ZJan), Raven FACs directed a successful strike against a truck park and storage area which accounted for 14 trucks and 3 tanks destroyed. The enemy is obviously preparing for a massive push, and General Vang Pao's forces, although highly skilled and motivated, may be severely hurt.

5. SUMMARY VIEW: Request this information be passed through your channels to DOD ASAP.

34

Letter, typewritten on AIRA stationery, addressed to Major Blake, dated 13 January.

Bill:

When you go down south tomorrow for your T-28 checkout, I want you to see if you can't get some time with Col. Lunderberg, the DO [Director of Operations] there. Report in to him as the new Chief Raven and let him know what's going on. Above all, stress the need for more sorties, and ask him to use whatever influence he has with 7AF to get them. I fully understand 7AF's problem—they do a great job, under the circumstances, but they can't keep up with everything up here. It's a pissing contest all the way, and they're leery (as I think you should know by now) of releasing sorties unless they can get quantifiable results for their computer. *That* we can't give them, yet, but I've asked Company intell to make sure they report all possible effects of bombing.

This is most important, so pull out all the stops, but don't tell Lunderberg I told you to come to him. We've known each other a long time and, for reasons I won't go into, don't quite see eye to eye on many matters. Tell me what he says when you get back.

Barnes

PS: Attached is a copy of a memo I sent out today, FYI [For Your Information].

35

Memo, AIRA to ARMA, 13 January.

Dear Henry:

How about a truce? We've got a war to fight, and if we continue to butt heads, we're in trouble. I saw your report the other day about Phou Nok Kok, and you know damn well we're not trying to usurp the prerogative of the Army by "using airpower as artillery." It's not only the guns they need, it's the trained gun crews, and that is your job. If you can coerce anyone to send some men up there, I'll see if I can get the Company to fly them in, but until you can guarantee that they'll go in the first place and then not spook, there's no point in it.

Also, how about getting your ground intell reports to me by 0700 instead of waiting until the Country Team meeting? I could certainly use them for my own 0730 briefing.

Thanks,
JB

36

Memo, ARMA to AIRA, 13 January.

Dear Jake:

I am sorry if you feel we're butting heads. That's the last thing I want to do. I think the problem lies in a conflict of missions: we're training the Lao as ground soldiers, but as soon as we get someone in the field ready to go, your airplanes come along and save the day. At least that's what the foot soldier thinks. The generals think of air as their magic wand—all they have to do is wave it and the enemy will go away—but we're preparing them for a day when the United States is not going to be around, and that posture hopefully doesn't include F-4s, F-105s, and whatever other miracle weapons you guys work with.

As you also know, we don't command. We only suggest, and if the FAR doesn't want to go, it won't. Don't forget the long-term animosity between the regular troops and the mountain tribesmen. It's just like the lowland Vietnamese and the Montagnards. Talk about butting heads, remind me to tell you a story or two about my days as a major with Special Forces there. And we didn't have airpower then, either.

About the briefings. Sure, you can have our ground intell, if you'll make it a point to direct your AOC commanders to teach the little guys to use proper targeting procedures and leave area saturation to artillery. We're a hell of a lot more accurate, you have to admit. And about those 155s for Phou Nok Kok, let's forget the idea—it's too late now, I'm afraid.

See you tomorrow. Sorry I can't drop by today and discuss this with you, but I've got to go over and review the new graduating class from the Lao Military Academy. As you know, it's an all-day affair, unlike our graduation. When was that? A hundred years ago?

Regards,
Hank

37

Letter, Blake to AIRA, 15 January.

Dear Col. Barnes:
 Mr. Jenkins is due down in an hour to pick up a bird from periodic inspection. He'll carry this back to you. I tried to get you on secure telephone, but as usual it didn't work too well, and when I did get through, you were out. I'll be back up on Saturday, all checked out.
 I saw Col. Lunderberg today and we had a good talk. He seems to agree that more sorties could be used, but he gave me a slightly different slant on the subject. He feels you have more power than he, or even the General here does, in getting resources. He'd like nothing better than to turn every airplane we've got loose on enemy troops "once and for all," and he says he's been requesting this so often that 7AF just laughs at him.
 He agrees that the PDJ should be defended and discounts the intelligence reports about the big NVA buildup. He claims there are only a "few thousand NVA in all northern Laos." According to him, if the Lao will stand and fight, they can hold at least the fringes of the Plain until the wet season comes back. I suggested that you and he get together and coordinate your requests, but he didn't seem too responsive to the idea. He said you'd tell me about the background.
 Between flights I'm going to spend some time in the Project CHECO [Contemporary Historical Examination of Combat Operations] office here (I'm using their typewriter). They've got some interesting reports on Air Force operations in the area, dating all the way back to the beginning. I'll see if I can bring some up to you.

Respectfully,
[signed] William Blake

38

Draft copy of teletype message, Horowitz, Vientiane, to Bryan, Washington, 16 January. Contained in folder noted in item 21.

1. Ref msg 160843ZJan I sent this morning to Saigon, urging that all available pressure be put on USAF to supply maximum air support to our withdrawal plan (transmitted to you on 23 December). Vang Pao is in agreement with our objectives, and I think he'll go along, even though he's muttering again about the "Grands Seigneurs" of Vientiane who will not give him the regular troop commitments he needs the minute he asks for them.

2. Ravens are able to handle increased sorties and will be at full strength by next week. Blake taking hold slowly but nicely, and seems to have the approval of the Ambassador, who said nice things about him after Country Team meeting of last Wednesday. If he works out, what do you think about pushing for an extension if he can be talked into asking for it?

3. Otherwise, we are all waiting to see what the enemy will do. If you plan to send anyone out, tell them to bring a bathing suit, even though the weather's strangely cool this year. Horowitz.

39

Blake, *Journal*, pp. 41–55.

Sunday, 18 January— I have to write this down. Why? God knows. Maybe in preparation for the RBI [Reply By Indorsement] from Barnes, if it ever gets out. Perhaps it won't, though—it may be the kind of experience nobody talks about. There are many of those up here.

Anyway, I suppose it all began because Jenkins had a birthday, and I, gregarious son of a bitch that I am, decided to give him a party. I wasn't trying to play the role of corrupter, and anyway Jenkins can't, I think, be corrupted. Except for an occasional foray (as an observer), he's one of the straightest guys I know. Loves music. Plays the guitar. Reads a lot (says he plans to get out of the Air Force when his commitment is up and go to law school). His only real condescension to the war is his habit of wearing those ridiculous scarves—different colors, one for each day of the week. Calls it his Red Baron complex.

Yesterday he was 25 (when I was 25 I had three children—wonder what would have happened if I'd been here then?)—and I, the middle-big Chief, decided it was time to honor one of our own. Told Weird—he said shit hot. Said he'd take care of the guest list and arrangements. Van and I got some balloons and extra goodies.

At 6:30 Valerie arrived in a black cocktail dress (I never realized how thin she is—no, not thin—slim. Really dark hair. Must weigh about 110 pounds. Heavy makeup. Said afterwards she felt Oriental last night.) A few minutes later Sheila Brown bumbled in (I say bumbled because she'd obviously been sipping for some time). Brought a "friend," which was the start of the screw-ups. A man whose name I don't think I ever really got. He does something down south, had come up to visit Barnes—and was a friend of Sheila's. Only thing I really remember is that he reminded us to call him Mister, not Colonel—with a smile. He obviously had one goal in mind—to get in Sheila's pants. We drank—lots. Jenkins was surprised. Relaxed quite a bit from his normal stiff self (maybe he's just shy)—I wonder if Valerie's ever gotten to him? He hasn't said. Neither has she, so I guess she hasn't.

Weird kept looking at his watch and pulling at his red mustache, which curls like a water buffalo's horn. Finally took me aside and said that a couple of the other "guests" were apparently not going to show—that we'd better eat and play the rest of the evening by ear (which we were on, by then). Living-room picture: Couch at far end (stage center) with Mr. —— and Sheila, the latter crushed in the corner with Mr. —— pressing. Jenkins on the other side (right) playing his guitar. Weird and Valerie looking through tapes farther to the right (Weird's equipment)—and at one time there was acid rock, Jenkins' guitar, and Mr. —— all playing at once.

Dinner was great, but fuzzy. Van kept the wine coming. Weird kept looking at his watch. Many toasts. Ladies were all over Jenkins, and Mr. —— fumed and guzzled. At the table, Sheila and Valerie on either side of our birthday boy, keeping his glass filled, leaning over and whispering, etc.

After dinner same scenario as before, but with brandy. Then Weird, pulling at his mustache again, announced that the festivities would have to be shifted because of an unforeseen scheduling difficulty. "We're all going to Lulu's," he said. Valerie choked, then howled. Jenkins blushed. Mr. —— frowned.

Sheila asked, "What's Lulu's?"

"You mean you've been here almost a year and you don't know what Lulu's is?" Valerie said, standing. "Boy, are you ever out of it." (I wonder what's between *them*—maybe it's because they're the only two good-looking Caucasian females in Laos.)

"Don't sweat it," Weird said. He turned off the tape. "It's a good place to go for a drink. It's Dave Jenkins' party."

Mr. ——: "Why not, whatever it is. Anything's better than just sitting around here."

Valerie wanted to drive. I said no. Weird gave me directions. It was a clammy night. Six of us in the jeep, somehow.

Lulu's, *the* Lulu's—a private house in an area of Vientiane which reminds me of Carmel, California, with overhanging and drooping trees, high walls, and dim lights glowing through growth. Only difference is that the wooden houses are pure Zanesville, Ohio, circa 1915, except they're made of teak. A stone walk from the gate to the porch (wooden), then a plain old door entering into (really) a parlor, like a Kansas farm home. Linoleum floor, sagging couch to the left, three lunch-counter tables and chairs (aluminum legs) and a two-seat carved wooden bar in the far corner. The room very bright—glints on the floor and the table legs, reflections from the single large bulb hanging from the exact center of the ceiling. Five little brown girls (definitely not LBFMs, not here) seated at two of the tables, one of them asleep, her head in her arms.

And Lulu—bouncing in from what turned out to be the kitchen when she heard the jingle of the little bell on the door. Lulu—if Valerie is the pearl of the Orient, Lulu's the oyster. Indeterminate age (Weird swears she's sixty)—a little over five feet, dumpy, blonde hair straggling down over her flowered mumu, big red lips—a shrunken Mae West. Told me later that she'd once owned whorehouses in Paris, Madrid, Beirut, Saigon, and Bangkok. She shuffled toward Weird and hugged him, then Jenkins (who flinched), then me. She smelled sweaty. I swear her hair crunched.

She must be quite nearsighted, because she did not apparently see the ladies until a couple of the girls at the table started giggling and pointing. Two of them ran out of the room, holding hands. "Oh," Lulu said. "Welcome to my home." Introductions followed.

Mr. —— said, "Come on, Sheila, let's get out of here."

"Why don't you shut up, old boy," Sheila said.

"I know your father," Lulu said to Valerie, leading her over to the couch. To the girls at the table: *"Départez—vite, vite."* They scurried out. "This is, how you say, quite an occasion, *mes amis*. We drink to the birthday boy."

Weird was the bartender. Jenkins straddled a bar stool and played his guitar. Mr. —— sat at one of the tables, glancing from time to time into the next room, where we could hear an occasional giggle. I stood, drinking very cold Singha (the best beer which produces the worst hangovers in the world), watching the three women talk on the couch. With slim Valerie, fat Lulu (in the center), and magnificent Sheila, they looked like a child's pounding toy as they shifted slightly, leaned back, or moved toward each other. Hazy smoke, and once I bumped into the light bulb and the shadows spun crazily.

"Welcome," Weird said, "to the finest house of its kind in Southeast Asia." He hit a beer bottle with a spoon and raised his glass. "Happy twenty-fifth to good old 53." Jenkins smiled, nodding. I could see he was quite drunk. I think someone started to sing "Happy Birthday," but Mr. —— (who had four empty glasses in front of him at the table) turned toward the couch and said in a loud, thick voice, "Just what the hell kind of a place *is* this, anyway? What in the hell goes on here?"

Silence. Weird pulled at both ends of his mustache. Jenkins looked down at his guitar. Lulu glanced from side to side, then shrugged. "We specialize," Lulu said, rising slowly and walking over to Mr. ——, her hands where I suppose her hips should be, "in the blow jobs, *par excellence*."

Silence. Weird's elbows on the bar now, his head in his hands, his shoulders shaking. Jenkins hit a minor chord. "Right," he said. "Right on."

Valerie started to laugh, her head thrown back on the couch. Then Sheila started, a low chuckle which became louder. Then we were all roaring, and I could hear a chorus of high-pitched titters echoing from the back room. Weird pounded on the bar top.

Mr. —— scowled. "I'm getting the hell out of here," he said. "You people are all crazy."

"What's the matter, *chéri?*" Lulu said. "You want a girl?"

"What?" Mr. —— said, leaning back in the chair, "What in hell are you talking about? I don't want your kind of girls." We were all watching him.

"Why not," Lulu said. "You think there is something wrong with what Lulu does?" Under the light the scene looked like a police interrogation.

Mr. —— just shook his head, eyes wide. "Come on, Sheila," he said, "let's get out of here."

"Who are *you?*" Lulu shouted. "What are *you* to talk about my kind of girls. You Americans and your—*moralité*." The rouge spots on her cheeks seemed redder. "You tell me your name and exactly what *you* are doing here, then. You know who I am and what *I* do, *n'est-ce pas?* At least I am honest. And you—but you are my guest—so I ask you to hold your tongue."

"And she'll have her girls hold theirs," Valerie said loudly, getting up and going over to the bar. "Now what, old Weird," she said, holding out her glass, "what do we do for an encore?"

"Maybe you should take him to the White Rose," Lulu said, "for *his* kind of girls." She tossed her head and shuffled over to the bar. "What one does around here, my friend, is hardly a measure of what one is. These people know that, eh?"

Silence again. Weird poured more Singha from the brown full-liter bottles.

"What the hell," Mr. —— said. He shook his head, holding out a glass. "Gimme a drink." [Marginal holograph comment: "Sheila later said he left her alone for the rest of the night."]

"I've never been to the White Rose, either," Sheila said.

"What the hell," Mr. —— said. "Let's go to the White Rose, whatever the hell that is."

"You would like the White Rose better," Lulu said.

"How would you know?" Mr. —— said. "Who runs *that* place—your sister?"

"You insult me," Lulu said. "I have never set foot in that diseased place. My *sister? Sacré vache.* I prefer not to admit that the White Rose exists."

Mr. —— stood up, leering down at Lulu. "Well I'll tell you what, Miss Lulu. Let's *all* go to the White Rose. Let's have a summit conference at the White Rose."

I hope I've reconstructed that conversation as it really was, but my headache tells me that I probably missed something. I knew I missed a lot later. Weird must have either phoned the Rose or had one of Lulu's girls call, because when the seven of us (Lulu in front, the other five crammed in the back of the jeep) arrived, the entrance to the White Rose looked like a formal receiving line. Two rows of LBFMs stood on either side of the flagstone walk which leads into the low, dark stucco house, and when Lulu puffed her way out of the jeep, an Oriental woman in a white—yes, white—dress strutted slowly down the walk. I don't know her name. For a moment she looked regal. It was as if Lulu was paying a visit of state. When they embraced, all the LBFMs giggled and crowded around, and the six of us, still in the jeep, said nothing until Mr. —— growled, "What the hell. Let's go in. And Sheila, if that's your crotch my hand is in, it doesn't mean a thing."

"It's *my* crotch," Valerie said.

"Well it still doesn't mean a thing," Mr. —— said.

"That's too bad," Valerie said.

I did not talk to Lulu again. She and her counterpart sat at the largest booth in what turned out to be a fairly standard bar—sunken floor with a space for dancing, dim lights, tables and booths. I don't know what the two madames talked about, or even which language they used. Valerie danced with Jenkins (there was a juke box with American rock), LBFMs danced alone and together, and I drank too much. I remember at least one show with the lights made even dimmer and a naked girl strutting around with cigarettes (how many? Sheila said five) sticking out from between her legs, and she stopped in front of occupied booths and made the cigarettes glow. I remember a wild dance when the LBFMs started doing impromptu strip teases, getting down to nothing rather quickly, and then Sheila was dancing and one of the little girls was helping her off with her sweater. [Marginal holograph comment: "Weird told me later that one of the girls had come up to Sheila, put both hands on her own breasts, then on Sheila's, and said, 'Me no hab—you hab mach mach. Maybe you cheat.' Sheila rose to the challenge. I'm sorry I missed it. Weird said they were both incredible."] Jenkins went to sleep with his arms around his guitar—I must have joined him shortly afterward—and Weird is still in the sack this soggy Sunday morning, so I can't find out yet exactly what happened. Lulu at the White Rose—the first communication established between the greatest professional rivals in the Orient—and I think, just for the hell of it, that I'll go to church. Maybe someone up there still likes me.

40

Memo (file copy), Blake to all Ravens, 20 January.

SUBJECT: Raven Policies.

1. OK, troops, it's time. Please don't think this memo indicates a ton of paper to follow. It does not. Because I can't see all of you at once, I'll be sending notes like this one from time to time. Bear with me.

2. I've heard reports that you've been flying too much—

like 120 hours a month. Cut it down and plan a regular flying schedule. There's an inspection trip in the wind, and if the big boys find out you've been pressing so hard, they'll cut us all off.

3. I've talked to the MR II Ravens about the worsening situation—but all the rest should also watch out for an increase in enemy activity, especially around Savannakhet, Pakse, Saravane, and Attopeu. Keep your eyes open.

4. Re Company relations: let's work with them. No more backbiting. If worst comes to worst, get to me directly, especially if you hear about operations being planned. I know what their policy is and their sensitivity to leaks, but we've got to know what's being considered so we can go in for sorties.

5. Re liaison with the AOC commanders—no matter what the rank, you can't tell them what to do—so *ask,* beg, talk, but communicate. They'll get pissed off because you fly regularly and they aren't supposed to—but if you'll help them, they'll help you.

6. Mickey Mouse Item: When we first started here, we were supposed to be inconspicuous—blend in, and all that. Now you can spot a Raven ten miles away. Clean up. Case in point: if Weird can do it, so can you. Let's be reasonable.

7. Watch the bar talk when you go south. Enough said.

8. I'll be down to see each of you from time to time. In return, please check in with me when you get up to Vientiane.

9. Sawadee.

[signed] Blake
R-01 [Raven-01: the commander]

41

Blake, *Journal*, pp. 56–57.

Wed, 21 January—I'm going to try and keep a daily log—even if I can't write much. Things are beginning to pop, and I may have to really account for some of the things I want to do. But it's time—. Don't forget: the sight of Weird (what a sweet guy) after he shaved his handlebars to conform, as he said, with "official Air Force standards" (i.e., "mustaches not extending beyond the edges of the mouth"). Now Weird's wearing a flaming red walrus tusk. He just cut the handlebars off, so he resembles a bushy Hitler with stubby ears (which no one could see before, either). No real problem.

Unlike other areas—weather, communication, purpose. Horowitz looked at me strangely today. I suppose he's seen my memo (I intended that he should), and I've told him what I think about his boys not communicating with USAF. I want cards on the table. Told him I would let him know if I hear anything he doesn't tell me first. Good talk, though, about "Big Al," as they call him, up at Alternate. Have Horowitz's blessing there. With VP being the strongest leader around, it's little wonder he develops such a clique. After all, he gets the job done. Hope to meet him next week.

Lousy weather. In addition to the smoke and haze, at night clouds are forming—low fog in the valleys. Not good. Spooky had a lot of action last night around Phou Nok Kok.

Hamilton; Hamilton; Hamilton. Wonder what would happen if I asked Barnes to move him to another location? We'll see.

Enough. Dear Sheila, here I come. Will you have the lobster or the steak?

42

Letter from Mr. Jenkins to Mr. Blake, handwritten on lined 8×10" notepaper, dated 21 January.

Mr. Blake:

Sending this down in the morning (Thursday) by courier from 20A. Spent the night and am staging out of here again tomorrow. Debriefed all this to Company intell, but want you have a copy for the record, in case I don't see you for a couple of days.

First: Ravens only worked four sorties around Phou Nok Kok today due to weather. Fog held in until about 1000L, and low stratus moved in and out all day. Got a good look at the summit just once—a big hole—and my heart goes out to the little guys down there. Incoming all day long—we couldn't spot the mortars in the haze—and twice the choppers couldn't land because of mortar shells exploding on the landing pads. We had to divert fourteen flights elsewhere.

Second: Only really successful mission was a flight of four T-28s (VP's Meo). Guess who was in the lead? They got one DK-82 and a couple of secondaries. Hamilton told me not to tell you. I didn't say anything. Personally, when he flies the little guys will follow him anywhere.

Third: I'm going to carry a half load of flechettes today—smoke doesn't do any good if you don't have targets. OK? Just in case I see something.

Sincerely,
Jenkins—Raven 53

43

Letter (Xerox copy) from Major David Halbers to Colonel Lunderberg, dated 23 January. Attached is a DD Form 95, with the notation "For Mr. Blake, OUSAIRA, Vientiane."

SUBJECT: Phou Nok Kok

1. In response to your request of this morning, here is as detailed a report of last night's activities as I can give you. Where possible, exact times have been taken from our aircraft tape recorder.

Sequence of events
2330L: Spooky 23 [C-47 gunship] arrived on station at Phou Nok Kok, replacing Spooky 31, who reported no vi-

sual sightings of the enemy. In response to a request by Red Rose [the ground FAG at Phou Nok Kok], Spooky 31 had flared continuously and fired out against suspected enemy concentrations. Weather upon arrival was variable broken to overcast at about 500 feet (estimated by Red Rose). When Red Rose turned on his command post light for identification, I could barely see the glow through the cloud deck, and our first flare confirmed that the cloud cover was almost solid, with thin layers and heavy fog in the valleys.

2351: Red Rose informed Spooky 23 that a perimeter outpost reported hearing noises about 150 meters away. Attempts to see his flashlight failed. Red Rose advised us not to fire without seeing flashlight.

0016: Red Rose asked us to fire a marking burst into valley at base of hill, approximately 500 meters to the north. Dropped one flare, then fired upon Red Rose confirmation of location. Red Rose said he could not see our tracers hit because of fog.

0023: Red Rose called: "Bad guys come. Bad guys come. You shoot, Spooky. You shoot good." I requested that Spooky 26, then on station near the PDJ, be diverted to our assistance. Immediately communication became difficult, with many voices talking in what I think was Lao, but some could have been Vietnamese. I do not know if the talking was done by friendly or enemy forces, and because no one on board spoke Lao, we could not understand what was being said. Three more flares showed only cloud tops.

0027: There was a large explosion about 200 meters from Red Rose's command post, followed by an intense mortar barrage. We could see the shells exploding through the clouds, too numerous to count. Red Rose called: "Where big bomb go off—perimeter wire. You shoot there, Spooky—you shoot like hell." We complied, expending about 2000 rounds in that area of the explosion where a fire still burned.

0029: Red Rose said, "You get plenty bad guys, Spooky. Number One."

0035: Spooky 26 called and said he would be on station at 0055.

0037: With the mortar barrage continuing, there was

The Laotian Fragments

another large explosion to the south of the command post. We were then about 800 feet directly above, and through a small hole in the overcast I could see what appeared to be hundreds of enemy moving over and through the coils of concertina wire. Most appeared to be wearing uniforms. Some were climbing over the bodies of others lying on the wire. We managed to fire about 300 rounds before the hole closed in.

0041: Red Rose called (I think it was a different voice), said, "Bad guys come through wire. You shoot now, Spooky. You shoot everywhere." There were no mortar rounds observed after this time. I did not think I should fire closer than 100 meters from the command post light, which we could now barely see through the clouds. We held our orbit and fired nearly continuously until our ammunition was expended at 0049, then continued flaring. We could see nothing but the tops of clouds until the flare dropped below them; then only a dim glow until the flare went out.

0053: Spooky 26 arrived on station. All attempts to contact Red Rose failed, although there was still some chatter on the radio. Without any contact with the ground, Spooky 26 decided not to fire, but dropped flares instead. We could still see an occasional flash, probably from small-arms fire, until 0103, when all activity ceased.

0107: Spooky 23 departed station for base.

0115: Spooky 26 ordered by Nightowl [the night airborne USAF command post] to fire out in the blind as close to the summit as possible.

0200: Just before changing radio frequencies when crossing the fence, I heard Nightowl direct a flight of F-4s to bomb the summit of Phou Nok Kok, using radar if necessary.

> Respectfully submitted,
> David Halbers, Major, USAF
> Spooky 23 Commander

44

DIA Summary (Xerox copy), OUSAIRA, Vientiane, to DIA, Washington, 24 January.

1. With the fall of Phou Nok Kok, Royal Lao Government officials are already asking about our intentions regarding Long Tieng. Their assumption seems to be that the government positions in the Plain of Jars are untenable, and while the Neutralist commander claims that his forces will fight to the death for Muong Soui, no one really takes him seriously. There has been a special meeting called of the Lao Cabinet, to which the Ambassador has not been invited but will attempt to secure access. Should Long Tieng go, and General Vang Pao's forces be defeated, AIRA suspects that there may well be a major crisis which would perhaps even lead to a decision to reach accommodation with the North Vietnamese and the Pathet Lao.

2. Reports are still incomplete from Phou Nok Kok, but some of the defenders have begun straggling into Lima 22 (Xieng Khouang). Preliminary evidence shows that the NVA attack was in multi-battalion strength, and after sapper squads placed charges on two areas of the perimeter wire, the friendly forces could not withstand the final mass charge. Unfortunately, Lt. Vangsana, the commander, was killed in the early stages of the mortar barrage, and without his leadership the remainder of the friendly soldiers thought it expeditious to evacuate the site. Exact casualties are not known but are estimated to be heavy.

3. Of importance for the record is that USAF air did all it could to prevent the loss of Phou Nok Kok. Only when the weather deteriorated below workable minimums were the enemy able to achieve success. Spooky gunships were on station and available, and no doubt hurt the enemy badly. Follow-up intelligence photos show that all equipment, including the 105 howitzers, ammunition, and communications gear, were destroyed by subsequent air

tacks when the position was declared lost. If the weather had remained good, it is AIRA's opinion that Phou Nok Kok could have been held much longer, if not indefinitely.

4. Also important to note is the role of the RLAF, whose T-28s did a heroic job of defending the position. We see great strides in their effectiveness.

45

Memo (carbon copy), OUSAIRA to Horowitz, Vientiane, 24 January.

SUBJECT: Phou Nok Kok
Abe:

Tried to call, but you were understandably out. Please drop by ASAP. I would not like to get the Ambassador involved unless necessary. I have some serious reservations about the fiasco Thursday night, especially in regard to the haste with which the friendlies departed the area. Damn it, we can't defend anyone who won't stay around long enough to be defended—and you know it. Do we have a problem here?

Barnes

46

Memo, Horowitz, Vientiane, to OUSAIRA, 24 January.

Dear Jake:

Now calm down. Your note was given to me as I boarded a plane for Luang Prabang, where I'll be for three days. I'll call you when I return. In the meantime, my assistant will be holding down the fort, so check with him if you've got questions.

As implied by your memo, though, the ground troops did not just walk out (you've said this before). They were outnumbered 20 to 1, and because you people have not yet developed a perfect means of close ground support through clouds, they made what I think was the right tactical decision. How would you have liked it up there Thursday night? Anytime the great fire-breathing USAF sky dragon fails to spew forth destruction, the little guys get understandably scared.

We've got some withdrawal ideas, however, which are pretty well firmed up now, and I'll give you a briefing when I get back. Don't get unduly agitated, my friend—it's always this way this time of year, or have you forgotten? Remember the first time Muong Soui fell? Or Site 36? Or good old "impregnable" Phou Pa Tai? Keep your chins up.

Regards,
Horowitz

PS: How about letting me know if the good Mr. Blake pays any attention to my daughter while I'm gone. A father speaking, you know. Thanks.

47

Teletype message, OUSAIRA, Vientiane, to 7AF, Saigon, 251130ZJan.

SUBJECT: Future Plans

1. Ref your msg 250200ZJan, Subject, "Withdrawal Plan," regret that this office cannot, repeat, cannot yet provide your headquarters with a precise scenario similar to a 7AF OPLAN. Suggest you contact Company officials in Saigon and Bangkok for possible assistance.

2. I have been promised notification as soon as possible whenever such a plan is developed and will forward it to you through proper channels. Also, visit to our headquarters by new Deputy Commander next month should help clarify matters. We will be down in two weeks for our regular planning meeting. Barnes.

48

Letter on standard business stationery, with letterhead reading "Barringer and Brophy, Attorneys at Law, 243 South Mansfield Ave., Brockton, Maryland," dated January 20.

Dear Major Blake:
 We have been retained by your wife in the matter of her suit for divorce, a copy of which complaint is attached (atch #1). As noted in the particulars of the bill, you have twenty (20) days in which to reply, preferably through an attorney of your choice.
 May we hear from you at your earliest convenience?

Most sincerely,

[signed] James T. Barringer, Esq.

Barringer and Brophy

49

Letter (carbon copy) from Major Blake to Ernest D. LaMora, Attorney at Law, 43 Main Street, Big Spring, Texas, dated 28 January.

Dear Ernie:
 Forgive the abruptness of this request, but the enclosed is self-explanatory. I'm asking you for help because, quite frankly, you're the only lawyer I know. You'll remember, I think, the land purchase you so kindly drew up for us when I was stationed out at the Air Base. I've contacted the Judge Advocate General's office in Thailand, and their advice was to get a civilian attorney.
 I really don't have too much time to screw around, unfortunately—you may have read about a little war

we've got going over here, and I'm in the middle of it, right up to my ears. Frankly, I don't know whether I want the divorce or not, but I do know that I can't concern myself with the problem every day. Will you take this case for me? See if you can get some kind of a delay, or something, or at least protect what few interests I seem to have left. I suppose there should be something about support, visitation, etc., but in any event, I'll trust your judgment.

Sorry about all the distance problems—but somehow a divorce case with the lawyer in Texas and the principals in Southeast Asia and Maryland seems about par for the course.

> My deepest thanks.
> [signed] Bill Blake
> William Blake, Major, USAF

50

Blake, *Journal*, pp. 58-68:

29 January, Thursday— Over a week since my last entry, in which I promised myself to make a daily log. Where does it all go? Straight to shit. A month now since I got up here—what to show for it? 32 more missions (only 18 count for air medals because you can't log more than one a day for awards and decs.)—one major battle lost—a wife who wants out—Sheila who wants me in (wonder what the hell Valerie's game is?). What a fucked-up life I'm leading, even if the job is starting to get a bit straightened out. In a funny way, thank God for Jenkins. At least he didn't strangle in his ridiculous WWI six-foot fringed scarf.

The weather's down again up country—supposed to stay that way tomorrow (I'm not flying anyway)—told Van to keep a pitcher of martinis full. Why not?

OK—so here goes:

21 January, Wednesday—Picked up Sheila at 7:00. Black and yellow flowery dress with most of those magnificent boobs peeking out over the top. She must be about an

inch taller (with heels) than I am (said she hoped I didn't mind—I don't). Said right off the bat that she didn't want to go to the White Rose (hah!)—so we had dinner at the Concorde. Somehow, so much here seems vestigal [*sic*]—the whole city is a walking reminiscence of what might used to have maybe been, or could have been. The Concorde—old paneling, dark booths, ornate carvings all over (no doubt hacked out by Lao who were in turn being gouged by the French). New, splitting naugahyde on the seats. Good dinner (Sheila did have the lobster—me too—but it turned out to be crayfish). She's an interesting girl (girl? mid thirties?)—has been with Horowitz for a hundred years, she says. Looks harder on the outside than she really is. Married once, no children (claims she found out she had a child a month after she married him—the only way she could wean him was to throw him out). Talked and danced, then went back to her apartment (I don't exactly remember where it was). Had too much to drink. Made love. Very good indeed. It's nice to fuck without getting all tangled up in attached strings. Didn't talk about my wife—come to think of it, Sheila didn't even ask. Remarkable girl.

22 January, Thursday: Flew up to Alternate in hopes of seeing Vang Pao. No luck. He was up somewhere on the PDJ with Hamilton. Picked up a backseater and put in strikes along Route 7 near the area where Hamilton and I found the big storage area. NVR all the way. Waited for Jenkins to return to 20A, chewed him out about using flechettes. Told him he was a FAC, not a fighter pilot anymore, and that his job was to mark targets, not to try and hit them (guess I didn't do a good enough job). Landed back at Vientiane just after dark. Valerie had called, Van said. Returned her call but she was out. So was Sheila. Almost finished Dommen's *Conflict*. A frightening book. Wonder if he really knows what he's talking about. I suspect he does. Thought about telling Barnes that Hamilton was flying again; decided not to. I'll talk with him. Fell asleep about the time Phou Nok Kok fell.

23 January, Friday: All hell broke loose at the office. Everybody seemed to know that Phou Nok Kok was bound to go—but we all hoped it wouldn't. American romanticism, I suppose. The first I knew was when Col. Barnes called me and said to be sure to make the early briefing

and not to fly, even if I was scheduled. Did so. Reports were that USAF had nicely decimated what was left on top of Phou Nok Kok and was continuing to do so, just in case. We sure can hit our own stuff. Weather not too bad. Intell reports of trucks moving up by the Ban Ban T. No contact by strike aircraft. Barnes was crushed—said he'd just about gotten private assurances of enough air to defend Phou Nok Kok. Barnes went south for a confab. I stayed in the AOC, coordinating. At 1143 the word came that Jenkins was down, right near Phou Nok Kok. Brickbat reported he'd requested a strike flight with CBUs, had seen people moving in the bunkers around the command post. Couldn't wait ten minutes—said he had some anti-personnel ordnance (want to bet they were flechettes?) on board—next thing anyone knew a Thud flight reported seeing an O-1 down and burning. SAR [search and rescue] effort successful, despite heavy groundfire. Only problem was that they were both dead, Jenkins and the Lao backseater. Jolly Green crew said there were dozens of holes in the aircraft and occupants. *Dumb shit* [underlined twice]. Wrote his mother, "Dear Mrs. Jenkins—Your son was a hero..." Bullshit. He was a dumb shit. But a nice dumb shit who *was* really a hero—every day except on Friday, January 23. His replacement's due in on Tuesday (Remember—shift Browning up from Pakse—tell Burr to check him out at Alternate). Valerie called again at the office, but I told her I didn't want to talk to her. PM: Got Jenkins' things squared away and out of the house, then Weird and I went out and got drunk.

24 January, Saturday: Two missions out of Lima 22, one way up north at Site 32, where VP's uncle has his small kingdom. Amazing place. Clusters of houses grouped around a vaguely defined dirt strip. Hard to pick out the runway from among the rice paddies. Small natural bowl (about a mile across) formed by surrounding ridges and hills, each with gun emplacements and circular fighting trenches carved out of the dirt. Steep sides on the outward banks of the hills. Completely surrounded, supplied by air. Seems to be heating up, but everyone's betting on VP's uncle, who's considered almost as tough as the General himself. What a hell of a way to live.

Sunday, 25 January: Had a small service for Jenkins in the USAID chapel. Both Valerie and Sheila there, on opposite sides of the aisle. Talked with Valerie for a minute afterward. She's going to Australia for a couple of weeks. Said she heard Phou Nok Kok go on her radio. Wrote final reports on Jenkins and two ERs (for Barnes' signature) on Ravens who are going home. Did busy work at the office in the PM (too hot to go outside).

Monday, 26 January: Inspection trip to the south and east. AOCs are in good shape, and no one seems upset about getting haircuts. How we magnify the inconsequential. Told by Barnes that the new Major General is coming up on 18 February. Plans to take him up to Alternate to talk with VP. Wonder if Big Al will let him in. Hah! First look at the Trail around Tchepone from this side. Craters of the moon. Saw where the bad guys are using some of the big craters to store oil drums in. One of the FACs told me about the tactic the NVA uses of piling empty drums in an exposed crater—when a gunship or fighter comes in after them they get hosed down by 23s or 37s, zeroed in and firing from caves in the karst. They take a lot more shit down there. Spent the night in Savannakhet—returned Tuesday at noon.

Tuesday, 27 January: Not much accomplished. Hot and humid, but the first really sunny day we've had for some time. *Dry* season? Even the weather's fucked up. Strange, though, everything can be bright and clear in Vientiane, but as soon as you cross the ridgeline south of Alternate and the PDJ, the weather can do an about face and clobber in. I wonder if this meteorological phenomenon has any effect on the political climate. Went over to talk to Horowitz, but he was still in Luang Prabang.

Wednesday, 28 January: Received letter from my wife's attorney. Wrote Ernie LaMora, the crook, for help. He was known as the most nearly dishonest lawyer in town. Mary, Mary, quite contrary, how does your garden grow? Ans: Not worth a shit. Horowitz still not back; Sheila said he had gone to Pakse for two days. Barnes in Bangkok. The Ambassador out with a bunch of reporters inspecting a new USAID miracle rice crop north of the city. Sheila cooked dinner for me at her place, and I spent the night. Marvelous, simply marvelous. It's a hell of a war.

Thursday (today)— Woke up at 5:00 AM, Sheila gave me the right kind of sendoff, and I made the morning briefing with three minutes to spare. Nothing really new at all. Intell says the bad guys usually lay low after a major victory to regroup and resupply. Wonder what my counterpart on the other side is doing tonight in his dirty little underground bunker somewhere under the great, gray-green greasy jungle canopy. I'll bet he's a hell of a lot more satisfied than I am.

51

Poem, draft holograph copy, on lined notebook paper. Inscription reads: "Bill, I wanted you to have this. I wrote it last night while you were out. It was for the T-28 guys, but it sort of sums everything all up. Weird, 29 January."

Words for Dave Jenkins: KIA, 23 Jan

Half a century gone. An image persists, born
When Spads and Fokkers dueled (they rarely really fought):
Men with tiny airplanes, shined boots, smiles and scarves;
Whine of wound-up engines, torque, smell and chatter of guns;
Watching for whims of weather or a blown jug.

Now, technology intrudes.
Pilots in their airconditioned world seem far above all that.
Sometimes.

There are still a few who strap into small birds,
Call "Clear," cough from backfire smoke,
Groan off the ground and shudder skyward,
Bombs rigged with baling wire and wood blocks,
Hanging upon a prop.

These could care less about refueling tracks or radar plots.

Their need is to dodge thunderstorms, skim peaks, keep
  lead in sight.
Bomb-laden, to climb above the clouds is to stagger on the
  edge of a stall.
It is enough to reach the target, hit it, and return.

Their textbook written for an older war,
These pilots fight, and sometimes die, in this one.
It is good to know that some men
Still fly with scarves and laughter
As real pilots always have
And always will.

Added on the back: "Bill, If I were writing this just for Dave, I suppose I should change it. But I won't. It's for all of us. W."

FEBRUARY

52

Memo (Xerox copy) from AMEMB (American Embassy), Vientiane, for "Standard Distribution," dated 2 February.

Gentlemen:
 1. With the fall of Phou Nok Kok, the position of the Royal Lao Government forces in northern Laos seems worse than it actually is, and I wish to exhort each one of you to continue your sincerely spectacular efforts in behalf of our mission here. Please make certain that your communications reflect no undue alarm. It is ironic, I suppose, that along with redou-

bled enemy efforts in the field, our cause is also receiving increased criticism, as well as funding cuts, at home, accounts of which you have no doubt read in the newspapers. Despite these rather unsettling attacks from all quarters, I can assure you that our goals remain unchanged. To cite an old adage: "Where there's a will there's a way."

2. Do not let these temporary setbacks discourage you or diminish your efforts. Across my desk daily come dozens of reports which indicate that each member of each command and/or agency, whether in the field or behind the lines, is accomplishing Herculean tasks in the face of a determined and capable enemy. Keep this up. Know that your government and your commanders wholeheartedly support your efforts. In the weeks and months ahead, know also that with God's help, we will not fail.

[signed] Stark

53

Teletype message, AOC 20A to OUSAIRA, Vientiane, 3 February.

SUBJECT: Weekly Operations Report

1. Most of the Phou Nok Kok force has straggled back in, surprisingly in better shape than previous reports had indicated. Of the 137 men, 16 are known to have been KIA (including the commander), 30 were wounded, and 10 are missing. In all, 97 are fit for battle and are being reassigned to units at Xieng Khouang (L22), Muong Soui, and here at Long Tieng.

2. According to one sergeant, they did not run in the face of the attack, but withdrew just before the enemy broke through the wire. Lt. Vangsana had given them this order, to be carried out in case of his being killed or severely wounded. They all followed preplanned escape routes and experienced no contact with the enemy during their retreat. Many of them had participated in the withdrawal from Site 36 last year, and as happened then, the

enemy seemed to have three sides well covered but left one corridor open for the friendlies to use, if they should choose to do so. They chose. All men retained their personal weapons and seem in quite good spirits. Those with families at Long Tieng returned here and are delighted with the opportunity for a reunion. Vang Pao praises their courage, and at a bauci last night decorated everyone. Is there any way we can, even if covertly, award Lt. Vangsana a posthumous medal? I would recommend at least the Bronze, if not the Silver Star. He was, as you know, 22 years old.

3. There is also evidence that the enemy is building a new road westward from North Vietnam toward Xieng Khouangville. Raven 23 spotted light equipment and what appeared to be fresh bulldozer tracks about 10 kilometers inside the Lao border. Recce of this area should continue. Suggest you request through channels that more big bombs be allocated for probing attacks to uncover truck parks, storage areas, and the like. The bad guys are getting more clever than ever.

4. Thanks for the heater. Unfortunately, it was wired for the wrong voltage. One of our maintenance men has rewired it. Hamilton.

54

Letter from Project CHECO office, Udorn, Thailand, to Mr. Blake, OUSAIRA, Vientiane, dated 3 February. The attachment, "Taped Interview," is included as item 55.

Dear Bill:

Nice to have met you last month, and thanks for stopping by. As you know, we maintain files here of classified reports of all aspects of our operations. Some of them are quite good, but unfortunately, very few people here read them. I suppose that the copies we send to Washington are at least looked at. I hope so. Perhaps Col. Lunderberg's new policy of having his staff members do some background reading will pay off.

Speaking of Lunderberg, I interviewed him the other day for a report I'm working on, and during the course of the conversation, realized that much of what we were talking about bore directly on aspects of your operation. I began taping halfway through. Here's the result, sent along with the Colonel's blessing. I asked if he would mind your having it; he said, and I quote, "I don't give a shit who hears it."

My very best,
[signed] Monty
L. Cranston, Major, USAF
Chief, Project CHECO, Thailand

55

Tape, Sony cassette, one side recorded, the other blank. Written on cover: "CHECO-Lunderberg, 29 January."

Lunderberg: . . . and I can't get north of the river when I want to, so there's no real use in speculating.

Cranston: Why not?

Lunderberg: Because it's all one happy family up there. And big daddy says no. Never mind. Seriously, I can do a lot of good down here, but they'll never win a war their way. About the only thing I accomplished up there was to get my ass fired.

Cranston: When were you up there?

Lunderberg: About a year and a half ago. I was Barnes' assistant attache. His DO [Director of Operations], I guess you'd say. The job that new guy—what's his name?—Vonnegut's got. You want to know why I got fired?

Cranston: Sure.

Lunderberg: Because I put myself in for a silver star. One day I had the U-17 out by Xieng Khouangville, where the good guys had taken a lot of shit the night before, and I saw one little guy running along the road. I made a low pass and the guy waved at me and I could see it was probably one of VP's boys, so I landed on the road and picked him up. It was Captain Sisouk. He showed me exactly where an NVA headquarters was, we validated the target, I called in a bunch of Thuds, we got a whole fireworks display when the ammo went off and at least 25 confirmed KBA. Took about ten hits in the left wing. Only problem was that a couple of days later some pinko reporter took pictures of the huts we burned up and it turned into a major flap. Said we'd strafed a village. Barnes got the newspapers and the citation for the silver star at the same time. Guess who lost.

Cranston: Then how did you get down here?

Lunderberg: The general who was here then agreed with me, even though Barnes wouldn't back me up. My new boss—well, I don't know him yet. He's only been here a couple of weeks.

Cranston: How do you think the war is going now?

Lunderberg: What war? We haven't got a war here. It's a fucked-up series of little engagements. The NVA runs the show—they're all over the place, but it's not a war like in Vietnam. The NVA can hit wherever it wants to at a time of its own choosing, and there's not a goddamn thing we can do about it—not the way we're fighting now. These fucking rules of engagement—we can't bomb here and can't bomb there—and if we blew up a hut it becomes a village and we're slaughtering civilians. "Let us win your hearts and your minds"—bullshit. The only way we can do that is to burn down their goddamn huts first. Shit. You just watch. If they want to take Long Tieng, they'll do it, and then we won't be able to bomb it because it is a village, therefore off limits. The only time we can bomb a house is before the bad guys move into it. As soon as they take a group of huts, they send for that Australian Commie Burchette guy [Wilfred Burchette, one of the few Western newsmen to be allowed access to northern Laos] and he writes an article about how the proud people of Laos are defending their homeland against the Yankee aggressor. You see his last report? About how the peasants were shooting down all those Yankee airplanes with hand-held rifles? Bullshit. I know the area he's writing about, and there haven't been any "peasants" there for three years. And "hand-held rifles"? They use 23 and 37 millimeter triple A with NVA crews. You know what else they do? They'll send in a couple of "deserters" into a government stronghold with word of a multi-battalion attack in a couple of days—then, when the time comes, good guys are so spooked that all the NVA has to do is beat a few drums and everyone takes off. Then the NVA lets out word that they're establishing a regimental headquarters in the village—we blow it up and accidentally kill a couple of civilians whom the NVA has forced to remain—and we've got another international incident. I kind of feel sorry for Barnes; he's too nice a guy. This job's going to kill that poor weak bastard.

Cranston: He seems to get along well with everybody.

Lunderberg: Sure he does, because he won't cross them. I didn't put up with any of their shit. My job was to help the Lao win a war, whether they wanted to or not. Some of them do—Captain Chantisak, for one—but the Lao power structure has got them so tied up they can't move. You know about Chantisak? He got railroaded onto a C-47 last year on a flight to Saigon. Ordered by the Lao brass to be a co-pilot at the last minute. When the bird landed, guess what the waiting customs found—that's right—gold and opium—about eight million dollars' worth. Chantisak swears he didn't know anything about it—and I believe him—but he got busted a grade in rank. The pilot, a Lao colonel, was given a month's house arrest and then got his job back. The South Vietnamese confiscated, if that's the right word, the goods. Chantisak's over at Savannakhet now—has the job of both T-28 *and* C-47 squadron commander. Flies his ass off night and day and does good work, but it's only a matter of time. He takes too many chances—flies too much. He gets tired. And even if he lives, he'll never be a real commander. He's not a member of the right family. Then again, neither am I. I didn't go to West Point. Maybe we're two of a kind.

Cranston: So what's the solution?

Lunderberg: Solution: That's a word we don't use around here. If it were up to me, I'd blow the bastards off the map—all the bad guys on both sides. No—not really, but you see what I mean. At least I'd stop the silly game we play where the only people who don't know what's going on are the commanders and the people back home. If you're going to fight a war—but shit, you know what I think. I just hate to see great guys—my guys—hang their ass out for nothing. What the shit, I'm retiring in three months anyway. But I'm going to do one thing before I go. If the bad guys really hit Long Tieng, I'm going to get all the goddamn airplanes in Southeast Asia up there to help Vang Pao if I have to lie, cheat, and steal and it costs me my ass. VP gets his share for supporting us, but goddamn it, he's a soldier, and I'll be fucked if he's going to get left standing on a ridgeline with his finger up his rectum.

Cranston: I think Blake and the Ravens will agree.

Lunderberg: Blake. There's another guy who's got some good ideas, but he can't win. If the bad guys don't get him, the system or the computer will. Horowitz is a master, and Barnes won't do a goddamn thing to stop it.

Cranston: What about the Ambassador?

Lunderberg: He's—now wait a minute, what are you going to do with this tape?

Cranston: Anything you say.

Lunderberg: Never mind. I don't give a shit anymore, anyway. I'm just going to do the best job I can. I don't know what the Ambassador will do, and I suppose I shouldn't even guess. If Blake can really get something done he'll have to walk across a rice paddy and not get wet to do it. But I'll be the first one to buy him a drink on the other side. Speaking of a drink, it's quitting time. Come on over to the club and we'll listen to Dang talk about her pussy— "you bet your sweet ass." OK?

56

Teletype message, Bryan, Washington, to Horowitz, Vientiane, 3 February.

SUBJECT: Senate Hearings

To squelch possible rumors, it is true that Senate Foreign Relations Committee will, repeat, will declassify a great portion of hearings on Laos. Military aspects only, however, will be published with DOD and Company approval. Watch for possible reactions from newsmen, the general public, and maybe even some of our uniformed brethren. Advise me of any problems. PS: Martha's bracelet appraised at $800.00. Thanks. WJB.

57

Blake, *Journal,* p. 69.

Tues, 3 Feb. I can't write every day, damn it. Fri, Sat, Sun, nothing happened. It's too quiet on the northern front. No people targets, so USAF is concentrating on selected interdiction on the routes, as if they think the NVA will come marching down in columns, four abreast. They won't. They hide behind the stone walls and fire at the redcoats (now there's a nice comparison. Who are the cowboys and who are the Indians? Did I think this one up myself?). Finished Dommen Saturday night. Wheels within wheels. It's all a circle, like a drum which different people keep beating to the same tune. Sunday Sheila took me for a ride out into the country. Found a neat place for a picnic under what I swear was a banyan tree. Love in the shade, and then we found a scorpion under the blanket. There's always a scorpion somewhere. Sheila's getting damned important to me. Must not let it happen. There's a job to do. At least the guys out in the foxholes don't have to worry about distractions like Sheila. *Don't Forget:* what it was like in the northern highlands of Vietnam, sleeping on the ground under the O-1's wing and eating C rations.

Am tempted to talk to Barnes about Lunderberg—but suppose I'd better not. They're both colonels. I wonder if it's a case of crossed transactions—parent v. child—or maybe children. Don't know. Suppose I'd better just hold out and see what I can accomplish, knowing as much of the story as I do.

Tomorrow: going down south for a general conference. Remember to take notebook. Sawadee, book. See you mañana.

58

Teletype message (Xerox copy), AMEMB, Vientiane, to SEC-STATE, Washington, 6 February.

Mr. Secretary:
Here's an update report on our little war. Don't believe what you read in the papers. It's not quite that bad. The RLG is a bit shaky, and the old Phoumists [the right-wing faction] are grumbling, but I don't think we're in for a major attempt at a coup. Any rumors you may have heard about Ma's return are false [General Ma, former Lao Air Force Commander, had fled to Thailand after an abortive coup attempt].

I think we've got a well-functioning group here, and we're as ready as can be for the rest of the dry season. As far as we can tell, the fighting odds are about even, with 50,000 of us and 50,000 of them. If the NVA would commit all their troops, we could really do a job. Only major question mark is how the various Lao factions will cooperate when the chips are down, but Souvanna seems still able to walk a tightrope among them. I don't see how he does it, after all these years. There's a rumor going around here that he may be considering a meeting with his half brother, the Pathet Lao chief, but I don't have anything on that yet.

Souvanna told me a funny story the other day—about the King's reaction to the NVN Ambassador's recurrent plea to order us to stop bombing in Laos. Said the King asked him how many NVA regulars were operating along the Trail, to which the NVN Ambassador answered, "The People's Republic of North Vietnam does not have any soldiers in Laos." King mused a moment, then told the NVN Ambassador a story: seems that there was this ancient king in the Setthathirath dynasty who was surrounded by people giving him advice, one of whom was a traitor. One day the old king was informed that this particular advisor was hiding behind a curtain, waiting to assassinate him. The king drew his sword, walked toward the curtain, and called out, "Anybody there?" No answer. He asked again, "Is anybody there?" After a minute or two of silence, the king jabbed through the curtain. There was a loud scream. The king jabbed again, and the body of the would-be assassin came tumbling through. End of story. After he had finished, the present King looked at the North Vietnamese Ambassador and said, "If there are no North Vietnamese hiding in Laos, why do you always scream out so loud when the Americans jab you?"

Yes, I think we're ready. Phou Nok Kok was a sad loss, but there is a concentration of forces in and around the PDJ which should give the enemy a very bad time indeed. Horowitz assures me that his people are on top of the situation, and I know that the Ravens will do a spectacular job. They're back at full strength again, and their new commander seems to be doing a nice job of welding them together. [Holograph marginal comment: "Sheila—Put this in Blake's file. H."]

Please let me know how projected funding cuts are going to affect our war here. Saigon is already feeling the pinch, and I've asked all my people to cut back on their travel funds. It would be nice to know what the big plans are—on either side. Stark.

59

Article, *The New York Times*. Major Blake cut out part of a longer article, as well as an advertisement. The three-column headline reads: "Hanoi Confirms Ban on Secret Talks."

PARIS, Feb. 12—Xuan Thuy, chief of the North Vietnamese delegation to the Paris peace talks, confirmed tonight

The Laotian Fragments

that there would be no secret talks as long as the United States maintained Philip C. Habib as acting head of its delegation. A spokesman for Mr. Thuy had hinted at this policy during press briefings following last week's plenary sessions. Asked at a reception this evening whether this was indeed Hanoi's attitude, Mr. Thuy nodded and said, "That is correct."

Mr. Thuy has boycotted the plenary sessions since Dec. 11 as a protest against alleged "sabotage" of the talks by the United States. . . . The United States has emphasized all along that Mr. Habib is fully authorized to negotiate on any point. . . .

[The advertisement is affixed here with Scotch tape.] The Bangle Belt by Duchess/Wear it on your hips or slip it around your waist. Looks fabulous with those new clingy knits. It's definitely the hip new fashion look. Has an adjustable closing so it fits.

Holograph comment: "Or you can simply shove the personality-ridden mess up your ass."

60

Memo on DD Form 95, written in pencil, undated. The handwriting is Major Blake's.

Note: What would Lincoln (whose next week birthday's no longer a national holiday) have done here? What did it take for him to fire his number-one general and replace him with that sonofabitch Grant? And who remembers Grant's birthday? But he won the war. Or did he? Just who does win a war? Or should the question be "Just what wins a war?" Or, "Just what does a war win?"

Note for tomorrow: Horowitz, 1030 (lunch)—drop by ARMA in afternoon and get the ground view. Formal briefings just don't give people the info they need.

61

Teletype message, AOC 20A to OUSAIRA, Vientiane, 12 February.

SUBJECT: Weekly Operations Report

1. New supplies received in good condition along with replacement parts for T-28s. Ordnance on hand is satisfactory.

2. On 5 February the first of the Lao reinforcements landed at L-22 in the Plain of Jars. Looked like the same Neuts who came up for the Prime Minister's canceled visit. Colonel Bounlouth now says there are about 1200 troops available on station, roughly divided equally between the FAR, SGU, and Neuts. My eyeball estimate confirms this number. The SGUs are patrolling occasionally and report no clashes with the enemy. The little guys seem OK, but no one's hanging pictures on their bunkers.

3. Big problem is still weather. Haze and smoke are very bad, even in and around the PDJ. Is there any way we could get a portable GCA [radar ground-controlled approach] unit up there? I know we can't use one at 20A because of the mountains, but Xieng Khouang is wide open for so many miles. Or would that be too politically sensitive? After all, you got a couple of air-conditioned trailers up for the allied generals. Please advise.

4. Important subject: read your report regarding the success of interdiction on routes 7 and 61. Please congratulate USAF on closing both roads. Unfortunately, there have been no reports of any NVA starving to death or running out of ammunition for the past five years. VP is grumbling a bit about fewer sorties available for his patrols, and he says the NVA can get through all the stuff it wants on the trails under the canopy. He says he'll send more men out on the ground if USAF will commit more airplanes to area preparation, but you say the aircraft

won't be available until more ground troops are out. Better resolve this little paradox.

5. New Raven 26 in place and flying. Good man. No problems with a pilot as experienced as this one.

6. PS: I'm dead serious about paragraph #4, above. The only way to stop these supplies is to hit them at the other end, hard enough so that the gradual withdrawal plan now in effect will work. If you cut one road, they'll just build another one—or else double the number of porters. Hamilton.

62

Teletype message, OUSAIRA, Vientiane, to AOC 20A, 13 February.

1. Appreciate your comments regarding close air support versus interdiction. Sorry. Recent published reports show that interdiction efforts have stopped major percentage of NVA resupply effort both on the trail and in northern Laos; therefore, decision is to continue keeping roads closed. Tell the General that we're ready whenever he needs us, and urge him to get as many of his men out into the field as possible. If you can substantiate with hard facts any claims that the enemy is getting heavy stuff through, please advise. Otherwise AIRA cannot make a case based upon your intuition (which, by the way, Dante, I do value).

2. No GCA unit possible. You know why.

3. New item: by authorization of Horowitz and RLG officials, you are to give Mr. Blake all assistance and cooperation from now on. Mr. Morrinello will receive similar instructions through his channels. Barnes.

63

Notes, written in pencil on standard 8×10½" typewriter paper in Major Blake's hand, undated. Title centered in capital letters, "THE WITHDRAWAL PLAN," with the comment, "at last."

Postmortem notes for the record: Horowitz directing the scenario, replete with purple pants, white fringed shirt, and appropriate steely-eyed flunky flipping the pages of the giant tablet mounted on the easel. In attendance: Me, Col. Barnes, Lt. Col. Raphael (Army guy), "Big Al," and a couple of others I didn't recognize. Plan to be briefed to Thai-based commanders next week (Thurs, 19 Feb?) after session up here with General what's-his-name on the 18th. Then he'll take it to Saigon and brief them the following week. No notes permitted at meeting—these are recapitulation.

Overall idea one of hopping from mountaintop to mountaintop—transport by chopper with heavy air cover (available?)—leave the valleys to the bad guys but keep pressure on them at all times. Control access routes with mortar and howitzer fire from the high ground. Series of lines (three? four?) represented by linked dots, tightening in phases around Long Tieng. Each phase outlined in a different color—we hold five or six key positions at a time—then, if the situation becomes untenable, hop all forces back to the next line. Phou Nok Kok the pivot of the first line (interesting—it was scratched off in grease pencil)—Lima 22 (Xieng Khouang) the center of line 3. Everything looks like rough ripples going out from 20A. Big fight, if necessary, for Lima 22, but Horowitz seems not to think there will be much of a problem because of open terrain. "If they'll stand and fight," says Horowitz, "we can stop the enemy cold, especially if he brings in armor and heavy guns." —if—if— "If the army will do its job." (My unasked question: How can the NVA bring in armor and heavy

The Laotian Fragments

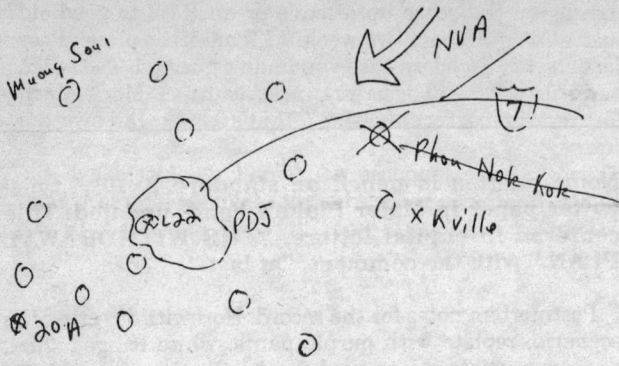

The rough sketch above appears on the verso of page 1 of Major Blake's notes. Compare previous map, pages 50–51.

guns if we've got the roads blocked, as our own reports say. Maybe we should declassify the reports and publish them so the enemy will know how hopeless their cause is.) Basic theme: Every mountaintop a Phou Nok Kok—chew the bad guys up—nibble away at them.

Asked question: Is it our intention to hold the PDJ? Answer: We'll have to play it by ear and see what happens.

64

Letter addressed to Major Blake, dated February 8. Envelope postmarked Melbourne, Australia. Assuming a five-day transit period, Major Blake probably received this letter on February 13.

Hi sweetie,
 Just a note from an old admirer who's been lying in the sun and wondering what's going on back home. Any

chance you can scare up a leave or an R&R to good old Australia in the next two weeks? I'll meet the plane. Poor old Valerie's bored, in case you hadn't guessed. Too much competition here. These girls are beautiful. Mach Mach GIs "resting and recuperating" (that's a laugh) all over the place.

Then again, I suppose you won't want to leave the mighty Sheila (see enclosed letter). I don't care, really, just so there's enough left for me. And don't mind Daddy—he's just a bit overprotective.

Love,
V (for victory)

65

Letter from Mr. Abraham Horowitz to Miss Valerie Horowitz, care of the Alexandra Club, 139 Collins St., Melbourne, Australia, dated February 2. Enclosure to item 64.

My Dear Valerie:

I trust that your vacation is going well, and please know that your mother and I miss you. A postcard would certainly help.

Your mother and I were talking the other day about the future, and you, of course, figured prominently in the discussion. I think you should start giving serious thought to a career—to something a bit more permanent than the life you have often of necessity been forced to live until now because of my job. I gather that you don't plan to return to the university—that's fine, dear—but I would like you to have some alternative in mind. You just can't keep running forever. Soon you'll have to stand up and face things. I'm sorry I sound trite, but it's true.

Perhaps the main reason I'm writing this is because of your attraction to Bill Blake. I know you've seen him more than a few times, and if a father's judgment is any criterion at all, you've rather tumbled for him on very short notice. I think you may be barking up the wrong tree. He's quite securely married, you know, but in addition seems to have succumbed to the Oriental atmosphere, as do so many others who have come over here. I do not, as you know, ever lecture on "morality," as such—nor do I believe that a man's private life is of any concern as long as he does his job (which Bill does very well indeed). However, he does make frequent forays to the local establishments, and in addition has been paying no little attention to our Sheila, who as you know has almost become an older sister to you during these past few years.

I have talked to her, and she assures me that everything is aboveboard, so far, and that she likes Bill as a friend, no more. But you know as well as I do what might happen. After all, Sheila has never carried on with any man since her divorce, and I suppose she has natural impulses, just as I'm certain you do. You should bear this all in mind when you decide on your future, whether it be here or back in the States (which, by the way, wouldn't be too bad an idea. If you wish, I can help you get a very good job in Washington).

Please forgive a father for rambling on, but your mother and I do love you very much, and want only the best for you. Have a good time, and let us know how you are.

Affectionately,
Daddy

66

Blake, *Journal*, pp. 70–83.

Saturday—Happy Valentine's Day. Dropped some candy by Sheila's but she was working (called later). Says Horowitz has got the whole office going full blast on a crash project that she couldn't mention on the phone. That happens. Our office was dead today. Very, very little going on. Even the command post radio was quiet most of the day.

Routine calls. Flew a nothing mission this morning up to Luang Prabang. Very little to report there.

The incredible contrasts of it all—the paradox—so quiet one moment, so intensely brutal the next. Like the river—the mighty Mekong. Like flying over Phou Nok Kok last week (Tuesday?) and seeing absolutely nothing at all. No ground fire—no signs of movement. The bunkers and trenches looking very much intact. What was I expecting—the Argonne Forest? I was tempted to drop down low and slow and take a good look, but decided not to. Probably a good idea. There were some strikes going in up on Route 7. Flew over one of the interdiction points where the dirt road snakes along a rather steep hill, like the old Pikes Peak highway. You can see where tracks cross a small stream and then disappear into a landslide of rubble for about a hundred yards (the Thuds have been dropping 2000 pounders on the top of the hill). Nothing can get through there, except an occasional foot soldier or two. There's a wreck of a bulldozer on its back where the road used to be. Once, apparently, the bad guys tried to clear the road after a slide, but the bulldozer got stuck and we hit it the next morning. I wonder how many times that bulldozer has been killed. Pilots need a target to shoot at.

Weird's out showing our FNG [Fucking New Guy] the town. Hope he can hack the hardship. Seems nice enough. I learned of his coming about three days before he got here (everything handled from Saigon, re assignments, etc.). Hope he's not like Donahue, whom we had to fire last week. Got too shaky. Said to Barnes and me in our final interview that the real reason he'd volunteered for this program was that he'd heard via the grapevine that we had a neat war going on up here, that the Ravens took 50% casualties, and that we all carried cyanide pills in case of capture. A real Steve Canyon type. I hate to think this, but Valerie was right again. She got going one night at a party and told me that underneath it all Donahue really didn't have any balls and had no staying power. Maybe we should make her our personnel officer. Maybe she is already.

I'd read—but there isn't much more to read. The classified CHECO reports document the Air Force's role from the beginning, but there's a definite blue suit flavor in all but a few. The Army doesn't have a comparable series of reports—at least not here (or else they won't show me—but I think they're being straight, despite what Barnes says). No one gets into the Company files. I wonder if they keep records here, anyway. I'd guess it's all in Washington. I sure hope they're microfilming everything. They don't set up permanent facilities—unlike the military who build officers' clubs and exchanges and BOQs. Wonder if the cost of tearing all those buildings down affects the decisions whether to pull out or not?

As for the civilian stuff, except for a few, the analyses are superficial. I had hoped that by reading both classified and unclassified publications I could, in a sense, fit two combs together, but I can't. There are still great gaps. Dommen is by far the best, but only for the early stuff, and he's just too cute at times. Gets carried away with neat stories and startling facts. He does know his subject, though. Hilsman is too petulant. You get the idea that he's pissed off because Kennedy didn't take his advice all the time. Hoopes [Townsend Hoopes, *The Limits of Intervention*] just ignores Laos—a serious flaw. You can't understand Southeast Asia country by country. They're all intermixed. We're refashioning the same wheel in Laos that we labored so to build in Vietnam during the '60s. Who's next? Thailand? Cambodia? No, not Cambodia. Everyone says that. Sihanouk's too strong. And the others—the Dooley books (what a passionate man), masterpieces of frustrated evangelism—Larteguy [Jean Lartéguy, *Les Tambours de Bronze (The Bronze Drums)*] and even Champassak [Sisouk na Champassak, *Tempête sur le Laos (Storm over Laos)*] are articulate, but extremely subjective and fragmentary. They take a thesis and find the facts to support it. And no one really has access to all the facts, anyway. I've combed the British Information Service Library, the Bibliothèque Nationale, and the USIS Library. Everyone thought I was a spy. Wish Pop Buell would write a book, but he's too busy saving lives [see item 81].

I wonder why I'm doing all this? I'm reminded of a movie I saw some time ago, Aldo Ray in *The Night They Robbed the Bank of England*—there was a British captain, the chief bank guard, played by someone I forget, who figured out that the vault was going to be robbed and was frustrated in getting all the officials together to open it up on a national bank holiday. Great scene, with the bad guys burning their way up through the steel floor inside the vault, while outside the senior bank official was telling the captain, "You're crazy. No one can rob the Bank of England. You think too much for a military man." Maybe that's my problem, too—and maybe that's why this reflective piece of writing sounds more like a paper for old Professor Harding's class than it does a journal entry.

Anyway, it's been a good afternoon and evening. Van did some fantastic giant shrimp in garlic butter when I got back from a walk—then I went down along the river and watched the sun set. The water level's going down. You can almost see the river shrink. There is much less flotsam now, and at times the water looks almost clear in places. The Mekong, the Volga, the Mississippi, the Amazon—great rivers about which great books have been written. Even if you don't care for rivers as symbols (which I don't), you can't help sensing something. Example: the Lao side of the Mekong is shaggy and undeveloped (except right around Vientiane), with little brush clumps and muddy, swirled beaches (seems like a perpetual beach side). The bank side, Thailand, looks quite regular, with neat little houses, some with thatched roofs, others with shining tin ones, lining the waterfront. Trees grow there, right down to the riverbank. We are at war here—they (officially) are not. Then of course, I was only looking at a piece of the river. Must remember to see if this comparison holds all the way down stream to Cambodia.

Also walked by the beach where one of the Lao pilots killed himself last week buzzing his girl friend's house. Returning from a combat mission—decided to give the folks at home a thrill—clobbered on his second pass. Hamilton said it was quite a funeral. All the Lao pilots attended, including the RLAF Commanding General, and no one in the RLAF flew any missions that day in respect to the dead. Wonder what the North Vietnamese were doing.

Hell—I suppose I'd better get to sleep, keeping my fingers crossed that Weird doesn't take it into his head to bring me home another present. I confess that the mystery of the Orient has worn somewhat thin for me. Four and a half months to go. But then what? Enough.

67

Teletype message, AOC 20A to OUSAIRA, Vientiane, 15 February.

Re the withdrawal from Xieng Khouangville last night, General Vang Pao says that he has not abandoned the village. His intelligence sources confirm enemy activity a few kilometers down the trail to the east, and VP has decided not to keep his forces in the town at night, when the enemy usually attacks. Consequently, he plans to occupy Xieng Khouangville during the daylight hours only. His troops will deploy on the surrounding peaks at night to protect the artillery. He requests increased airstrikes in the valleys east of Xieng Khouangville, round the clock. Hamilton.

68

Teletype message, 7AF, Saigon, to OUSAIRA, Vientiane, 16 February.

SUBJECT: Airstrikes in Laos

1. Regret that your request of 15 Feb for additional sorties east of Xieng Khouangville must be denied. Photorecce and all-source intelligence do not, repeat, do not confirm increased enemy buildup in that area. Furthermore, it is impossible from our resources to divert aircraft based upon one man's opinion, regardless of his rank.

2. Seriously, Jake, I know you've been up there a long time and know the situation better than perhaps anyone else in the world. But we've got indications that the NVA

are planning a big push down here for Tet, and we must concentrate on the Trail. Of course, TIC [Troops in Contact] will take first priority, when and if it develops, but we just cannot assign half our fleet to blowing up trees in hopes a limb or two will fall on the enemy. Suggest that you pressure the RLAF to concentrate T-28s in that area, and if anything really develops, we'll support you. Please try and explain this to Vang Pao, with our apologies. I wish we could all fight a war the way the little general wants it fought, but we've got a lot of different pressures to contend with, not the least of which is the pending scaledown of forces. Above all, we don't act; we react. OK? I will explain more about this next week when you come down on Wednesday. Please try to make it—it's my last planning conference before going back to the (ugh) Pentagon.

69

Memo, Barnes to Blake, 16 February.

Bill:

Once again, the attached message [item 68] speaks for itself. I can't really blame them, but we're faced with a dilemma, here and all the way up the line. In this war, any commander who makes his own decision is subject to excoriation from above—perhaps that's why there are so few real decisions made. We know the raw data from our own experience—in this case, that Vang Pao's brother-in-law or someone says the bad guys are moving around. So we call for air—bombs get dropped—and nothing can be verified to satisfy the pound-of-flesh per pound-of-bomb analysts who have to report to *their* superiors about cost effectiveness and results. So we get cut back on airplanes. As a result, what happens is that what you think or I think or even Vang Pao, for that matter, thinks gets lost in the computer and nothing gets done.

So we've got to give them some results. It's the only way. From now on, I want you and your Ravens to report everything possible that could conceivably be evidence of enemy troop movements. I know there are only 21 of you—and it means extra flying. If necessary, "forget" to log some of your missions. I know that there are increased numbers of jet FACs [F-4 aircraft] operating up north now, but they go too fast to spot what we need to see. And when you put in a strike, the benefit of doubt should be given to the possibility that there *was* something there. If what you see even *seems* like a hard target, report it as such. Note: I am not, repeat, am *not* telling you directly to lie. Remember that, and when you get through reading this memo, burn it before eating the ashes.

Barnes

PS: And tell your boys down south to keep their eyes open too. Something's brewing. Exactly what, I'm not sure. The Lao Military Region Commander just sent his family to Thailand for a "vacation." I suppose the only fact we do know is that we don't know—and, short of invoking Buddha, there's not a damn thing we can do until the enemy moves.

70

Memo (carbon copy) from Blake to Horowitz, dated 16 February.

Mr. Horowitz:

This note is in the form of a plea. Because of the increasingly precarious situation, I would like to request that you or one of your intelligence people notify me directly, either in person or by secure phone, of any significant information relative to enemy troop or supply movements. That way our USAF intelligence reports to Saigon can back up yours, and vice versa, and at least our requests will stem from similar facts. In return I'll ask my Ravens to debrief your people immediately along with ours.

Suggest also that you try to ring in the Army intell people on this as well. Their ground reports are also most important, but until now the daily dog and pony show briefings have been the only source of information, and what with the individual briefings at 0730, then the Country Team meetings later in the morning, by the time we get to use any of the material it's time for lunch and the Lao siesta. OK?

Thank you.

Blake

Holograph comment in Major Blake's hand: "OK—confirmed by phone. H. says to be careful, though. Careful of what?"

71

Teletype message, OUSAIRA, Vientiane, to AOC 20A, 17 February.

SUBJECT: High-level Visit

Re our previous discussions and messages, your visitors will arrive with me tomorrow morning on the 0900 shuttle. In addition to the expected new out-of-country Deputy Commander, I have been informed that there will also be a ranking representative from home. Act accordingly and make certain they are afforded every courtesy. Tell General Vang Pao it is a very important day. Barnes.

72

Letter, typewritten and double spaced, from Dante Hamilton to Bill Blake. No date. The editor has emended where necessary to correct misspellings, typographical errors, strikeovers, and the like. The letter was obviously written in haste.

The Laotian Fragments

Dear Bill:

One of the Company chopper pilots will bring this down to you ASAP. He's got a 0530 takeoff for Vientiane. But I want you to get the straight scoop before you get the official word. It's 0400 now—I'm in the command post—and it's been a hell of a night. Everybody's asleep, and they're due to leave at 0900.

First of all—no one threw the General's aide in the bear cage behind the Ice House. That slimy little non-rated son of a bitch deserved it—but there was only talk, not action. And Vang Pao did not order him shot for taking pictures with his brand new Rolex. It was one of VP's guards who raised his rifle when he saw a stranger standing there in front of the compound with all his lenses hanging out. Didn't anyone tell him about cameras at Alternate? What did he think he was—a tourist? Remember what VP tried to do to that reporter who sneaked in here last year?

Here's how it all happened. The Air America C-123 brought the group up, and VP, plus his whole staff, met them at 1100. Morrinello, myself, and Burr were there too. I thought they had been well briefed, but when the General and the Senator got off the plane, they looked as if they thought we were all crew chiefs, or parking attendants, or something. You know how short VP is. He was wearing his favorite baseball cap with the braid and his initials on the back, but I swear he'd at least had his fatigues pressed. We were all in civvies, of course. Problem always is that VP looks about fifteen years old—and even when Barnes pointed him out to the visitors, they seemed to stare right by him. Mach Mach loss of face.

We went directly from the Company compound to VP's house—and I think that was the first time the big boys realized who they were with. They seemed impressed with the fact that the house was the only "modern" one in the valley (except for the King's palace on the hill, which they couldn't see because of the haze)—and they sort of marched up, and when VP's bodyguards saluted they all saluted back, even the Senator. Our General's aide kept looking around as if he were an FBI man searching for assassins.

Bill—when this happens again, please tell our guys to eat before they come—then be polite and sample each part of a meal when they get here. And tell them about VP's scotch bit. They all seemed surprised when there was a bottle of White Horse for each of them—and no ice—and VP's boys kept filling up the GI water glasses with warm scotch—and by 1300 the whole day was shot. VP gauges people by the way they react to him. He's king here—by law and by tradition. Our General was OK—he didn't drink that much, but everyone else, including Barnes, was on their ear. What's bugging Barnes, anyway? I've never seen him like this.

About 1500 VP began strutting, as only he can do, and he led us all on a tour of the valley. He'd gotten the shops to stay open, and we lost the Senator for a while when he was bargaining with a little girl for some silver. We walked all over hell—even up the mountain to the King's palace, which VP said he was guarding for his country, and down again, and by the time VP turned the group over to the Company people for their part of the show, our guests were damn near dead. I think the General took a short nap somewhere. The Senator was last seen throwing up.

Then it was time for cocktails about 7:00 PM back at VP's house. He'd gotten in some hill tribe dancers—and we ate and drank—and by 9:00 the General's aide was dancing with the girls, the Senator was pounding on the table, and Barnes looked just plain green. Jesus, imagine this scene (you've been in VP's living room)—it looked like some kind of a Roman orgy, with his highness VP reigning and calling the shots. Goddamn it, Bill, he's just like any other Asiatic—he'll wear you down to see what you're made of—then he'll bargain. Remember the drinking contest I won? VP set up the glasses of scotch, said the guy before me had downed 17 half-full water tumblers, and let me know that I could try to beat his record if I wanted to. I hit 18—and puked for three days, but I didn't let VP know it.

VP plays the game to the hilt—and when he nodded to our General that it was time to talk, old dumbass Burr, *your* boy, *your* head Raven up here, took it into his head to start shooting off his mouth about how to really win the war—about how the General didn't have any idea what was really going on and that he, Burr, was going to tell him because he only had three weeks left on his assignment and he wanted to set the record straight. Damn it all, if they ever really find out what's going on they'll change it. Burr was so drunk he missed the General's order to see him in the morning, and he kept standing behind where the General was sitting, yapping. Then the General's aide came over and told *Major* Burr that the *General* wanted his ass out of there, on the double, and Burr told him that he'd better shut up or VP would have him shot (that's where the story got going). The aide said that he, Burr, didn't have that kind of authority, to which Burr replied, looking at the General, "You've got two stars, but I've got a bigger combat command than you do. I can get a hell of a lot more done in this war than you can."

Morrinello jumped in then, standing up and nodding to a couple of his boys, and they got Burr out of there, and the General told his aide to sit down. Then VP started laughing and called for more scotch—the music kept on going—and Al and I went back to his room and cried. It takes a lot to shake Al, he's been here 5 years, but this one did. Fortunately, the Senator was drunk enough to have missed it all, but I don't know about a couple of his icy assistants who'll probably tell him in the morning what he ought to remember about last night.

Oh yes—somewhere during the afternoon the General's aide said how he envied all the people up here killing North Vietnamese, how he'd love to be able to kill the enemy, and VP said, "You want to kill NVA? Good." He said something to a sergeant standing beside him (I think we were down by the hospital then, just east of the runway), and in about five minutes the sergeant returned with the scraggliest-looking prisoner I'd ever seen. He looked about eighty pounds and his hands were tied behind his back. VP pulled his pearl-handled .45 out of the holster, turned it around and offered it to the aide, then said, "You want to kill NVA? OK. You do it. Right now. Or I set him free." Only the aide's dark glasses kept his eyeballs from falling on the ground. We were all frozen for a minute or two, with the NVA guy looking quickly from one to the other of us, and then Al started laughing and clapped VP on the back. "Number-one joke, General," he said. "Number-one," and he took the .45 and gave it back to VP. VP just smiled, and we continued our tour. I don't know if he set the prisoner free or not.

Anyway, these are the highlights. I'm sure there is a lot more which Barnes will tell you—if he remembers, that is. Honestly, I'm surprised at the way he acted—I've known him for a long time, and even though you know I think he's a candyass, he's still been as straight as can be. At least he lets you do your job, unofficially.

But stand by for the blast—and you'd better start looking for a replacement for Burr earlier than you'd planned. If he gets fired tomorrow, I can handle his job up here as well as mine—for a while, anyway.

Good luck,
Dante

73

Memo from Office of the United States Air Attache, Vientiane, Laos, to the following addressees: RLAF Commander; The Major, Air Commanding Officer of RLAF Vientiane Air Base; The General Managers of Air Companies: RAL, Lao Airlines, Lao Air Transport, Thai Airways, Air Vietnam, Xieng Khouang Air Transport; His Royal Highness, the Director of Civil Aviation. Dated 20 February.

Gentlemen:

The Attache regrets to inform you that from now on the *Guide to Airfields and Approach Facilities, Laos* should reflect UFN (Unfriendly) status for the Lima Site at Xieng Khouangville. As of this morning, Friday, 20 February, field reports indicate that the enemy now holds the town and the adjacent airstrip.

[signed] J. Barnes, Col. USAF

74

Teletype message, AOC 20A to OUSAIRA, Vientiane, 20 February. Priority, FLASH.

Reliable reports from ground teams report 20, repeat 20, enemy APC [Armored Personnel Carrier] vehicles, plus an undetermined number of PT76 tanks sighted five miles south, repeat, south of the main interdiction point on Route 7, heading general vicinity of PDJ. Source is ground team who observed vehicles just before dawn today, then withdrew when enemy patrols approached. Source said that all APCs appeared filled with troops and that there may have been some wheel mounted artillery and/or AAA weapons. Ground team exfilled by chopper and on way back now. No friendly forces in area. Three Ravens airborne at first light for recce. Hamilton.

75

Tape recording, Sony cassette, no title, no date. Identification of speakers made by internal evidence.

Blake (I): . . . so maybe this is it?

Hamilton (I): Maybe. You can't tell with these guys. And maybe there were only a couple of trucks.

Blake (I): You take the left side, I'll scan the right.

Hamilton (I): OK. By the way, I like your idea of grid searching. We usually just go up and look.

Blake (I): It's something we used to do in-country.

Hamilton (I): Well . . . look, I apologize for the shit I've been giving you. OK?

Blake (I): No sweat. Let's get to work. See anything at all?

Hamilton (I): Negative.

Brickbat: Raven 01, Brickbat, over.

Blake: Go ahead, Brickbat.

Brickbat: Raven 01, Home Plate advises aircraft you requested are authorized and available, providing targets assured. Advise when needed.

Blake: Wilco, Brickbat. Raven 01 out.

Hamilton (I): Providing targets assured. There's the clinker.

Blake (I): We'll find them.

Hamilton (I): Want to bet? Lemme tell you something, my friend. Look at that trail down there, for example. Would it support tanks?

Blake (I): Sure, but nothing's been over it. We're only a thousand feet above it now, and it hasn't been used.

Hamilton (I): Bullshit. Let me have the bird. Got any guts?

Blake (I): Your aircraft. Lead on.

Hamilton (I): *Now* look, Bill. You can see under the trees. See all the room they've got?

Blake (I): You've got fifteen feet of clearance on this side.

Hamilton (I): Rog. I live down here most of the time. Look at the road surface. See any tracks? You won't, and that's what's funny. No footprints, no animal tracks, no nothing. We're going up now.

Blake (I): You just set the "G" force record for the O-1.

Hamilton (I): I'd just be breaking my own, babes. Now—suppose they sent some stuff through at night and then swept the road afterward. Suppose they've got a series of little way stations *under* the triple canopy that they've had prepared for months, with backpacked gas and spare parts. Suppose they only want to move two–three miles a day. It's only a few weeks from North Vietnam that way.

Blake (I): Wouldn't their engines be picked up by radar—or whatever super scopes we've got up here at night?

Hamilton (I): Maybe, if the birds happened to be in the right place at the right time. I don't know what kind of stuff they've got up here at night, anyway. Nobody tells me the details. Anyway, they could pull the APCs and the guns down by hand, to use them just for the big push at the end. With their engines off, they wouldn't show up on any scope.

Blake (I): I see. So where are we?

Hamilton (I): Right where we've been for years—flying down in the weeds hoping to spot something—a mistake, maybe—praying that some bad guy got drunk last night and forgot to push his truck all the way under the camouflage net.

Blake (I): What about using sensors up here—like they have on the trail?

Hamilton (I): Maybe they do, but I think they probably don't. Look at the terrain—wide open in spots, mountains and jungles in other places. You'd have to put sensors every four feet over the whole damn country to do any good. It's not like the Trail, where there are only certain routes and passes the enemy can use. Up here, they could come from anywhere, and I think it would just cost too damn much to blanket the area. See anything? It's a hell of a clear day, for a change.

Blake (I): Negative. Let's swing down by Xieng Khouangville. Weird said a long time ago that he suspected they'd come in through there, from the east—and the bad guys own it now.

Hamilton (I): Nobody owns it, I think. VP pulled back a little ways. If he can sucker the bad guys into the town, he can chew them up with artillery from the peaks. But I don't think they'll bite. Let's go. The other four Ravens can hack the grids. I'm glad you laid on this extra flight. By the way, have you heard my favorite story about sensors—about the lieutenant and the nurse?

Blake (I): No. I laid on the extra flight because I wanted to see what's up, myself. Weird's holding down the fort.

Hamilton (I): He's a good man. Anyway, it seems they dropped one of those gadgets near a bivouac area, and when they turned it on, they picked up a conversation between an NVA lieutenant and a nurse. He was putting the make on her, and she was being coy like all women anywhere, telling him about Uncle Ho's instructions that women should put the country above sex, and all that. Then she reminded him of his wife and family back home who thought he was fighting gloriously for freedom in South Vietnam, and so on. Nevertheless, he finally scored, and the damned sensors recorded it all. They've got a tape. The funny thing was that the next day some colonel with a sense of humor had some leaflets made up (we couldn't bomb them, because it was a village then), and a couple of guys flew up and saturated the area with paper. The leaflets gave the whole seduction story, complete with names and the conversations. We laughed about that one for weeks. I'd love to know what happened.

Blake (I): My favorite is the one about the NVA guy who spotted one of the sensors hanging in a tree. Apparently he climbed up to get it and couldn't, so he decided to saw off the limb it was on. There's a lot of talk back and forth between him and the guys on the ground—"hand me the saw," and so on—and you can hear sounds of sawing, swearing, I think he dropped the saw once, much breaking of branches—and then suddenly there's a loud cracking noise and a piercing scream, followed by a thud. The intell people conclude that he sawed the limb off all right, but inboard from where he was sitting.

Hamilton (I): I hadn't heard that one. You'd think with all that sophistication we'd be doing better than we are.

Blake (I): No comment.

Hamilton (I): Rog.

Brickbat: Raven 01, Brickbat, over.

Blake: Go ahead, Brickbat.

Brickbat: Roger, Raven. I've got two flights for you, if you can use them. Negative reports from the other four Ravens.

Blake: Negative here too, Brickbat. Send them to their alternate targets.

Brickbat: Roger, Raven. Sorry.

Blake: I'm sorry too, Brickbat.

Hamilton (I): Why don't we put them in somewhere, just to shake up the bad guys' siesta.

Blake (I): I don't think we'd better. It's touchy enough as it is, and I don't want to piss any of our bosses. We've got a few sorties for probing anyway, so let's wait until we really need the others. A couple of confirmed tanks will go a long way.

Hamilton (I): OK. You're right. That's Ban Don down there, about fifteen clicks east of Xieng Khouangville. It's all bad guy territory.

Blake (I): It looks so goddamn peaceful.

Hamilton (I): You know, Bill, I really love this country. I really do.

Blake (I): So do I.

76

Notes from a planning conference, dated 24 February, on plain 8×10½" bond; interleaved between pages 83 and 84 of Major Blake's *Journal*. There is a great amount of marginal doodling and underlining of certain phrases.

I'm jotting notes, waiting for the conference to start. Normal periodic meeting of all participants on our side, except this time everyone looks a little more somber. Let's see—reps from the A-1, F-4, and F-105 outfits—all in flight suits. The A-1 guys still have their mustaches. Major Johnson from Saigon (frag shop), some headquarters weenies, and a few others I don't recognize (the faces change so rapidly as people rotate in and out). Two colonels from Intelligence, one a new guy (replacement?). Barnes and Vonnegut (the new Lt. Col. who's his assistant attache—wonder if his SAC background means anything). And me for the Ravens. About 18–20 in all, sitting around and beside the General's big planning table in his conference room. It's nice and cool. Interesting contrast in colors—civilian clothes (mainly white shirts), HQ weenies in khaki, pilots in olive drab flight suits, a few men in special jungle fatigues. Enter the General and Horowitz—let the meeting begin (Christ, is Horowitz wearing *spats?* No—just two-tone shoes).

Gen. K——: says good morning—big agenda—let's get down to business.

Intell Report by Col. Gabriel (slides in big screen): Let's begin with the situation in Military Region 1, up here to the northwest. I'll take the first part of the briefing, then Mr. Horowitz will take over. In MR I—relatively quiet northwest of Luang Prabang—enemy still holds Nam

Tha—light probing attacks—no excessive boat traffic on the Nam Tha and other rivers—little to say (droning on, he's done this a thousand times)—security at Luang Prabang Airport no problem—enemy same number of troops as last time. Chinese Road keeps heading south—another kilometer completed.

Now down to MR IV—Pakse, Attopeu, Saravane—little activity there either. Bases on Bolovens Plateau relatively quiet—NVA defectors say regular cadres badly hurt by American airstrikes along lower Trail—tells story about NVA truck driver who was captured—he was asked how they avoid being hit by air—said (swears it's true) that if they hear a propeller-driven aircraft (A-1, gunship) they drive for the nearest tree and try to hide—but if they hear a jet they stop in the middle of the road and hide under the truck—HAH—A-1 boys laughing and applauding and cheering, while the jet jocks look at each other and frown. Bad day for the blowtorches. Reports that southern NVA forces depleted by demands in South Vietnam. Morale good.

Same with MR III around Savannakhet, although friendly troops not out very far from the lines around the city. B-52 strikes doing heavy damage on the Trail below the passes—no signs of SAMs—AAA increasing as it always does this time of year.

MR V (right around Vientiane)—nothing except one rice-burning action against PL [Pathet Lao] rice fields—no contact with enemy—active training of FAR troops—counterinsurgency measures seem to be working well. Now to MR II—Mr. Horowitz will brief.

Horowitz: I wouldn't put too much stock in that MR V PL rice burning, George. We think that was our General Phanasouk trying to eliminate some competition. He's in the rice business too. And there's one more thing about MR I—you know that Highway 13 north to Luang Prabang has been open, surprisingly, for some time. We think we've found out why. Under the terms of the USAID agreement with Laos, the Lao military can't fly supplies up for free—they have to go in by private carrier to stimulate private enterprise. Well, the RLAF Commanding General got angry over the price the single company (owned by a Lao two-star Army general) was charging to get food up by truck, so he authorized a couple of C-47s to fly in rice. The trucking company went on strike, and the next day some bad guys ambushed one convoy of army replacements. We've asked the RLAF to stop flying their own stuff in. Problem should be taken care of soon.

About MR II: You've all heard the report about the tanks and APCs. There's been no follow-up intelligence to speak of, but we suspect they're there, and the situation could break wide open at any time. When it does, we're going to ask for all the support you can give us—here's what we envision (Oh Christ, it's the withdrawal plan again—this time Xieng Khouangville is crossed off too—with another grease-penciled, colored X—when these guys release a plan, they beat it to death—). Estimate the enemy convoy to be about here (just north of the 7/71 split—bullshit, didn't see a thing yesterday)—asks for maximum effort by USAF air in that general area.

General K——: Do you think that a relatively small saturation attack might do some good?—or at least reveal something?

Horowitz: Sure do.

General K——: Then let's do it.

7AF Major (a *major*—here we go again): When?

General K——: How about tomorrow, Thursday?

7AF Major: No can do—"not programmed for that many sorties."

General K——: Bullshit (gets up, excuses self, leaves room—comes back in three quiet minutes—sits down)—Yes, we can do. I just talked with the boss on the phone. (I'll be damned—maybe this guy has something after all).

7AF Major (gulps): Yes, sir. We'll lay on three flights of four aircraft.

General K——: And let's get some results. Go ahead, Horowitz.

Horowitz: Thank you, General. We can use all the help we can get. Generally speaking, then, we expect the enemy to start nibbling away at our outposts, one by one, and we want to hold each one as long as we can. General Vang Pao has assured me that with proper support from the regular troops, his SGUs will fight for every inch of ground, and that when this dry season ends in May, the Royal Lao Government will be holding more territory than it has in years. Thank you, gentlemen (he's always so goddamn formal in public).

Col. Lunderberg: What's next? Any questions from Intell?

USAF Col (I haven't got his name): Yes Sir; Mr. Horowitz, you mention that we plan to hop from mountaintop to mountaintop. What happens if the enemy tries a massive frontal assault on, say, Lima 22 or Long Tieng—cutting behind your present line. What then? (Here we go—Clausewitz and the Maginot line.)

Horowitz: He's never done that before. He's always preferred small, intense actions.

USAF Col: Yes, but what if he does? Do we have an alternate plan?

Horowitz: We think he'll wait until Long Tieng—if he gets that far—for his big push. Remember, he lost a thousand men at Phou Nok Kok, thanks to your excellent air support (God—what a politician)—and we think he'll save his main forces for an all-out assault on Vang Pao's Headquarters. As you know, VP's been a thorn in the NVA's side for years, and they figure if they can get him, they'll be able to get anything else they want.

USAF Col: Yes, but what if? . . .

Horowitz: This whole war's an "if," Colonel. If we knew what they were going to do we'd make sure they wouldn't do it, now wouldn't we?

Col. Lunderberg: . . . (I was watching the other colonel and Horowitz try to eye each other down, the colonel frowning and Horowitz looking serene and knowledgeable) . . . something about a new code proposal.

Young Captain (Communications, I think, non-rated): There's been a lot of idle chatter over the air—benefit to enemy—etc, etc (now he's passing out little wallet-sized cards—what the hell is *this*—pictures of trucks, tanks, AAA, each with a letter after it) . . . and so we thought we should change the transmission procedure. Example: instead of saying "I see two trucks," the FAC would say "two Alphas," for tanks we'd use "Bravo," for APCs "Charlie," and so on. This way, when the FAC calls in targets or reports BDA, the enemy won't be able to know exactly what he's talking about (individual discussion going on—much gabble—captain blushing breathlessly).

Col. Lunderberg: Any other comments? Here's what I think. I think it's a bunch of shit (here he goes—no wonder people have a hard time working with him). Two *bravos*? Shit, you ever try to fly an airplane and look at a code card at the same time? And how would we fool the enemy? A FAC says "I've got two six-wheeled Bravos rolling down the road at thirty miles per hour," or "There's a 37 mm Delta shooting at me," or "You got the five floating Foxtrots tied up to the dock. Come on, Captain, be sensible." (Captain sits down, really red in face. I feel sorry for the poor guy. All he was trying to do was help win the war his way.)

(That sort of ends the festivities—big group breaks up for individual discussions—I'm to go meet the new General with Lunderberg.)

77

Teletype message, AOC 20A to OUSAIRA, Vientiane, 25 February.

SUBJECT: Special BDA Report

1. Concentrated airstrike flown this morning on coordinates as briefed on suspected truck park and storage areas, TX 202425 and 204137. Although initial BDA assessment was NVR due to smoke and haze, follow-up FAC reports one truck destroyed and one damaged, sixteen road cuts, and one military structure destroyed.

2. However, use caution in assessing above report. Area struck has been hit repeatedly before, and it is possible that observed results were from previous strikes. Visibility over target was so bad at time of attack that drops were made mainly by radar. No reported groundfire. They moved a lot of dirt around, though. Hamilton.

78

Letter from Mr. Ernest D. LaMora, Attorney at Law, to Major William Blake, dated 18 February.

Dear Major Blake:

Of course I remember you, and I am sorry to hear of your marital difficulties. Please accept my sympathy.

I would be happy to represent you at any time, but unfortunately there is a problem in this instance. Because you are not a resident of Texas, and because the civil suit has been initiated in another state, one of which you incidentally are not a resident either—and neither is your wife, because by law a military wife must accept the residence of her husband—there is nothing formal that I can do for you. If you should wish to declare Texas as your permanent domicile, I might be able to help, but that would involve having a residence here to which you plan either to return or retire into. Should you desire to do this, I will be happy to start the necessary proceedings.

However, I really do not think you have much to worry about. Under the World War II Soldiers and Sailors Relief Act, which is still in effect, I doubt very seriously that you can be sued for divorce while overseas in a combat zone. My advice to you is just to ignore the whole thing, saying or doing nothing which would prejudice your case. To be binding, papers must be served upon you in person, and I would suggest that you take no notice of any correspondence which comes your way. I suspect that your wife did not fully acquaint her attorney with the facts of the case—or else she has retained an attorney who is not experienced in military domicile.

Should you wish me to do anything further in your behalf, please do not hesitate to communicate with me.

                            Sincerely,
                            [signed] Ernest D. LaMora

79

DIA Summary (Xerox copy), OUSAIRA, Vientiane, to DIA, Washington, 26 February.

SUBJECT: Situation in the Plain of Jars

1. Although last night's action saw Royal Lao Government forces suffer their worst defeat so far this year, it was not because of lack of fighting spirit or an absence of U.S. airpower. Combined circumstances, along with an unexpectedly superior enemy force using heavy artillery and tanks, completely surprised the defenders of Lima 22 (Xieng Khouang) and overwhelmed them. The Plain of Jars now belongs to the enemy.

2. Here is as complete a report as is possible at this time, pending updates by some field sources which are at present out of contact with this office. Until 2330 local time, no enemy activity had been observed, and the approximately 1000 government forces were in their normal positions both inside and outside the perimeter wires. Two AC-47 gunships were on station, one of which had responded to a brief call for support from Red Tiger, about 15 kilometers from Lima 22. As you are aware, there had been absolutely no ground contact in and around the PDJ for nearly three weeks (see DIA Summary 192145Z February). At 2335 an outpost four miles north of Lima 22 reported what he thought were engine sounds. One of the Spookies was diverted to him, but nothing else was heard or seen, and because of the possibility of firing upon friendly forces, no ammunition was expended. Nevertheless, the entire base at Lima 22 was put on alert. At midnight one Spooky reported off station to return for fuel and relayed back to Nightowl that his replacement would be delayed one-half hour because of guns maintenance problems (he was due on station at 0030). At 0018, White Tiger FAG, on a hilltop just north of Xieng Khouangville, 20 kilometers to the east, reported heavy troops in contact and

that the enemy was at his perimeter wire. The long AC-47 headed toward him and commenced firing almost immediately upon arrival. About two minutes after the Spooky called from White Tiger, at 0034, the enemy launched his attack on Lima 22, coming from the north, east, and west, preceded by an extremely heavy mortar barrage and assisted by what one observer claims were "numerous" 23mm antiaircraft guns firing directly into the base from nearby hills. As you know, these guns possess the most rapid rate of fire in the enemy's arsenal, and their effect must have been devastating. Estimates are that about one-third of the Lima 22 defenders were either killed or wounded by the initial barrage, and the troops around the outer perimeter panicked, fleeing back into, through, and over the wire. Some of them ran through the mine fields, setting off their own mines. The fires and explosions could be seen by the Nightowl crew roughly 30 kilometers away because of the absolutely perfect visibility.

3. A few minutes after the initial assault and before the friendly troops could get reorganized, an undetermined number of tanks and/or APCs breached the wire at the north end of the perimeter, and despite some losses to deflected 105 howitzers firing at point-blank range, some enemy troops had reached the runway by 0050, 16 minutes after initiating the attack. One estimate was that the tanks were traveling 40 miles an hour when they reached the wire. At the sight of the enemy seemingly all around them, some of the defenders attempted to retreat to the south. They were led, we are told, by one of their comanders. Unfortunately, the NVA had established a blocking force to the south as well, and when the friendly troops ran into them, enemy fire caused a large number of casualties. The retreating troops then ran back into the camp, where it is reported that the remaining defenders mistook them for attacking NVA. Finally, the survivors massed together and succeeded in breaking out to the west toward Muong Soui. At 0110 there was a series of massive explosions, and everything became quiet. The AC-47 who had been diverted to White Tiger was recalled at 0055, but he had expended his ammunition and flares against what was apparently a most successful diversion. Two more AC-47s

arrived on station at 0115 and 0120 respectively, but reported no signs of the enemy.

4. Morning reconnaissance reported no signs of life at Lima 22, and surprisingly few bodies in and around the bunkers and trenches. Raven FACs reported numerous new tank tracks crisscrossing the open Plain and that there were at least five additional wrecked tanks and the hulks of three APCs which had not been there the day before. Unfortunately, the five repaired PT76 tanks which friendly forces had been using were missing from their parking spaces, so it is assumed that the enemy about broke even on his armor losses. Part of the POL dump had been destroyed, but the bomb dump and ammunition storage were intact. Consequently, USAF F-4 aircraft were called in at 1000 local to destroy the remaining usable stores. With excellent accuracy, they achieved numerous secondary fires and explosions and denied this valuable resource to the enemy.

5. By afternoon the first stragglers began appearing at Muong Soui, and plans are being formulated for a stand there. It is the last major town north of Long Tieng remaining in friendly hands, and is of great symbolic value to the Lao, being as it is the original Neutralist capital. All other outposts on the defensive lines reported in this morning that they had seen no enemy, and even White Tiger reported that all was quiet there as well.

6. We are all too stunned at this moment for a reasoned assessment of what this all means, but General Vang Pao has flown down to Vientiane for consultations with the Regular Government Forces. We will forward further information as soon as possible.

80

Blake, *Journal*, pp. 84–91.

28 February. If it were leap year, this would be the next to last day of the month. By the looks on some of the faces

here, it may be the last day of the world. Horowitz is unavailable, Barnes is down in Saigon, Sheila won't speak to me for some reason, and I've just finished outprocessing Burr. He's about as chagrined as VP must feel (or is he?—VP, I mean). And Weird leaves next week—he wants to stay, bless him, but there's no real point. He's put in his time, done shit hot work, and it's someone else's turn. Oh hell, Valerie's due in tomorrow—she and the NVA arrive at the same time—like the plague.

Lima 22—looked so quiet this morning . . . and I felt so sterile and disassociated, even when I buzzed the runway the way Hamilton did on our first trip up there. Many men died on the ground two nights ago, but to me it seemed as if the little guys would come running out of their spider holes and start shooting straight up again and waving their hats. I felt like calling out, "Where is everybody?" or landing just for the hell of it and asking someone for a cup of coffee or a cold Singha. Absolutely no sign of anyone—not along the runway—not in the few remaining (about five, I think) structures—not in the trenches which snake around all over the place—I'd guess there are about ten miles of trenches and bunkers in the complex. And the whole base set squat in the middle of the gently rolling Plain of Jars—burned brown and pockmarked from sun and fire and bombs. The nearest hill is about a mile away—it must have been from there that the NVA shot their 23mm—God, what a job that can do—mach-mach rounds per minute with its four barrels. I'll bet those NVA gunners felt like some of our Spooky crewmen do, looking down on the darkling plain and blasting away. More airplanes around today than I've ever seen—7AF sure made good on its promise. Looks like O'Hare International Airport during rush hour. Some wag reported to Brickbat that he was over the North Laos Gunnery Range. I don't think I'd like to be down there now—we're pounding every tree in sight, especially between the PDJ and Muong Soui—can't bomb west of Muong Soui because of the refugees—mainly women and children—leaving town. I guess they believed the government propaganda—for a while.

So where are we? In a mess, I suppose, and I'd love to see

The Laotian Fragments

all the reports that are going out of here these days—to Washington, to Saigon, to Bangkok, to Hawaii, to God knows where else. I wonder if I should take Burr's job myself—not enough time to get a good replacement who knows the terrain and who can work with Hamilton. (Hamilton's really angry today—has a strange look about him—claims that the NVA didn't fight fair by putting that blocking force in, something they've never done before.) No accurate body count, either—some of the troops headed straight for Long Tieng, others went to Muong Soui, others simply vanished. No, not yet. Browning's a good man. I'll put him in Burr's slot at Alternate. He'll be number one up there.

It's not because my going up to Alternate would piss off the ladies. Bah. My having Sheila around is like the guys who flew in Korea—living in Japan and taking off for their daily derring-do against the CHICOMs—and then returning home at night to screaming kids and a wife who wanted to know why hubby was late again. Or at least *most* of them returned. What a hell of a war *that* must have been.

So, I'll take my new copy of *Playboy* to bed. Who the hell is Asa Baber, and how does he know so much about Laos? [No doubt a reference to Asa Baber's novel *The Land of a Million Elephants*, first serialized in *Playboy*, then published in book form.] My fingers are crossed.

Above all, I think I'd better really start recording this whole show, somehow. The new General down south seems real, but he's unfamiliar with this war and I'm an old head (two months—what a veteran). I think I'll cull the files and rathole some of the good stuff—for good old posterity—or a book—or something. *Drums along the Mekong*—there's a good title. Or how about "Down among the Sweltering Napalms" or "Saigon, It's Been Good to Blow Ya"—hell, I'm getting silly. Maybe Sheila would condescend to one more Sawadee screw if I told her I was really going off to fight her Boss's war.

MARCH

81

Article from *The Washington Post*, March 5, entitled "The Meos: 100,000 Have Died in Nine Years of Laos Warfare."

Sam Thong [a village about ten miles west of Long Tieng; it is the official Government capital of the province], Laos (AP)—Covered with dust, a three-day growth of beard on his chin, Edgar "Pop" Buell stood in the door of his house and watched an American helicopter bring in a wounded Meo soldier, only 14.

"They can't take it much more," he said. "Do you know there have been so many young Meos killed that girls are having difficulties finding husbands? The soldiers are getting younger and younger."

"Pop," as he is known to Americans and Meos alike, has been in these hills around the Plain of Jars for nine years.

A retired farmer from Hamilton, Ind., he came to Laos as a $60-a-month volunteer with the International Voluntary Service. He is now U.S. Aid coordinator for the northeast region of Laos, where a powerful North Vietnamese force is pushing the Laotian army back from the Plain of Jars.

Buell, 57, is responsible for feeding and caring for some 350,000 people, about half of them Meo tribesmen who live in the hills and valleys around here. He has seen their number dwindle—through war, hunger, massacres and disease—by about 100,000.

The Laotian Fragments

Buell has accompanied the Meos as they have been pushed back by North Vietnamese forces from the mountains east of the Plain of Jars. After nine years, they are near the edge of the plain.

The Meos have two choices, Buell said. They can remain in the mountains if the North Vietnamese take over or they can flee. Until now, they have always chosen to flee. Less than 10 per cent stayed behind when the North Vietnamese and Pathet Lao, the Laotian guerrillas, took over other areas of their homeland.

The Meos are a nomadic tribe that migrated out of China by way of Vietnam. One group settled in the mountains of what is now Laos about 70 years ago. Other Meos pushed into Thailand. There they are having trouble with the Thai government because of their dislike of authority and a definite liking for growing opium poppy.

Buell thinks the current fighting, in which the Meos are taking most of the casualties, may be their last stand. They have carried most of the brunt of the battle against the North Vietnamese and Pathet Lao for years.

The military leader of the Meos, who also commands Laotian troops in this military region, is Gen. Vang Pao, a tough guerrilla fighter. Buell calls him the "best man I've ever met."

But Buell is pessimistic about the likelihood of stopping the North Vietnamese offensive and the fate of the Meos. An attack on Sam Thong is becoming more likely, he said. North Vietnamese soldiers have probed to within eight miles of here.

"Last year's offensive was not as big as this," he said.

"This time they've got more units, bigger units."

Transcript of tape recording, with title entry "A. Horowitz and W. Blake, 4 Mar," in the manila folder noted in item 21.

Mr. H: This is a recording of a conversation between myself and Major William Blake, Chief Raven FAC, in my office, Vientiane, Laos, 4 March, at 1030 hours. I have asked Major Blake to meet with me to define and outline future policies relative to U.S. Operations in Laos for the remainder of this dry season.

Blake: Good morning, sir.

Mr. H: Good Morning, Bill. Thanks for dropping by. Have a seat. No, not over there. Here. I may want to use some maps. Right. Slide over beside me. Miss Brown will have some coffee soon. Now . . . that was a good meeting last week.

Blake: Yes. I'm impressed with the new General.

Mr. H: He's a go-getter, that's certain. I wonder if he's bucking for his third star.

Blake: He seems sincerely interested in getting the job done.

Mr. H: True, but he wants it *his* way. He thinks airpower can work miracles.

Blake: He's not alone in that.

Mr. H: You're right—and that's one reason I wanted to talk with you today. We have a very delicate situation developing here, and you're caught right in the middle of it. Let me recap for you. I think you know, don't you, about the relationship between Barnes and Lunderberg—it goes back a long time—and our new General is going to be heavily influenced by what Lunderberg has to say—you know, blow them all to hell, and so on. I'm more than a little concerned that some of your good boys in blue may try to do just that—with results which prove to be in opposition to U.S. policy here. Remember last year, when Vang Pao's SGUs covered so much territory during the wet season? And how the USAF received so much praise for sustaining him with air support? Actually, he just wanted to visit his home town near the NVN border—just once, to show that it could be done—but what happened was that the publicity turned his trek into a major invasion of Pathet Lao territory. We think the North Vietnamese are just trying to pay him back this spring for disturbing the status quo—to regain lost face, for instance. All they really want is to keep the Ho Chi Minh Trail open to supply their forces in South Vietnam—*that's* where their main interests lie.

Blake: Wait a minute, sir. Are you saying that the NVA does not want to take over Laos, as they do South Vietnam?

Mr. H: Not exactly—well—almost, but not quite. Don't forget, they're primarily interested in using the Trail, and the Lao Government isn't strong enough to stop them. The right wingers would try to cut the NVA off, and there isn't enough support in Laos for a Communist dominated government. Also, neither the Thais nor the Americans would presumably let the latter happen. With either a right-wing or a left-wing government, we'd probably be forced to take extremely strong measures, either out of necessity or by request.

Blake: I'm a little confused.

Mr. H: I don't blame you. After all, you've only been here two months. Barnes used to understand the whole thing pretty well.

Blake: Used to?

Mr. H: Maybe he still does—but I think, just between you and me, that he's getting tired. A lot depends on the results of the promotion board. He may be worried about what the triumvirate will think—you know, Congress, the JCS, and the President.

Blake: I'm not sure I agree with you, sir.

Mr. H: Why not?

Blake: I think Colonel Barnes is one of the most dedicated, professional officers I've ever known—and I can't believe he's bucking for rank.

Mr. H: I didn't say that, Bill. His job here calls for a colonel, not a brigadier, and he could be promoted out of his present assignment—by regulation.

Blake: I see.

Mr. H: Anyway, there *is* that lure of power—we're all afflicted with it. Poor Jake's caught between the desire for advancement and the opportunity to stay and run his own little war. You don't get a chance to do that very often anymore. I should know. I turned down a Home Office job to come back here. (I brought in the coffee here, Mr. H. Sorry I couldn't find the real cream. Sheila.) Now, let's get down to business. What I want you to do is help the General modify his plans a little—not to call him off—but emphasize close air support to troops instead of interdiction—and hard targets. He's the kind of guy who's just liable to buck for "unleashing the force," so to speak—maybe as far north as resupply depots in Military Region I, where we've never bombed *en masse,* or even on the Chinese Road. *That's* a politically sensitive area, by the way. If the North Vietnamese think we're going to go all out, then they will too, and they could take damn near any piece of territory in Laos that they want to. And all the airpower alone in the world couldn't stop them, if they were willing to pay the price.

Blake: Why don't *you* tell the General this?

Mr. H: I can't, don't you see? It would be like my telling him we don't need his airplanes, which we do, but not in the way he wants to use them. He's more liable to listen to you, being a blue-suiter too.

Blake: But his way is, you might say, the classic military way—to destroy the enemy.

Mr. H: True, but we know we can't destroy the NVA completely—and neither do we really want to. We just want to destroy those elements which are trying to destroy us.

Blake: Jesus Christ, Abe. I'm sorry, but it's a big fucking circle.

Mr. H: Now calm down, Bill.

Blake: I'm sorry, sir.

Mr. H: Look, Bill. It's like parents and children. When your boy grows up, he may turn into something you don't like, but there comes a certain time when he's effectively beyond your control. You can beat him, whip him, chain him up—but he'll get out. And if you've angered him enough, even for the right reasons, he'll find a way to pay you back. So you have to be patient. Youth has staying power—and the North Vietnamese are younger than we are. Right or wrong, they're trying to change the world—while we're trying to preserve it. About all we can hope is that we can hold them back long enough so they can grow up. Meanwhile, we just have to understand them.

Blake: Are you saying that we shouldn't try to stop the enemy?

Mr. H: Not at all. We have to stop him, but we can't really destroy him. That's all I'm trying to say.

Blake: Then we might as well use rubber bullets and tear gas.

Mr. H: Hah, hah. Don't get cynical. Remember when we tried to use tear gas in South Vietnam? When there was a group of NVA who'd taken women and children into a cave complex? It was a couple of years ago, I think, and the local U.S. commander authorized tear gas—flushed a lot of them out and they were taken prisoner—and then someone published the fact that we were using gas in contravention to the Geneva Accords and the Army colonel was reprimanded. So what did he do? Ordered his troops to clean out the caves with flame throwers. Killed about thirty "enemy," some of whom were rather young and some who had quite well-developed breasts.

Blake: Sir, you're asking me to do an awful lot.

Mr. H: I realize that. But you're the only man in northern Laos who has access to all commands and agencies at all levels—and who also, I might add, is rather universally respected. And you've no axe to grind—no vested interests. By the way, congratulations on your promotion. Barnes told me your name was on the lieutenant colonels' list.

Blake: Thank you. It won't be effective for a long, long time. I'm way down on the totem pole.

Mr. H: Well, it's good to have in your pocket, so to speak.

Blake: Look, sir. I'm going to have to think about this one. If you don't mind.

Mr. H: I do mind.

Blake: Why?

Mr. H: Because time's running out. We're doing all we can to keep Vang Pao on those ridgelines, and if he doesn't see airplanes up there all the time, he won't stay, even if those same airplanes are blowing big holes in roads farther up the pike or supposedly destroying tons of enemy supplies. VP's a field commander, not a military analyst, and he's concerned about his men. What he wants is a curtain of lead between him and the enemy—American lead, coming from the sky.

Blake: But he can't have it. There's no way.

Mr. H: You know that, and I know that—but try and convince the little General of it. I dare you.

Blake: Sure, but there's more to this war than just Vang Pao, Abe.

Mr. H: Not to me there isn't. Not now. This is my area of responsibility—northern Laos—up here—and this is where I'm going to do my job.

Blake: But what about Saravane, Attopeu—southern Laos?

Mr. H: That's Wellington's territory—you know Wellington?—he acts as British as his name. He was our man in Malaya before he came here. That's his war down there.

Blake: Barnes wants me to keep a special eye on southern Laos.

Mr. H: I'm sorry about Barnes. He's beginning to become too concerned with his own version of the Big Picture, in capital letters. Right now the Plain of Jars is where the action is—the real action.

Blake: I don't know, sir. I just don't know.

Mr. H: Don't give me any of that stuff about your being just a FAC, Bill—just a major who's doing his job. You volunteered your ass into this mess—just as I did—and there's no turning back.

Blake: I'm beginning to see that. Well . . . about all I can say is that I'll do the best I can.

Mr. H: I'm counting on you, boy.

Blake: Is there anything else, sir.

Mr. H: Not now—well, not really—no—never mind.

Blake: What is it.

Mr. H: Well—it's about Valerie.

Blake: What about her.

Mr. H: Well—she—you know—thinks quite a bit of you, and I . . .

Blake: Please know one thing, sir—and no offense, please—she's a fine person, but under the circumstances—under all the circumstances—I wouldn't touch her with a ten-foot pole.

Mr. H: Now I didn't mean that, Bill.

Blake: I think we understand each other, sir. Let me know what else you'd like me to do. Good day.

Mr. H: Good day.

Postscript to interview: Blake looks as if he's lost weight —Sheila: please write General and Mrs. Phitsanolouk in Bangkok—see if their beach cottage at Pattaya is available in a week or two. I'd like to send Major Blake down for an R&R—and no, you can't go with him—not that you'd want to, anyway. Your turn next month. Take a week and go to Japan. OK?

83

Teletype message, AOC 20A to OUSAIRA, Vientiane, 9 March.

SUBJECT: Weekly Operations Report

1. The situation can only be described as extremely tense. Muong Soui has become the focal point now. The town resembles a dusty, Midwest bus station during rodeo week. Refugees are leaving in droves as soldiers pour in. Estimate that most if not all of the residents have departed, along with many of the friendly troops, who have paused only long enough to steal a chicken or two. Pop Buell reports that some people have started leaving Sam Thong—the wealthy —those who can afford bus tickets. No outward sign here of deteriorating morale, but there are not as many smiles as usual.

2. Have not been able to sit down with Vang Pao for any policy discussions—neither have Company men. He has been on the go almost constantly, and has traded his well-known personal helicopter for one of the ordinary H-34s to avoid being spotted. Has apparently been going back and forth to outlying posts talking to his men.

3. Re Muong Soui: the airstrip is still intact and a few T-28s refueled and rearmed there yesterday, as did Ravens. No sign of enemy activity—yet.

4. Of major concern to all, however, is the report that at least two of the forward positions manned by SGUs have been evacuated and/or abandoned. All posts have experienced extremely sporadic enemy probes, but none has been actually attacked. Company officials claim they have no knowledge of pre-planned withdrawals of this nature. Will advise as soon as hard information is available. Hamilton.

84

Article from the Bangkok *Star*. March 10, p. 1. Banner headline reads: "Last Major Lao City in Plaine of Jars Falls to Reds."

Following up their recent success at the market town of Xieng Khouang, Communist forces succeeded in forcing the last government defender from the strategically important city of Muong Soui, a few kilometres west of the Plaine des Jarres. According to one eyewitness, who claimed to be part of the last contingent to leave, there was never really any doubt that the town would fall. "We received no instructions to stay and fight," he is quoted as saying. "None of the commanders stayed, so we all went away too."

There are no reports of a battle for Muong Soui, the last sizeable habitation between the Plaine des Jarres and the Mekong heartland to the west. Although both American and Lao sources had been predicting an enemy attack at any time, none had actually materialized as of yesterday, 9 March. Only the fact that the stream of refugees fleeing west and southward began to slow to a trickle gave observers indications that all the defenders had left. Muong Soui itself is now a ghost town. There are reports of a few fires in and around the marketplace.

One spokesman in Vientiane stated that if Muong Soui had definitely fallen, plans would no doubt be made to retake it as soon as possible. Noting that the village was once the seat of General Kong Le's Neutralist Government, the official continued, "To let the Communists keep Muong Soui would be grievous sin." He then repeated an earlier statement that there would be an official government comment on the subject "before very long."

85

Blake, *Journal*, pp. 93–98.

10 Mar—Muong Soui day. Had the U-17 up (two of the O-1s are out for maintenance)—received request from Brickbat to land at Muong Soui to pick up a couple of Vang Pao's officers who were at the airstrip. No one knew that it had "fallen"—including, I suspect, the enemy. Apparently everything snowballed—the retreating soldiers touched off a panic with their stories about thousands of NVA and hundreds of tanks, and once the cattle started stampeding, no one could head them off at the pass. First real indication was when Raven 26 wanted to land for fuel at about noon—no answer from the runway control—he buzzed the field, saw no one, and decided he'd better not land. Limped into Alternate on fumes. Repeated attempts to raise anyone failed, until Brickbat said they'd gotten a call from Moonglow FAG requesting pickup. Authentication was OK, and I was the closest one around who could take a couple of passengers. Moonglow had said there were enemy all around, but none in the city as yet, and no sounds of shooting. My observer and I came in fast from the west, touched down long, turned around at the south end by the bomb dumps and were about to take off again when two scraggly, dusty little guys came hopping out from between the piles of 250 pound bombs and raced like hell for the U-17, waving their hats and rifles. My observer got the door open—they scrambled aboard—and we got off in a big hurry. No sign of anyone else. Moonglow turned out to be a Lt. Sayorith, who'd been recently promoted, given a crash English course, and sent back into the field. He'd been a sergeant at Phou Nok Kok, and was the man who'd taken over the radio when his boss was killed. He was furious at the retreat. Said it wasn't Vang Pao's fault but that of the "city troops who know only how to run away, not to fight." I asked him about the SGUs leaving the hilltops—he re-

plied only, "What we do in the mountains is different from what they do in the valleys." Didn't say much else from then on. He got airsick soon after.

I'd like to walk around Muong Soui sometime—when this is all over. There's a beautiful lake (looks artificially made), and it's the only town up here which appears to have been laid out. There are definable streets and even blocks, with dozens of little tin-roofed houses and even a two-story building or two. Very few signs of war. The story goes that the bad guys blew it up first some years ago with 105 howitzers, then rebuilt it a little when they held it for a year. Then the good guys blew it up and recaptured it; then the Americans blew it up when the good guys lost it again. This time, however, it's been almost completely rebuilt—and looks permanent. I hope the bad guys don't move back in. If they don't, maybe we won't have to blow it up again.

One fire burning in the center of town—but my observer said it wasn't because of the enemy. Said one of the friendlies probably tipped over a stove while he was running away. Wonder if he was named O'Leary. I hoped that Moonglow could help spot some of the NVA, but he said he hadn't seen anything—that he'd walked through town for about two hours. Saw no one. Said the only inhabitants were a few dogs and many, many bad Phi.

Because of the pickup, had to cancel my part of the really big show just north of the PDJ. Left Browning in charge of FACing the first strikes. Hope they really get something tonight—otherwise Horowitz will start breathing very hard indeed. I don't even want to think about him or anything right now.

86

Teletype message, AOC 20A to OUSAIRA, Vientiane, 11 March.

SUBJECT: Special Strike

Composite BDA reports from yesterday afternoon's and

last night's special missions flown north of the PDJ indicate major damage to enemy supplies and storage. Numerous secondary explosions and fires raged most of the night with black smoke still visible this morning through haze and broken cloud deck. Follow-up strikes planned today, and if the weather clears enough, more accurate assessment will be forwarded ASAP. Hamilton.

87

Memo from Horowitz to Blake, dated 11 March.

Mr. Blake:

Despite encouraging reports, if last night's strike indicates a new trend, it reflects the opposite of our understanding. I have instructed my people to make absolutely certain all their reports on damage and the increasing number of enemy are completely accurate—repeat—accurate. We cannot diminish support to the men on the ground.

Horowitz

88

Memo (Xerox copy) from OUSAIRA, Vientiane, to Horowitz, dated 11 March.

Abe:

Bill Blake has outlined the substance of your discussion with him a week ago Wednesday. Please understand me—I will not permit subterfuge—or any clandestine juggling. U.S. policy here is to defeat the enemy. Don't forget that. Will you and your people kindly stop playing your silly games and get on with the business of prosecuting this war?

> Thanks,
> Jake

89

Teletype message, OUSAIRA, Vientiane, to 7AF, Saigon; 7/13AF, and numerous other addressees, 12 March.

SUBJECT: Loss Report
 Pilot Name: Hamilton, Dante (NMI [No Middle Initial])
 Serial No.: FR52176
 Grade: Major
 Type Aircraft: T-28D
 Location: Northeast Laos
 Date and Time: 12 March—1031 local
 Mission: Observation
 Weather: 1500 foot broken to overcast; poor visibility in smoke and haze
 Remarks: Aircraft hit by probable ZPU groundfire and crashed two miles south of target. One good chute sighted; beeper received. SAR effort initiated at 1045 local. No voice contact with pilot or allied observer, but beeper signals continue intermittently. Area of SAR considered extremely high threat because of numerous enemy ground forces.

90

Tape recording, Sony cassette, no date. Apparently recorded 12 March by Captain Robert Browning and Major Blake.

 Blake: Sandy Lead, this is Raven 01, over.
 Sandy Lead: Go ahead, Raven.

Blake: Roger, Sandy. What's your position?

Sandy Lead: Two clicks due south of the "T"—there's a small stream which goes through a north-south valley. We're at 10 grand [10,000 feet] now.

Blake: Who's with you?

Sandy Lead: I've got a flight of four A-1s—another flight orbiting east for backup. High and low Jollies [rescue helicopters] in position and ready to go if contact is made.

Blake: Any other Ravens?

Sandy Lead: Negative. Raven 24 had to leave with low fuel. The bird's been down two hours.

Blake: Any sightings? Voice contact?

Sandy Lead: Negative on that, Raven.

Blake: Got you in sight, Sandy. I'm at your seven o'clock. Where do you want me?

Sandy Lead: Search just south of the valley where the stream goes into the trees. Prevailing wind is from the northwest. Last report was that one of the guys had a good chute—visual sighting by Dingbat 31—but he lost contact when the chute entered the clouds.

Blake: Roger. Negative on two chutes. You're only looking for one guy. Any reported groundfire?

Sandy Lead: Negative. Not yet. This guy a friend of yours?

Blake: Roger, Sandy. Get him out.

Sandy Lead: Will do.

Browning (I): He was going after that cave complex—you know the one just north of the "T" where the truck tracks go in one cave and come out another?

Blake (I): I know it.

Browning (I): The other T-28s are OK, I think. They were landing just as we took off.

Blake (I): Rog. Keep your eyes open. We're going down.

Browning (I): I'm glad it cleared up, anyway.

Blake (I): Me too. It's the screwiest weather I've ever seen.

Foxy Lead: Sandy Lead, this is Foxy, over.

Sandy Lead: Go ahead, Foxy.

Foxy Lead: Got a flight of F-4s here. Need any help?

Sandy Lead: Negative, Foxy. Monitor this frequency. I'll call you.

Foxy Lead: Wilco.

Prince [a USAF aircraft which was the overall rescue coordinator]: Sandy Lead, this is Prince. Got a possible two-way fix on the beeper. Check coordinates TG132765—I say again—TG132765.

Sandy Lead: Copy TG132765. Go that, Raven?

Browning (I): It's just a little bit south of where we are—probably the other side of that ridge—the one with the three big trees on top.

Blake: Roger, Sandy. Dante, Raven 01 [thirty-second pause]. Dante, Raven 01, over.

Browning (I): Do a 180, Bill. Is that a chute, half collapsed on that big rock?

Blake (I): Sure is, babes. Sure is. [Transmission]: Sandy Lead, Raven 01. Got a visual on a chute. About one-niner-zero from you at five clicks.

Sandy Lead: Have you in sight, Raven.

Jolly Green 20: Jolly has a tally too, Sandy.

Sandy Lead: Hold out for one, Jolly 20. Got the chute, guys?

[Staccato replies]: Two, Three, Four.

Sandy Lead: Let's go daisy chain, Sandy. First pass dry. Watch your ass.

[Answers]: Two, Three, Four.

Blake: Raven's clear. Got get 'em, Sandy. I don't see a thing down there.

Sandy Lead: Lead's off right. Any action, Raven?

Blake: Negative.

[Multiple transmissions]: Two's off right, Three's off right, Four's off right.

Sandy Lead: OK, Jolly, you're cleared in from the south.

Jolly 20: We're going in.

Blake (I): Watch out, Jolly. It's too goddamn quiet down there.

Browning (I): Do you think he's still alive?

Blake (I): I don't know.

Jolly 20: Have the chute, now. We're right over it. It's collapsed, looks like it's partially buried right between two big rocks and small clump of trees. The harness is empty.

Sandy Lead: Can you land, Jolly?

Jolly 20: Negative. Too much slope. We'll send down a PJ [crewmember who would be lowered to assist an incapacitated pilot] on the penetrator.

The Laotian Fragments

Sandy Lead: Any footprints?

Jolly 20: We're kicking up too much dust to see.

Foxy Lead: Sandy Lead, Sandy Lead, Foxy 20, over.

Sandy Lead: Stay off the air, Foxy. SAR in progress.

Browning (I): Those Jollies have got balls the size of watermelons.

Blake (I): Rog.

Jolly 20: PJ's down. Absolutely no sign of anyone. PJ's in the trees now.

Browning (I): See that, Bill? About half a mile down the stream?

Blake (I): Sure do. [Transmission]: Sandy Lead, Raven 01. You got some bad guys half a click away. Can't tell how many, but they're moving in.

Sandy Lead: Roger, Raven. You copy, Jolly?

Jolly 20: Roger, Sandy. PJ's coming back now. He's shaking his head.

Sandy Lead: Come on up out of there, Jolly.

Jolly 20: We could move down the hill.

Sandy Lead: Negative, Jolly. If at first you don't succeed, get your ass out of there until the next time.

Jolly 20: Wilco.

Prince: Sandy Lead, this is Prince, over.

Sandy Lead: Go ahead, Prince.

Prince: Brickbat reports survivor picked up fifteen minutes ago by Company chopper, one mile from you, in good condition. Terminate SAR. You can go home. Survivor says thanks anyway.

Browning (I): Well I'll be a sonofabitch.

Sandy Lead: Thanks, Prince. You copy, Jolly?

Jolly 20: Rog. I'm glad he's OK.

Sandy Lead: Raven 01, Sandy Lead. Hey, Bill, you looking for work?

Blake: Sure am, Sandy. Let's go. I'll put my smoke where I last saw the . . . [Tape ends.]

DIA Summary (Xerox copy), OUSAIRA, Vientiane, to DIA, Washington, 12 March.

SUBJECT: Laos Situation Report

1. It has become obvious during the past week that the enemy has intensified his offensive not only in the Plain of Jars but all over Laos as well. In the north at least two NVA divisions have carried out successful attacks upon numerous government positions and towns, and the enemy now seems to be regrouping for what is expected to be a final, massive assault on Long Tieng. In the south renewed attacks upon friendly positions on the Bolovens Plateau preceded the investiture of Attopeu on 11 March by an estimated three battalions of NVA. Thus the enemy now controls the approaches to the Bolovens and, more important, the Sekong River entrances to Cambodia and South Vietnam.

2. The political situation here is grave. There have been almost daily "crisis" meetings of the cabinet, with each faction disagreeing as to the reasons for the situation and the methods to solve the problems. General Vang Pao has been pressuring the FAR and Neutralist commanders for more troops to defend Long Tieng, but the lowland Lao are extremely reluctant to commit forces for the defense of the Meo, whom they have long regarded as lower-class bandits. The other day Vang Pao threatened to pull his entire tribe out of the war, a statement which left the other generals more than a little nonplused. Without the Meo buffer to the north, Vientiane and all its approaches are extremely vulnerable to attack, and while we are relatively certain that the regular troops will acquit themselves well if forced to defend their own territory, it is obvious that they would rather not have to do so. The major problem seems to be one of shortsightedness: the lowland Lao, relatively well educated (by Lao standards) and much more

well off, do not want the enemy to attack them directly—but neither are they willing to send their troops off to what they consider almost a foreign war—the NVA vs. the Meo. All this seems to be another variation of quite a well-known and familiar story.

3. In addition, there has been little hard intelligence regarding the enemy's real intentions. After the heavy bombing raids following the fall of Muong Soui, the Pathet Lao, through its embassy here, served notice that it would not send a representative to the annual birthday picnic for the King unless all "Yankee air activity" was stopped, and repeated again that the Pathet Lao had no territorial desires—that their only goal was a return to the 1962 Geneva accords. This restatement of their old position leads us to believe that they may be relishing their recent successes and are waiting to see what will happen at Long Tieng before making further proposals or engaging in discussions. Despite these claims, however, Vientiane is worried. If Long Tieng goes, it is only 40 short kilometers to the capital itself—and contingency plans for our first blackout and curfew since the beginning of the war are being drawn up. What the enemy really wants is anybody's guess.

4. USAF continues to provide airpower when necessary, and we are attempting to achieve as good a balance as possible between close air support and attacks on hard targets. Unfortunately, the unseasonable weather still hampers air operations, as does the elusiveness of the enemy. There is, however, a growing spirit of cooperation among all commands and agencies, and AIRA is certain that all concerned will do their very best to see this crisis through.

92

Blake, *Journal,* pp. 99–114.

16 March, Monday. Have been too busy to write much lately. Am sitting in Pakse, of all places, on the pot, waiting for a rocket attack. How's *that* for openers? As far as I

know, Vonnegut is still crouched beside his bed, holding his M-16 and looking at his watch. It's 1:30 in the morning, and intelligence reported that the bad guys were planning their first rocket attack ever on Pakse itself, to commence at 0145. I've been sitting here for half an hour blowing my insides out, and a peek through the door a couple of minutes ago revealed our hero Vonnegut preparing for war. I tried to talk him into flying up north with me last week, but all he said was that Barnes had forbidden him to fly combat—so he was sorry, but he just couldn't. Poor baby.

Came down to Pakse this morning with Barnes to look over the situation here and also to see about finding a job for Hamilton. Barnes wants to move him out of Alternate—I don't—but unless I can really show cause, his little fiasco of last week may have cost him his job. Horowitz was delighted that a Company chopper picked him up—and I wish Hamilton hadn't told him that his first move was to call for help on Company frequencies. What the hell did he expect? That no one would tell? He said he walked down the hill about a mile from where he hit, turned on his radio, contacted a chopper coming back from a resupply mission, and that was that. Never saw a bad guy, even the ones who shot him down. Horowitz is really gloating over this one.

Time—0140: Rocket attack minus five. Somehow, I can't believe the enemy sticks to this kind of a timetable. I suppose I'm as safe here as anywhere—furthermore, I can't really move. What a day *this* has been. I can see the headlines now: "Assistant to the U.S. Air Attache Killed While Sitting on the Crapper." What a laugh.

0145: Called out to Vonnegut, "See anything?" He told me to be quiet. I closed the door. He's new, I guess—maybe that's it. Came directly from the States. Boy, does his SAC background show. He sure believes in ETAs [Estimated Time of Arrival]. I hear springs creaking. Peek. Vonnegut's back in bed, his M-16 propped against the wall beside him.

The reason, dear reader, that I'm sitting on the toilet writing on an official U.S. Government clipboard is that I ate too much tonight, twice—once at dinner here with the FACs and AOC personnel, and then, two hours later, at a formal Lao feast. Barnes, Vonnegut, and I came down in the Attache's Apache this morning, and we were met not only by the Lao hierarchy of MR IV, but by the RLAF Commander and two generals from Vientiane who had arrived yesterday. The RLAF Commander, General Sourith, whom I know fairly well, told me he'd be honored to have me join him for dinner—then he and the other generals and Barnes went tearing off in a couple of jeeps, leaving me to show Vonnegut around. I didn't know whether to take his invitation seriously or not. Didn't get any lunch because the damn jeep broke down and the driver had to walk back for a distributor rotor—I spent most of the day under a shade tree listening to Vonnegut tell me how he plans to win the war. Would you believe he's even thinking about finding a bunch of P-47s, rebuilding them, and giving them to the Lao? Christ, the torque alone would break their right legs. Unfortunately, his new, tailor-made one-piece jump/flight suits (mocha brown) don't quite fit him in front, and I'm afraid I pissed him off the other day by giving him a spoon to put in his left sleeve pencil pocket. Just because all multi-engined pilots put a coffee spoon in their pencil slots doesn't mean that Vonnegut should get uptight. Oh well, I suppose I was unkind. But if he doesn't have a sense of humor around here, he'll never last.

Anyway, when I couldn't get anyone in the afternoon and early evening, I ate a really good steak with the FACs. Vonnegut had three. At 7:30, sitting with brandy and a newspaper, I got a call from Barnes, who said that the General's car would pick me up in fifteen minutes. Vonnegut looked delighted when I said he didn't have to go. Drove downtown with Barnes—a tiny city—no, not a city at all—looks like one of those little Mississippi River towns in the thirties—only the main street paved—lots of heavy hanging trees—and beside the town, the Mekong flowing by. The river's way down now, with caked mud flats on both sides.

We met the generals at Pakse's leading restaurant, or so Barnes said. Looks like a park pavilion for the local band concert, only larger. Waiters (Chinese?) bowing and scraping as we walked through the open-air dining room. None of the other customers looked at us. Drinks on a private porch in back, overlooking the town and eventually, I suppose, the river. The Lao drank Pernod and colored water (Kool-Aid?), Barnes had scotch, and bless them (although I was bloated already), someone had provided a bottle of Jim Beam, "for the Americans," General Sourith said.

Cast of characters: Me, Barnes, General Sourith, General Phasouk (the Vang Pao of southern Laos), General Ka from Vientiane (he looks as if he's got some Nung [a Chinese ethnic strain] blood in him), and two other Lao officers whom I did not know and whose names I missed. Oh yes—and Wellington—*the* Wellington—who sat gravely throughout the entire evening and never said a word. Not one word, except perhaps "Thank you" and "Pass the Plakaphong, please." Perhaps because the conversation was mostly in French, or maybe because he was losing his war too—must check with Horowitz and find out more about this guy.

We spoke French because General Phasouk refuses to speak English. It's as simple as that. Barnes claims he has as near perfect English as any Lao he knows, but Phasouk hates to lose face by mispronouncing a word. Educated in France during the late '40s—even a year at the Sorbonne in addition to a degree from L'École de L'Air [the French Air Force Academy]. An absolutely charming man, and as different from Vang Pao as night and day. Seems the French decided to take one of the "peasants," a tribal leader without inherited status, and make him into a general. They certainly succeeded. Much taller than Vang Pao, Phasouk is lean, very intense, and looks very much like a commander. The perfect picture of a perfect major general. Seems tired, though. I can see why. Last week Attopeu, and today Saravane (Phasouk's birthplace) was occupied by the NVA. Another case of pre-attack jitters, I think. The NVA announced they were coming; Phasouk ordered his troops out. Barnes says the Company is furious (maybe that's why Wellington didn't say anything), but Phasouk's logic is somehow unassailable: "I had two tired battalions," he said simply, puffing on a long black cigar. "They had three fresh battalions. I knew I could not win. Maybe next year." Then he added sadly, "But I did not want to lose Saravane town. Maybe I will take it back soon."

General Ka, the Vientiane staff man, was pushing for an aerial show of force. "You send up many, many F-105s," he said. "You fly low over the town. You make the sky black with your airplanes. That will show the enemy you mean business, and they will go home."

General Phasouk smiled. "We sent twenty T-28s today in one formation," he said. "They dropped leaflets (he showed me one, a short passage in Lao printed on flimsy paper) which said that the North Vietnamese should leave before they are all destroyed by the Government Forces. I do not know whether they will believe it or not."

"Our valiant T-28s are not enough," little General Ka said, leaning as far forward in the wicker chair as his stomach would permit. "What we need are hundreds of American F-105s," turning to me, "like you sent up to Hanoi and Haiphong."

I looked at General Phasouk, who smiled again and closed his eyes. We understood. I said only that I hoped for a change of fortune, soon.

Incredible dinner—all courses served at once and passed around the large oval table in a private dining room. A waiter (I *know* he was Chinese) brought my bottle of bourbon and set it beside my place. Sliced meats, rice and fish dishes, evil and powerful sticky and drippy things, and plates of vegetables: spinach, squash, tiny Lao sweet potatoes, tomatoes, Chinese cabbage (like iceberg lettuce), leeks, cauliflower, Chinese snow peas, and so on. (Maybe recapping all this will help my insides purge it all out—) Later, fruits: mangoes, lichee nuts, papaya, pineapple, breadfruit, guava, watermelon, rambutans—God knows what else. And a whole red snapper flown in from somewhere, from which we picked pieces.

I tried to nibble, but General Ka, stuffing himself beside me, kept filling up my plate. Once he complimented me on my French (which is really lousy). "You speak better French than I do English," he said. I agreed. "What other languages do you speak?" I told him none. "You do not speak Chinese?" he asked. I shook my head, trying to keep from crying because of the fiery mouthful that was dissolving my fillings and is now ripping up my gut. "You should learn to speak Chinese," he said, squeezing sliced limes over his heaped plate. "Everybody should speak Chinese around here—now."

0300: I've been here for almost two hours, and my butt feels as if it's got a perpetual ring engraved on it. Fortunately for long-term sitting, Lao toilets are built smaller than those made in America. I feel better-purged physically, anyway. Thank God, Barnes and I left early, about midnight. One of the generals suggested a ride downtown to Pakse's number-one massage parlor. We declined. I can just imagine what would have happened when some little LBFM started pounding on my stomach. Vonnegut snores like hell. Maybe I should tell him there was a rocket attack after all and he missed the whole thing. Better not—he'd probably believe it, and either way he'd never forgive me. Tomorrow it's back to the other war. So it goes.

93

Teletype message, AOC 20A to OUSAIRA, Vientiane, 16 March.

1. Last night, at 0200 local, an enemy sapper squad attempted to infiltrate Long Tieng for the first time. They were detected just after they crossed the ridgeline, a firefight ensued, and the last enemy was killed attempting to cross the runway. Apparently the six NVA were attempting to reach General Vang Pao's house, because no charges were placed on any aircraft and no other buildings were attacked. All six bodies, dressed in black pajamas, have been recovered. One defender was wounded.

2. Hold on to your hats, Vientiane—the entire squad consisted of NVA women—I say again—women, of ages ranging approximately from 18 to 25. We have no intelligent answer to the question why—maybe the NVA is running short of men because of our airstrikes—or maybe they've got a women's lib movement that just won't quit. Hamilton.

94

Teletype message, AOC 20A to OUSAIRA, Vientiane, 16 March.

1. This is a follow-up message to earlier one re sapper attack. One NVA female was still alive when captured, but died subsequently of wounds. All she said was that there were "many, many liberators," of which she was the first, and that they would attack "very, very soon."

2. Attempts to keep this information quiet have failed. I noticed many of the valley's inhabitants talking in clusters today, pointing up at the sky and along the ridgelines which surround Long Tieng. The haze and smoke were so bad I could not see if they were pointing at anything in particular. Everyone seems agitated. Suggest you alert Company from your end for possible evacuation airlift.

3. Concerning the weather, I flew a test hop yesterday and noted evidence of a dozen or so fires which seem to have originated upwind from Alternate along readily defined trails. It may be a coincidence, but I doubt it. I have never seen the visibility around here so poor. Please make certain that morning briefings to USAF pilots alert them to the unbelievably cruddy weather. Also, re pending plans to transfer some Lao pilots up—do not be too surprised if they refuse to come. If I had been given no instrument training, I wouldn't fly up here either. VP's three surviving Meo pilots are doing a S- - - Hot job. Hamilton.

95

Note in Major Blake's hand on 8×10½" typewriter paper, no date.

I record this item just for the hell of it. Yesterday, 15 March, President Thieu stated in Saigon that "the Pathet Lao proposal to end the fighting in Laos was the same as the Vietcong plan for ending the war in Vietnam." He was speaking to an "ethnic groups convention in the Central Highlands," whatever that was—or so the newspaper says. I quote: " 'The goal of Communists still is to invade Laos, and their stratagem still is to force the allied forces out of Laos and to establish a broadened coalition government in this country so as to bring in more Communist elements,' Mr. Thieu said." End quote.

Will wonders never cease.

96

Letter from Sheila Brown to Major William Blake, dated 17 March, written on standard typewriter paper, enclosed in an office-sized envelope, no stamp.

Dear Bill:

I'm sorry I have not answered or returned your calls. I confess that I have been here for some of them, but I just could not bring myself to talk to you. I'm sorry.

I'm going to have to end our relationship—now—before it goes any further. It's not because of your wife (Mr. H. told me all about her), even though I confess there is still a puritanical streak in me which cringes slightly. It's simply because I don't want to get really involved—not the way we were going.

I agonized, Bill, every time you took off to fly up there— and I just can't stand it anymore. The moments we had were grand—lots of fun—and I'll never forget them—but I'm incapable of going on that way. If I commit myself entirely to you as a human being, I know I would not be able to face life if I were to lose you. Consequently, my only alternative is to stop it all—right now—and allow us to go about our plain old lives without encumbrance.

Please understand, Bill. It's not that I don't care—it's

that I care too much. Maybe after all our big and little wars are taken care of—maybe then we can find another shady tree somewhere and see.

Sheila

97

Teletype message, AOC 20A to OUSAIRA, Vientiane, 17 March.

1. Last night saw the first enemy rocket attack on Long Tieng. At 0200 local, four 122mm rockets impacted almost simultaneously in the area, one near the runway, two on the side of the hill up from General Vang Pao's house, and one in the marketplace. No casualties and little significant damage. Patrols are out this morning attempting to determine the location of the launch site or sites.

2. As a result of this attack, apparently again aimed at General Vang Pao himself, the Lao General Staff has ordered Vang Pao not to spend nights in his quarters. Reluctantly he has agreed and will be coming up here only during the day. His exact whereabouts at night will be a carefully guarded secret.

3. Both AIRA and Company personnel have been alerted to possible evacuation notice. Word of this, along with Vang Pao's planned departure, has caused near panic among the villagers. Some are already starting to walk out on the road to Sam Thong; others are beginning to cluster down by the airfield any time a cargo bird comes in.

4. Weather remains lousy. What kind of a dry season is this anyway? Hamilton.

98

News release from the Office of the U.S. Air Attache, Vientiane, Laos, dated 18 March, stamped "For Immediate Release to All Wire Services."

Two U.S. Air Force officers were killed today when their light observation plane crashed into a mountainside while on a routine training mission near the Plain of Jars.

Captain Robert Browning, 34, from Terre Haute, Indiana, and 1st Lt. Harold Morgan, 26, of Big Bend, Wisconsin, both attached to the Air Attache's office here, were on an orientation mission over the scene of recent heavy fighting between Royal Lao Government troops and North Vietnamese Regulars. Captain Browning had been in Laos for five months. Lt. Morgan had just arrived and it was his first flight.

Both officers served as Forward Air Controllers (FAC) spotting enemy targets for airstrikes. Their aircraft crashed in a remote area, and according to other observers, there was no enemy activity at the time of the accident. Mechanical failure is being investigated.

99

Blake, *Journal*, p. 115.

19 Mar— "Beware the ides of March," someone said. How true. I'm sitting at my desk at 4:30 AM, bag packed, waiting for the weather to lift. It's bad today even down here—not low enough to keep us from taking off, but visibility at Alternate is zilch. We're on standby. Should improve soon. For the past three or four days, cumulus buildups follow the low stratus in—no rain—it never rains

The Laotian Fragments

in March (I wish it were late April—then we'd have some real rain). AOC will call me as soon as weather breaks and I can get off.

Gloomy Thursday—and it seems as if everything has come to a head in this past two-week period. Poor Browning. Poor Morgan, whoever he was. I hardly even got to meet him. I don't think they were shot down. One forgets, sometimes, that people can just screw up. Probably bumbling their way down a valley, looking at the sights (or what they could see through the haze), and blooey. No holes in the aircraft—no nothing. Interesting that we can now report casualties—Barnes got a copy of the message from Washington to the Ambassador. Hope this doesn't mean we'll be required to have a lot more losses.

But it's off to war—sort of—and even the Ice House isn't like the quarters (hah) I had in the Central Highlands of Vietnam. Barnes says I should go up to stay—and only if I ride herd on Hamilton will he let Dante keep his job. I don't know which will be rougher—controlling Dante or fighting the NVA. Barnes also wants me to write all the Operations Reports.

Letter from Weird yesterday—enclosed another poem. I like it, but who would have ever guessed old Weird was a poet? How little we really know about other human beings—from the inconclusive fragments that they let us see. Yet how much we *think* we know. Perhaps the real tragedy of today is that we mistake bits and pieces for fact. Too much information—thus massive ignorance. But we have to make decisions anyway. So what do we do? Flip coins. Roll dice. Guess. Ignorance breeding impulse: what grand ingredients for truth.

Phone rang—ceiling's up. Go.

Letter from Weird to Major Blake, dated 13 March, no return address, written in blue ink on standard white typewriter paper.

John Clark Pratt

Dear Bill:

Flight home was a drag—still no booze allowed on MAC [Military Airlift Command] charter flights—but it was worth it. Have adjusted to the time change—and am just lolling around the BOQ telling war stories to all the nurses. God it's good to see nothing but round-eyes again.

Speaking of round-eyes, had a moment of pathos at Udorn the night after I outprocessed. Remember that F-4 that went in on the Trail two days before I left? The guy in the front seat had been Dang's—you know, Super-Thai—Dang's tealoch [Thai word for lover]. She was just crushed—sort of moping around the bar. A few guys would talk to her, some offering condolences, others obviously trying to move in. I got smashed as usual—and the result is the enclosed. Maybe I should tell MPC [USAF Military Personnel Center] that I want to get out of the Military Airlift Command and start a Poetry Command. But seriously, there's a lot about this war—I mean your war, now—that no one's ever said—not yet, anyway. When you add what we think we *can't* say to what most of us *won't* say, it totals about 100%.

One more thing—say hello to everyone for me, and tell them I miss all their smiling faces but I don't miss the job one single bit. As for you, you sad bastard, all I can say is that working for you was a very definitely distinct gas.

Your friend,
[signed] Weird

101

Poem, enclosure to item 100, typed in elite type, double-spaced, on erasable bond paper. The editor has supplied a brief glossary at the end. At the bottom of the page is a note in Major Blake's hand: "Send this to *Grunt* magazine." *Grunt,* often called a "GI *Playboy,*" was a publication originating in Saigon for the American troops stationed in South-

The Laotian Fragments

east Asia. The editor has been unable to locate a complete file of this periodical in the United States, and none of the issues he has seen carries this particular poem.

Words and Thoughts

Hey, you, *you slant-eyed, luscious brown-skinned broad,*
Why you no smile tonight? What you no hab?
Where your zoomie tealoch-man who keep you,
Pay you, love you? He butterfly around again?

Maybe he go home States and send for you.
Big joke. It neber hoppen. He buddy me.
He hot jet jockey, sure, but he hab wife,
Three baby-san. He short-time. He speak lie.

No worry, babes, no sweat. I tell you true.
You have long legs, great calves, soft, rounded thighs.
You need no Hongkong bra. You number One.
You nice girl. You not nit-noy. You super-Thai.

I same-same. No hab mama-san like him.
You be my tealoch, I extend a year.
I make love good—always use balloon.
I long time love you mach mach—chai?

Don't cry, please. I'm so sorry. I no try
To hurt you. I just make damn silly joke.
I'm a lonely pilot, very far from home,
Who plays the game. I dumb GI.

Your tealoch good man. Marry you someday.
Please, what's the matter? What you say?
He shot down? He work Tchepone today?
I didn't know. Flew last night. Slept all day.

You loved that part of him he let you love, I know.
But so did we.
Please stop your crying and forgive us all,
As well as me.

[Line 4, *butterfly,* to be unfaithful; 8, *short-time,* about to be rotated home; 12, *nit-noy,* pidgin Thai for "small"; 16, *chai,* pidgin Thai for "true."]

102

Teletype message, AOC 20A to OUSAIRA, Vientiane, 19 March.

SUBJECT: Daily Operations Report

1. Raven 01 [Major Blake] arrived on station this morning to assume duties here. On hand are a total of six (6) FACs with four (4) O-1 and two (2) T-28 aircraft. If necessary, we have been informed we can use the Lao O-1 if it is not needed for artillery spotting. As of today, aircraft on the ground here will no longer be parked side by side in the refueling area; instead, they have been dispersed at random around the field.

2. Approaches to Long Tieng are still relatively quiet, but a patrol sighted "numerous" enemy troops to the west of us, apparently moving south in the direction of Sam Thong. Mr. Buell and other USAID officials were alerted. Meeting this morning between General Vang Pao, Ravens, and Company representatives was rather inconclusive, with the result not much more than an agreement to search out the enemy and try to get him to fight on our terms. VP seemed slightly evasive about exactly where his troops are and how many he has in the field, and he reiterated his requests for more airpower and more troops from Vientiane.

3. The refugee situation is about to break wide open. All over the valley, residents are beginning to pack up their things in preparation for a move. A few of the shops in the marketplace did not open today, and there are some families who seem to have taken up permanent daylight residence down by the airstrip. Understand that a number of C-123 aircraft have been programmed for evacuation alert, should the need arise. Suggest that all pilots and

U.S. personnel be briefed not to show any concern or alarm. There is a definite atmosphere of apprehension.

4. All FAC aircraft airborne on schedule today, but haze and smoke in the morning, then heavy cumulus in the afternoon forced diversion of twenty-seven (27) USAF sorties. Best results came from a strike at Red Dog's position, eight (8) kilometers northeast of Alternate, where we have four (4) 105mm howitzers. From coordinates supplied by Red Dog, eight (8) F-4s achieved six (6) secondary explosions and fires. The three Meo pilots flew six (6) short sorties apiece, with no verifiable BDA.

5. SUMMARY: This Thursday was almost normal, but everyone is gearing for a fight. Best estimate we can come up with is that Vang Pao has about 2000 combat troops in the area, against estimates of enemy strength which range from 1500 to 8000, with the latter figure the one most people are leaning on. We are delighted to hear that at least there have been preliminary assurances that additional FAR troops will be arriving, but all of us here will believe it when we see it. Blake.

Blake, *Journal,* pp. 116-124.

Thursday, 19 Mar (continued)— I think I've written more today than at any other time. What am I—a combat pilot or a journalist? Journal entry early this morning—then after a miserable flight in the AM wrote a couple of ordnance and part orders—then a short but thoroughly understanding (hah!) reply to Sheila—did the Ops Report (we're going daily for a while)—and now this. I've got blankets up on the windows and am using a red bulb. Reminds me of my prep school days, trying to cram for an exam after lights were supposed to be out. I can barely hear the click-clack of the teletype across the hall.

I couldn't sleep—tried—but a thousand thoughts keep coming—so it was time for a cold beer. Hamilton was right—there is a change in the valley. Everything seems so much darker and gloomier. It's not only the weather. I'll never forget my first sight of Alternate—a sparkling little bowl in the middle of miles of unbroken green. Looked like Sun Valley, Idaho, with trees. Hundreds of neat, tin-roofed little houses, some built part way up the steep sides of the surrounding ridges. The paved runway splits the valley and dominates it, and then the white lines and large numbers on the runway looked new and clean and welcoming (today I could barely see them). That was in January, right after the end of the monsoons. Everything was lush—flowers were brilliant—and the stall shops were filled with bright-colored garments and uncountable numbers of items made from gold, silver, and wood. People laughed, and little kids ran after you all the time. Once, there was even an honest-to-God carnival when I was up here—ferris wheels and all-loud, grating music blaring through loudspeakers—that was the day the A-1 came limping in, shot to hell on a SAR effort on Route 7. Just a piece of barely flying junk (they ended up stripping it for parts and throwing the rest away). We all met the pilot, who'd never been here before, and because he'd missed the last shuttle back south, he spent the night. I remember walking around the carnival with him—still wearing his flight suit—saying over and over again, "I don't believe it. I just don't believe it. This can't be happening to me." Or the time Lt. Po lost his brakes coming back from his first combat mission—came screaming down the runway like speed was going out of style and slid into the big stack of empty oil drums we use for a barrier (the Navy theory, I suppose)—the T-28 tilted up on its nose at a 45-degree angle and just balanced there, surrounded by dented and tipped oil drums, and Po (he's dead now) climbed out looking scared and sad until the ground crews and the other pilots started cheering and gave him the champagne they had ready—and we were all sitting around on the oil drums, laughing and drinking to old Po, who'd managed to bring his bird back alive. Or the time—shit, those were the bright days in a land of dreams—so various—so beautiful—so new.

Not so now. I could barely see the runway when I flew over the valley this morning, just clearing the ridgelines. Came up by way of Sam Thong, then homed in on the

TACAN [Tactical Air Navigation] until I almost hit the south ridge. There seem to be fires all over (I'm sure the bad guys are setting some of them), and the smoke layer tops out at more than 12,000 feet. In the smoke I saw large pieces of what looked like carbon paper sailing by—they must be burnt leaves—and the turbulence is distracting. It's like flying above a giant incinerator.

Could barely see the other end of the runway on touchdown—and what we call Titty Karst loomed dimly at the far end—the two breastlike rock formations that stick straight up like chicken croquettes. This smog makes Los Angeles seem like Colorado on a clear day.

And on the ground, what a difference . . . streets dusty and people walking around with bundles in their hands and on their heads. Passed five Meo ladies in their incredibly beautiful gold and silver stitched robes—their Sunday best (or whatever the Meo equivalent is)—and I smiled and said "Sabadee," but they just kept on walking. Shops are all boarded up. With no sun to reflect, the rooftops look dingy, and the grayish-brown teak buildings look like unused outhouses. There is concertina wire all over the place now, roll upon roll surrounding the airstrip, Vang Pao's house, and other strategic buildings. Men are digging trenches and gun emplacements. Standing on the Ice House porch, I could not see the artillery pads which dot the ridgelines, only about a mile away. It's comforting to know they're there, anyway. So what to do now? Here I am, field commander of a tiny group of pilots whose job it is to support an "army" of fifteen- and sixty-year-olds against a gigantic force of the best (so we are led to believe) North Vietnam has to offer. Met with Big Al and Hamilton briefly this afternoon, showed them the little piece of paper Barnes got me from the Ambassador telling all concerned that I was running the show for the duration of the crisis—they grumbled a bit but not much. If we're going to survive this one, we've got to do the job right. For the next few days, anyway, I'm the funnel for intelligence and orders—and if I can't get Barnes, then I'm on my own. This includes recommendations for strike targets, mission scheduling, sortie requests, and airborne liaison with Brickbat and USAF aircraft. It also means coordinating with VP (I'll go through Hamilton for this one) and finding out just what he does want—and where. Lunderberg should have this job—he's got a hundred years of operations experience, but he left for California last week. Then again, maybe his kind of smarts wouldn't work here either. Al said OK, no sweat—said he's also tired of Horowitz's effete (wonder where he learned that word) diplomacy. We all shook on it.

But I feel so damned isolated, as if this valley and this impending battle were the end all of everything. I've gotten used to hopping from one place to another, doing something here, a little there—getting my ass shot at for a few frightening minutes—then everything is calm and I go back to the bar for a cool one. Even Vietnam wasn't like this. Being an American, I felt a certain serenity in SVN, as if it really wasn't our war but that we were acting like traffic cops. Occasionally we had to arrest a speeder—and every once in a while we'd have to shoot it out with some guys who'd just robbed a bank.

Not here. We know that all the bad guys have to do is blow up our airplanes and we're at Long Tieng for the duration. The aircraft is our umbilical to safety, fragile as it is—and we may well end up as plain old foot soldiers trying to protect our own little foxhole. And unlike Vietnam, where we could usually count on American troops, out there, somewhere, to keep the enemy from overrunning our positions, here all we've got are some scraggly, evil-looking mountain tribesmen who've never even been taught to march—and we're not sure how many of them there are—exactly where they are—or for that matter, how long they'll stick around. Fair makes the mind real [sic], doesn't it? I wonder—maybe I can talk Vang Pao into sending a spoiling force back up to Xieng Khouang—just to keep the bad guys guessing. I wonder—

Midnight—the witching hour and all is well—I shall finish this cool one and . . . [The sentence ends abruptly here, with a heavy pencil line slanting diagonally down the page.]

Teletype message, AOC 20A to OUSAIRA, Vientiane, 20 March.

SUBJECT: Daily Operations Report

1. The NVA attack on the old ADF [Automatic Direction Finding radio transmitter] site last night was more than just a probe. Estimates are that at least two squads overran the two buildings at approximately 0015. Preceding this attack, two 122mm rockets impacted at 0005 about three hundred yards from our quarters. Fortunately, the enemy assault not only destroyed structures which had been scheduled for removal, but also alerted a nearby perimeter patrol, who quite effectively chewed up the NVA force as they withdrew. Apparently the NVA did not know we have not used the old ADF site for over a year, and it is heartening to see that perhaps they too can make mistakes. Six NVA bodies were recovered this morning, along with three AK-47 rifles. There were also indications that other enemy troops had been wounded.

2. Sorties still continue to be diverted, with only radar bombing being conducted against suspected enemy positions and storage areas between here and the PDJ. With the SGUs no longer patrolling in outlying areas, ground intelligence sources have become minimal. For some reason Red Dog's 105mm artillery site has remained very quiet. We do not know if this means the enemy has bypassed it or whether they have not yet reached it in force.

3. The refugee situation, however, is becoming critical. At first light what appeared to be hundreds of small groups began walking out toward Sam Thong, and a few others appear to have struck out across the mountains toward Vang Vieng, where they can still get bus transportation to Vientiane. Urge that you start refugee air evacuation as soon as possible. Company and Vang Pao

concur and are sending similar requests through their own channels.

4. Brief ground action recap: at 0801 a patrol reported light contact with an unknown-sized enemy force, six kilometers NW. No casualties. At 1000 seven mortar rounds impacted near one of the forward artillery positions about two kilometers to the north. The enemy may be starting daylight attacks. T-28 airstrikes were called in; no further incidents. At 1342 a patrol reported seeing a large number of foot tracks crossing a stream about five kilometers to the northeast. There has been no radio contact with this eight-man group since that time. All else has been relatively quiet.

5. Air action picked up early this afternoon as the weather broke for a few hours. In all, 84 USAF sorties struck storage and transshipment areas; Ravens FACd all but 22 of these. No close air support contact with the enemy. Raven 23 did take four small-arms hits in the left wing; aircraft repaired and fully serviceable at this time. Blake.

Teletype message, AOC 20A to OUSAIRA, Vientiane, 21 March.

1. Early Saturday (today) morning, at 0200, we received what is becoming our nightly rocket attack. Four 122mm rockets hit in pairs, about two minutes apart, bracketing the airstrip. One landed directly on top of the Lao O-1, destroying it and killing two guards who were posted nearby. No significant damage. In addition, during the early morning hours there were at least three brief clashes with enemy forces of unknown size within three miles of the valley. At 0415 fifteen enemy conducted a probing attack on the south ridgeline, getting to within two hundred yards of the summit before being driven off by a combina-

tion of mortar and AC-47 fire. No confirmed enemy dead. It was a relief to see those stars last night for a change.

2. In addition, reports have come in that a "large NVA force" has been sighted to the northwest, moving south, about halfway between here and Sam Thong. In a brief firefight, friendlies inflicted unknown casualties, suffering one KIA and two WIA of their own. Rumors which have been circulating for two days of another enemy force to the northeast were confirmed today when Raven 23 spotted glints from metallic objects in the general vicinity of TG163415. He received heavy groundfire, but the clouds closed in shortly and prevented further observation or visual airstrikes. Two radar-directed missions were conducted soon afterward, but our continuing game of aerial battleship produced no definite results.

3. As increasing casualties begin to trickle in to the hospital here, we were all relieved to see the air evacuation start. All day long C-123 aircraft successfully airlifted valley residents and wounded to prepared refugee camps in and around Vientiane. When the word got out, we were concerned about a possible attack as people began clustering around the airfield, packed so tightly at times that it was difficult for the aircraft to taxi. As of this afternoon, the guards surrounding the O-1 and T-28 aircraft have been instructed to protect the birds from the enemy at night and the friendlies by day. We lost count of the number of sorties or the number of refugees evacuated, but our guess is there were well over two thousand people flown to safety. Please commend all pilots for their humanitarian efforts in such rotten weather. Also to be commended are the control tower personnel. With minimum U.S. assistance they claim to have handled 243 takeoffs and landings, often with poor visibility and occasionally with two aircraft on the runway at the same time and a helicopter touching down to one side. We do suggest, however, that you contact Air America ASAP and inform them that it is not good practice for their Porters to take off opposite to traffic when incoming aircraft are touching down. Granted, they have a short field capability, but one of the Lao T-28s nearly veered off the runway when he saw someone else's propeller coming straight at him.

4. Targeting: I have approved and Mr. Morrinello has

passed through his channels Vang Pao's request for a significant airstrike around coordinates TG163415. Suggest maximum effort. Vang Pao is looking extremely worn down these days, and his growing gloom is reflected by his men, some of whom, it is rumored, have left with their families.

5. General: the situation is grave, still, and all are bracing themselves for the enemy to move, whenever and wherever he plans to. Vang Pao has apparently consolidated his forces in a tighter ring around Long Tieng—but he will not say exactly where or how many. This fact alone would make air support rather difficult, even if the pilots could see the ground.

6. Raven 01 is coming down tonight in General Vang Pao's aircraft as requested for meeting and to pick up replacement T-28. Blake.

Blake, *Journal*, p. 125.

Saturday, 21 March—a few quick notes. Tense meeting in Vientiane tonight with everybody. Barnes is very pale; even Horowitz looked as if his favorite tailor had just left town. Speaking of Horowitz, he had the gall—yes, gall—to pass out invitations at the meeting to a dinner party he's having next Saturday, the 28th, to celebrate the completion of his swimming pool, "at last." Jesus Christ! But then, on the other hand, why not? If the bad guys take Long Tieng and the Lao government collapses, he may never get another chance to use it.

Tomorrow morning a quick trip south for a big confab—some VIPs, no one would say who, coming in. Looks as if we've finally got some really high-level interest at last.

Wonder if Sheila would change her mind?—no—shit, I'm too tired anyway—what with Van's *Filet au Pommard* and my intense relief at not having to worry about incoming rockets, I'm just going to collapse.

107

Teletype message, JANAF, Vientiane, Summary of Operations, 22 March. The addressees on this report, emanating at regular intervals from the Joint Army, Navy, and Air Force Attaches in each country where an embassy is maintained, include the Secretary of State, the Joint Chiefs of Staff, the Defense Intelligence Agency, and the Department of Defense.

SUBJECT: Laotian Situation Report

1. The situation in northern Laos continues to worsen, and hardly by coincidence, we suspect, the enemy has increased probing attacks on the Bolovens Plateau and in the vicinity of Pakse and Savannakhet. The extent of the NVA's intention is not known, but we are beginning to believe that this is not just another limited dry-season offensive. Captured NVA have stated that their instructions are simply to "liberate Laos," and we suspect that the North Vietnamese intransigence in Paris is keyed directly to their success in this current campaign. They may impart more significance to Laos than we do.

2. Politically, the Royal Lao Government is in a schismatic state—with the liberal and conservative factions beginning to exert more pressure along their own lines. The Communist-oriented parties obviously want to see Vang Pao relieved of command, while one of the old Phoumist representatives has asked privately for American ground support similar to the White Star teams of 1960–61. There is also an uncorroborated but extremely alarming report that one of our AID personnel saw a large bank draft, in excess of 1,000,000 U.S. dollars, mailed for deposit to a Swiss bank. All of these indicators point to a shaky situation indeed.

3. In the war itself, today can be described only as frantic, but every one of our people did a magnificent job in the face of what are becoming almost impossible odds. Yester-

day (Saturday), "Pop" Buell received advance word that the enemy would hit Sam Thong in force; accordingly, extra aircraft were assigned to the refugee airlift, and all key and wounded personnel were removed from Sam Thong. His intelligence proved correct, because at 2300 local time an enemy force of unknown size entered the city and set fire to one warehouse and one wing of the nearly completed USAID hospital. There was some fighting in the streets, and at daybreak the friendly forces had withdrawn to the hills south of town, while the enemy apparently occupied mountain positions to the north. If the weather breaks at all, airstrikes will be conducted in an effort to dislodge them.

4. At Long Tieng the decision has been made to effect a full-scale evacuation of all, repeat, all personnel except for combat troops. Weather and enemy presence permitting, we will continue to fly up to Long Tieng during the day, but as of this morning, all efforts will be made to remove or destroy vital equipment and supplies. Logistically speaking, Long Tieng is no longer a permanent base; it has become another seasonal forward operating location. The evacuation order was given at 0430 this morning, just as a group of us were preparing to head south for the scheduled meeting (ref JCS Message 190845Z). Instead, all Raven FACs flew north and assisted other personnel in dismantling and loading equipment. A typical C-123 load might consist of half communications and crypto gear, half Meo refugees, who still line up in droves for transportation out. Weather remains very bad.

5. Except for sporadic mortar fire in areas surrounding Long Tieng, there was strangely little contact with the enemy today, and there were no significant nighttime incidents. Intelligence reports continue to show large enemy units maneuvering nearby, but we have no hard numbers to report. It is becoming apparent, however, that the enemy has probably committed the bulk of his forces in northern Laos to this campaign. In the face of this adversity, we are beginning to experience a degree of cooperation among all units not before possible in this war. At least we have something good to report.

Blake, *Journal*, p. 126.

Sunday nite. Vientiane— Quite a day—when you put in 18 hours, you get so geared up it's hard to quit. At least I don't have to worry about Ops Reports for a while—teletype's been shut down. I just handcarry notes down to Barnes, who puts his own version of them on the wire. We've got people sacked out all over the house—Van is frantic, claiming we should have given him more notice so that he could have bought more food at the morning market—promises a better dinner tomorrow.

Just a few random notes tonight—too tired to think—but I pray that one thing doesn't happen. Our civilian contract pilots have threatened a strike unless their wage demands are met. Honestly—that's about all I can say. Sure, they've had a continuing dispute with their management for months—and true, a possible strike has been in the offing—but Jesus Christ, there's a limit sometime, and we've reached it. Wonder what would happen if everyone went on strike—on both sides. Hah. But we can't do without them, and one pilot told me that his supervisor said he thought they'd get their raise and overtime, but that the decision had to come from the home office, and it might take a couple of days. We don't have a couple of days.

Ran into Cranston today from CHECO. Just for the hell of it, took him along—his first visit to Alternate. He wants to get the whole thing down on paper—I'd like that too—and it was such a milling-around mess that I don't think anyone noticed him. He did look funny, though, in his sports shirt, loafers, gray trousers, and a pistol belt, plus a Czech submachine gun which someone gave him at the last moment "just in case." I don't think he knew how to use it. Hope he got some good stuff.

Weather was just above minimums all day—but no bad guy attacks. Wonder what they're waiting for. Just before

I took the runway, I waved to Sgt. Champong, my favorite crew chief. For the first time, he didn't wave back. I understand. He's got to spend the night up there.

109

Teletype message, OUSAIRA, Vientiane, to 7AF, Saigon, 23 March.

According to General Vang Pao, results of special mission flown last night were spectacular, repeat, spectacular. He said that he had no idea the enemy had so many supplies so close to Long Tieng. Visual reports indicated secondary fires and explosions lasting well into the morning hours, and we suspect that one of the major enemy supply depots has been destroyed. Follow-up strikes in the same area continue by radar today. Thanks. Barnes.

110

Blake, *Journal*, pp. 131–142 (pp. 127–130 are blank). Major Blake's handwriting shows a marked change here. It is quite uneven and slants backward. Numerous words are crossed out and rewritten.

Monday, 23 March— Now I'm taking frustration out on paper. I suppose it's the best way. This whole show makes me want to hit someone. I thought yesterday's mess capped it—today was worse. When we finally got down here last night, no one knew what the flying schedule would be, and in the confusion I forgot to write down where everyone was staying. I had three or four Ravens in my house, others bunked with some of the Attache people. Hamilton took his boys somewhere else—so when Barnes gave me the poop late last night about today's activities, I had to find everyone this morning at 0400. Only problem was that the phones were all dead. They're never dependable anyway—but of all days. Left notes on doors, woke people up. Felt like Paul Revere—except I was driving a jeep.

Then we couldn't get to the airport. The 23rd of March, it seems (and no one told me), is Lao Armed Forces Day, and everybody and his brother turned out. It's a memorial celebration—but exactly what they have to celebrate I'll never know. There must have been 10,000 troops marching throughout the city—all FAR and Neuts—buckles polished, shoes shined, etc, and all the main streets were blocked. We tried to get down to the field the short way, through the marketplace, but even at 6:00 AM the parade was forming on the main street and we couldn't get through. In front of the vertical runway, waves of brown—jamming the streets, obscuring the sammlars. Everywhere (it seemed) that we tried to go there was an officious armed guard who told us we had to go some other way—finally got down to the airport almost an hour late.

This is the ultimate incongruity of it all. Forty miles away there's a battle shaping up which may determine the future of their country—and these guys down here don't seem to care. They'd rather parade around and put on a show of force for the home folks than they would get out and fight for them. Somehow reminds me of what happened in the U.S. early in the Vietnam war—when all the airline pilots who had been flying with the Air National Guard started bitching because they were called up with their units—and then they bitched some more when they were told either to fly for the airlines or with the National Guard, but not both. What the hell do people want these days, anyway?

With the teletype out between Alternate and Vientiane, we didn't find out that Sam Thong had gone until we got up to Long Tieng. As it turned out, I was the first to land. Some C-123s due in for air evac turned back because one of them picked up some groundfire on final approach. There's another bitch—first they talk about striking—now they won't fly because it isn't "safe." What the hell do they think a war is? I landed with no trouble at about 0830, cranked up the portable transmitter, and told everyone that the war could start now. Chewed out one of the Lao radio operators unjustly—he said he had no authorization to declare the field open until an American told him to, and I was the first one up that day. Remember to apologize.

Except for the fact that the T-28 bombloader broke and they had to load by hand (Vang Pao helped—he's pulling out all the old stops to keep his troops' morale up—but the strain shows), no real problems today—except for the weather. Not even a probe last night—no rocket attacks, either (maybe they've run out of rockets? Reminds me of the story about the NVA porter who was drafted in Hanoi, given two mortar shells to carry down the Trail—did so, surviving air attacks, malaria, and monsoons—arrived in the Delta three months later and reported to his commander that he had brought two mortar shells and wanted to do his bit for the cause. "Thank you," the NVA commander said, taking the shells and dropping them, one by one, into a mortar. Bloop, went one. Bloop, went the other. "Now Comrade Dong," the commander said, "go back and get two more").

I don't see too much of Hamilton these days—he's been busy getting his own stuff out and closing up his part of the show. Saw him down on the flightline haranguing a crewchief about a stack of supplies and asked him to join me for luncheon—he looked at me as if I was crazy—until I told him I'd found ten pounds of frozen prawns when we were cleaning out food supplies—and that I had made a command decision that they would not survive the trip down. He went screaming up to the Company cafeteria and stole some ketchup and horseradish, and we gorged ourselves with cold shrimp and cocktail sauce. Some of the other guys came in and there was plenty for all. We fed the multitudes.

Two or three incoming mortar shells today, I think—and a hell of a lot outgoing. The 105s boomed with regularity—I wonder if they know what they're shooting at—and how deserted the valley is beginning to look. Once they got going, our civilian friends did another beautiful job in getting refugees out. More went over the ridgeline southwest—because someone passed the word around that the NVA had promised not to harm them. They believed it. Score another one for the other side. Everybody's forgotten what the NVA did to the people of Hue, I guess, or maybe the news didn't get here. I just don't know.

Weather—weather—weather—weather. I wish we could control *that*—(I seem to be remembering stories tonight)—there was that time in Vietnam when some bright boy came up with the idea to burn out the bad guys in the U Minh forest, where we'd been bombing for weeks without visible results. The bombs would disappear under the jungle canopy, sucked in it seemed, like the shells from a lone patrol boat firing into a jungle shoreline—and this bright boy got the Air Force to retrofit some aircraft to drop used oil, like the slurry carriers on the West Coast do on forest fires. One of the rationales was that it cost money to dispose of all the used oil—thus they were killing a lot of birds with each stone. They dropped tons of the stuff in the jungle, then set it on fire with Willy Pete [White Phosphorus] rockets. Big Blaze—much smoke—for a few minutes until the abruptly rising heat formed a thunderstorm which put the fire out. The weather—maybe the great rain god in the sky is trying to tell us something. I heard we even tried cloud seeding on the Trail—authorization for which was given by a former boss with the words, "Let's do it. It's better to make mud, not war." There are so many stories like these—but no one tells them. There's no GI Joe—no Bill Mauldin—even Beetle Bailey never goes overseas. Are we all too self-conscious about this war? It's no different from any other one—not really—and it's the only one I know of which is being fought primarily for a principle by both sides. God help us when men refuse to die for a concept.

I'm just too exhausted to sleep. I find it not too bad to get along on four hours or so—with a little nap here and there. I've almost forgotten what it's like to FAC a visual airstrike—it seems like another era—about all we're doing is searching—searching—flying through muck you wouldn't believe, knowing we probably wouldn't see anything anyway, even if it were clear—but hoping. When I got up from lunch today, Hamilton said with all seriousness, "I want you to get the mail through, William, even if you have to fly at night to do it." I didn't catch on for a moment, then I laughed. We both roared. Hamilton's OK. Later, looking down at the jagged mountains and trying to figure out where I was in the haze, I thought of the early airmail pilots. We've sure come a long way. Sure.

I'm just babbling, I know. But it's a fucked-up mess. I'd guess that all wars—at this level—seem just as fucked up. Unfortunately, by the time the news reaches Washington, then the history books and tactics manuals, all the fuckedupness gets edited out, and battles that were won because someone read the wrong date on a calendar get reported as examples of a commander's master strategy. It's funny—when we're winning, we're properly executing the campaign plan, but like now, when we're about to get our ass kicked, it's the enemy whose strategy is superior. But each side keeps right on doing the same thing. I wonder if they're as fucked up as we are.

No—it's just the day which counts—and here, the individual battle. I see no overall sense of purpose reflected in the daily actions of the men, yet they do their jobs—and some die doing them—it's only when a *lack* of purpose from above starts shining through that the guys start fidgeting.

Enough—these are late-night thoughts, written by kerosene lantern in a flight suit (the electricity's off again). I do know one thing—I'm beginning to understand this war, and I know a hell of a lot more than anyone else around. Tomorrow we'll see. I may have gotten VP talked into a little caper we're not telling anyone about, yet——

111

Teletype message, JANAF Summary of Operations, 24 March.

1. With the loss of Sam Thong yesterday, the situation here has markedly worsened. Even though the enemy is in the town, we have acceded to requests from Mr. Buell of USAID and others that no air attacks be made against Sam Thong, and almost as if in return, the Royal Lao Government has dispatched FAR units from Vientiane and some SGU cadres from southern Laos to bolster the de-

fenses of Long Tieng. This is a first. Until now each Military Region has acted with feudal autonomy—but the gravity of the present threat has forced all friendly factions to at least begin to work together. It is too early to say whether a precedent has been established or not. If so, the NVA may have made a serious mistake by generating a threat large enough to unify the country.

2. Airlifted in by C-123 and other aircraft, the fresh Lao troops arrived at Long Tieng at 1000 today, Tuesday, and almost immediately were deployed around the perimeter. It is true that many of them had not been told where they were going—because of security reasons, we were informed —but once the situation was explained to them—that they were surrounded by the enemy and that they would have to fight their way out—the grumbling stopped and they seemed to accept their orders without further resistance. These additional troops will help fill the gaps which have been left because some of the Meo soldiers have fled with their families. The exact number of deserters is unknown but is hoped to be small.

3. Although we had also hoped the enemy had expended his 122mm rocket supply, last night eight (8) of the large missiles were fired. Two scored direct hits on buildings and one damaged General Vang Pao's house. An orbiting AC-47 Spooky saw the rockets fired and immediately attacked the observed launch sites, with no reportable results. Interestingly, the weather at night has been markedly better than during the day, but it is still exceedingly difficult to convince the friendly troops to undertake night actions.

4. A highlight of the day, however, was one action by General Vang Pao himself, as reported by personnel who saw it happen. About noon a small enemy force slipped in to the south ridgeline and, unobserved in the haze, set up a 12.7mm machine gun and began firing into the valley floor. General Vang Pao, who was down on the flight line, commandeered a mortar, and after firing one shot which was long, achieved a direct hit on the enemy machine gun and caused numerous secondary explosions as the ammunition went off. Observers could hear a rousing cheer go up all over the valley. A squad was sent immediately to the

site, and five enemy bodies were found. Score one for our side.

5. We are still awaiting the big push, as intelligence reports still indicate massive enemy resupply and reinforcement efforts. Airstrikes are keeping him off balance, we know, but whether we are hurting him enough is unknown. The fact that the NVA did occupy Sam Thong the day after the extremely successful special mission bodes ill.

112

Memo, OUSAIRA, Vientiane, to Blake, AOC 20A, 25 March.

Bill:
Horowitz informed me today that the Ambassador seemed to be somewhat distressed at the breakdown in the chain of command these past few days. He gave me no details, but he did seem concerned. I'm not certain what he means. Do you? Call me when you get in tonight, please.
Barnes

113

Notes for a report, hastily written in Major Blake's hand, dated 25 March.

For Col. Barnes:
1. Sorry I could not get to you last night (Tuesday)—don't worry about Horowitz. We don't have time.
2. Today very bad—Meo pilots set new record for sorties—Vongsaly flew 19; Kong Kha 18. Most flights lasted only 5–8 minutes—arm, takeoff, clear the ridgeline, drop, land. I made them at least shut their engines down while load-

ing—one of the little guys was almost killed by a spinning prop. USAF A-1s did get some work done—two artillery posts under daylight attack (a first)—both held, but took casualties—commend A-1 drivers. Jets couldn't work low — enough—we heard them above us all day, but they were diverted for radar drops.

3. Ask Horowitz what kind of a trade he wants to get the civilians to fly airplanes—they refused again to land early this morning because of groundfire. Christ, we'll take up a collection if it will help.

4. I don't know how many troops remain—the artillery seems to echo in the valley for first time—no more civilians left here at all—maybe enemy was waiting for this—don't know. Very few soldiers in the town itself—most are up on the ridgelines (if there are any still there at all)—couldn't find all our Lao maintenance men today—no one knew if the missing guys had been killed, been drafted into the front lines, or just deserted. Incoming mortar fire—more—reports that some big enemy guns (130mm?) sighted just south of the PDJ.

5. In a word, everything's going to shit.

Blake, *Journal*, p. 143.

Thursday, 5:00 PM—Vientiane. I should be up at Alternate with the little guys. All round-eyes ordered out early today—not given the option of staying if we wanted to (Hamilton and I tried)—weather forecast a factor—predicted no visibility whatever tonight—if we didn't get off then, we probably wouldn't at all.

We weren't the last ones out, either—just after noon some more reinforcements got in—don't know who they are—but they look better than the other groups—no insignia—helmets—no screwing around at all—formed ranks and marched off into the mist toward the King's palace.

Barnes called meeting for 6:00—don't know how long it

will last—shit—shit—shit. Helpless, hopeless feeling. Out of nowhere, today, appeared about a 60-man Meo group, wandering across the airstrip, some carrying musical instruments. The 20A Long Tieng military marching band, who'd been sort of waiting over by the hospital for orders to evacuate. A couple of Meo officers scarfed them up—passed out rifles, some of which looked like vintage World War I. Didn't see them again. For all I know, they're all we have left.

Leaving the valley, couldn't see anyone at all—gun emplacements shrouded in mist—all brown and gray—a painted town upon a painted jungle, where no birds sing.

115

Tape recording by Major William Blake, undated except by internal evidence. The frequent pauses in this monologue are indicated by ellipses.

It is too late, I fear, to sleep. My head swims, still . . . and Friday's dawn is due like thunder shortly . . . and the sun will come lethargically and abrasively burning through haze and smoke and clouds . . . and the real thunder will be on the ground. It's four AM, and I must fly soon.

I cannot believe last night. It is the culminating madness. I have slightly more than an hour until I must rejoin the real world . . . and the war. Where are you, Weird? Are you really gone, David? Do we all go to dusty death today?

Oh bullshit, Blake. Man, cool it. You're still drunk . . . of all the nights and days to be so drunk. Valerie still sleeping in your bed, and you in your crusty flight suit, damn near dead. Valerie and your zippers . . . looking down, Christ, there's a small blue bow on the bottom zipper, center front . . . "Keep it safe for me," she said. Keep what! "Just so," she said, tying the bow and cinching the zipper shut. "That's my brave lord." Then Valerie to sleep, and me, the stupid nut, still talking, much too drunk to write. For whom? And what could I really say? The truth? The facts, ma'am? The way it really was? Or is my goddamn drunk and heat-oppressed brain conjuring up another fucking fiction on this tape?

I cannot believe Barnes last night... but can I Valerie? I suppose I can believe anything, now. Who arrived here first, Valerie or Barnes?... think, you stupid idiot... it was Barnes, at ten o'clock... with eight (yes, count them), eight FACs just ending chow. Van perplexed... we'd mixed peanut butter sandwiches with his *coq au vin*... or whatever the hell he'd fixed. With all of us exhausted, a sorry meal indeed. Growth of beard... flight suits stained with white sweat... glaring eyes. Too tired to sleep, but what the hell... (Shit... I can't think straight today) ... All my Ravens: Bulkeley, Page, Brochowski, Hamner, Flint... names enough to make a Buddha flinch... looking at watches, each and all... blankets on the floor, on couches, Harrison sacked out on two chairs. We fly tomorrow (today!)... one flies east, one flies west... shit, we all fly north today.

Barnes arrived at ten... or thereabouts... two gaboons of scotch, one per hand... beating on the door, and then inside. Would you call him wild-eyed? Maybe so. Just beat... beat... beat... who's that knocking on my door? Saying, "What the hell *is* this, my boys? A wake?" Brochowski, napping on the couch, leaps up, sees Barnes, goes back to sleep. Barnes shouting, drunk, "My captains and my major..."

Shit, Blake, what in hell are you doing? You need sleep. Oh fuck it, babes. Who dies this day is quit. Quite.

Dawn... very red sky. Palmettos and mangoes and other great green growth outside the window turning pale with fright... (what made me say that?)...

Barnes at ten o'clock... weaving among us, pouring drinks... "A toast, you sad, heroic bastards. To all my sad captains," then to me, "and one poor major too. Give the bastards hell." Raised glasses... Van with ice, perked up because there was still laughter.

How many toasts? To what? I tried to shut Barnes up, but if you try to dam the Mekong, then you drown. We damn near did. And Valerie arrived soon after, white dress, slouching sleeves, said, "Fuck the midnight bell." Whence cometh she? Wake up, you idiot... you have a war to fight tomorrow . . . today . . . have you gone native with the rest? Never . . . never . . . neverland . . . never . . . nevermore.

I carry this recorder in my hand . . . sleep, Ravens . . . this is my unknown private self . . . you'll rise and fly so soon . . . in ancient, creaking crates that would make the Wrights weep. I will be pale and passionless as the dawn. Page snores . . . Flint farts . . . it's a sad dawning at best.

They dropped off one by one, exhausted (I'm in the kitchen now, pure water heating on the stove . . . need coffee . . . good French coffee, it says made in Cuba . . . CUBA . . . shit) . . . Flights of Ravens . . . good kids . . . and the last awake were Barnes, dear Valerie, and me.

"Call Horowitz," Barnes exclaimed.

"Oh goody." Valerie clapped her hands.

"Get out of here," I said.

"He wouldn't come, not Daddy." Valerie was stoned.

"You're right," Barnes said.

I groaned. "Goddamn it, Valerie . . . and Colonel Jake. Will you two leave and let us warriors get our tails to bed?"

"They're all sleeping—look," the Colonel said.

"Drinkie-poo," said Valerie, holding up her glass.

The Colonel: "Sure, you bet your everloving ass," then pouring, slopping on the floor.

The water's boiling . . . put it in the pot . . . don't spill . . . goddamn it's hot . . . Where are you, Weird? Still safe at home, your memories fading fast? . . . The goddamn incredulity of war. Do you really know?

What brought the Colonel and the broad last night? Subliminal frustration . . . last attempts to set things right? A mock-heroic gesture . . . or a damn despairing thrust? Aggression? No . . . my tongue burns . . . Christ, that's hot! . . . and bitter . . . and the sleeping Valerie, promising she'd get up to make us breakfast . . . sending the good boys off to war with bellies full . . . no, those weren't her words . . . I think she said she'd fuck us all, when Barnes had left . . . but she let all the sleeping birds lie lonely by simply passing out. I carried her to bed and let her lie . . . sent Barnes, his driver waiting . . . on his way . . . lay down . . . and then I couldn't sleep. Goddamn it Barnes, you blew it, coming here last night. There's no one left but me who knows enough to set this sad world right.

Take warning, pilots . . . the sky is red today . . . no, that's for sailors. Pray, you dumb shit, pray. Now the red sky's gone . . . it's gray . . . and it's raining . . . RAINING . . . Hey, you guys, wake up . . . It's pouring out today.

116

Blake, *Journal*, pp. 144-145.

Friday, 27 March. The rain keeps up. It never rains in March—never—never—never—but it is now, and it has been all day. Our weather prophets attribute it to a severe tropical depression in the atmosphere, a pattern which normally indicates the onset of the monsoons. They say it's too soon to tell if it's a fluke—or if the rainy season is really starting early. Can't tell if it's ever happened before—meteorological records in Vientiane go back only to 1937.

Today—we sat—and sat—and sat. Had the ceiling lifted, we would have gone up. Vang Pao tried to get in by chopper—no good. No radio contact with the north—no nothing. Brickbat tried to get Alternate to come up on every available frequency—no luck (the Thai bases have not yet been hit by the rains). Apparently the storms moved down from the north—weathermen estimate they must have hit Alternate just before midnight (along with the enemy?—God, I wish I knew). Lower atmosphere is super unstable, and the heat rising from the ground (NVA fires? Hah!) caused massive precipitation. Mekong doesn't show it yet, but the locals have ordered the summer beach squatters to move back to higher ground because of a possible flooding situation.

Made my daily message delivery run this morning to everyone—pouring rain, and the windshield wipers didn't work so I opened the front windshield and loved it—wet, stinging, sloppy, beautiful rain. Nothing at all happening in the command post—Barnes stuck out down south somewhere—so I came back and went to sleep. Valerie left some time in the morning. Woke up about noon, and Van fixed us the lightest, fluffiest cheese omelet I've ever seen. Periodic weather checks. No go at all. Four of us played bridge in the afternoon, then watched a movie. Thought we might generate a party, but no one (including myself) wanted to. Everyone got showers—changed clothes, shaved. How nice it all feels.

Banner headlines in the Bangkok papers about Long Tieng—as far as they're concerned, it's just about gone. Only a matter of days. Someone's requesting an emergency meeting of SEATO—someone else claims there are Red Chinese troops getting a piece of the action—many wild speculations.

All I know today is that driving off the main streets in Vientiane is almost impossible, even with four-wheel drive. Even the boulevards are running five inches deep, with Toyotas, Hondas, and an occasional American car splashing waves up on the sidewalk. The dirt roads are three feet of mud. Yesterday they were hard packed and dusty. Wonder what would have happened if it had rained on the Lao parade? What a gas.

But if it's like this down here, what's it like up north? My fingers are crossed. Anyway—if my newly devised alarm and notification system (ALNOT) works tomorrow morning, we should be down at the flightline at 0400, ready to go. Two jeeps, two bicycles, and three runners.

And an unbelievable report from Paris—says the paper —Saigon wants to release 343 NVA prisoners, but Hanoi drones on: "Both North Vietnam and the delegation representing the Vietcong preferred to focus attention on what they charged were efforts by the U.S. Administration to prolong the war in Vietnam and to extend it to Laos and Cambodia." What absolute horseshit! I wonder if they really know what their own troops are doing back home, or is their intelligence about a month late too?

Oh well—according to Van, the Lao New Year (Pi Mai) coincides with our Easter. This war's full of strange coincidences.

117

Teletype message, JANAF Summary of Operations, 28 March.

1. The unseasonally torrential rains continue today (Saturday). At least nine inches have fallen since yesterday, and there is no sign of a letup. This morning the intense storm system spread into Thailand, effectively halting all U.S. air operations until further notice. After numerous F-4 aircraft began having difficulty returning to base with unexpended ordnance, even radar and all-weather sorties were canceled.

2. As a consequence of the rains, there is absolutely nothing new to report at this time. We are all standing by, in actuality treading water, to see what is going to happen.

118

Blake, *Journal*, p. 146.

Saturday, 28 March—Nothing happened at all today. Phone lines are all down. We listened to Radio Hanoi for a while—no mention of the rains at all—according to them, Long Tieng has been taken and northern Laos is liberated. We'll see.

Don't even feel like writing tonight—everything is dripping wet—windowpanes fogged—sheets and pillows are soggy—today was to have been the day VP and I were (maybe) to have led the diversionary charge up the PDJ, thanks to Al M. and a few of his chopper guys who said they didn't believe in big unions either. We planned to leap into Xieng Khouang during early morning, shoot the hell out of the place, and get out at night—maybe—just to let the bad guys know we were still around. It seems that even the *worst* laid plans oft gang agley.

No initiative—no enthusiasm—I still feel rotten about the other night. Haven't seen Barnes since—nor Valerie. Wonder if I plant Valerie outside in the mud if she'll grow up a little? Outside—shit—tonight was Horowitz's party— and we all forgot about it. Wonder if anyone else got there? It's too late now.

Think I'll take a walk in the rain—just for the hell of it.

119

Teletype message (Xerox copy), JANAF Summary of Operations, 29 March.

1. When we were advised last night that weather satellite photos showed the storm system beginning to move out to the south, all aircraft and personnel were alerted to resume activities this morning (Sunday). Although Thailand bases were still experiencing low ceilings, no problems were encountered in launching sorties. The Plain of Jars cleared at about 0100—and Long Tieng broke wide open just before daylight.

2. Raven FACs flew a few trolling passes over the airstrip at Long Tieng before attempting to land, and when no groundfire was seen, touched down at approximately 0700. They were met by a group of soggy, but joyous friendlies, who stated that the situation was unchanged from the time the rains began. General Vang Pao arrived shortly thereafter and was seen to smile for the first time in many days.

3. Except for an occasional fair weather cumulus cloud, the sky was clear all day, and FAC's and strike aircraft flew a maximum number of sorties. All planned targets were hit, some with good results (see pertinent OPREP's [Operations Reports]), and there was very little sign of the enemy. A patrol entered Sam Thong at noon, and reported that the town was completely deserted. A probe toward the north of Sam Thong, however, did encounter some NVA

fire, and the friendly force withdrew to its position south of town for the night.

4. Long Tieng has been adequately resupplied—and two more battalions of friendly troops were airlifted in. It is far too early to tell if the siege of the valley has in fact been lifted. The enemy has shown no signs of withdrawing, for example, as their supply trails show no evidence of traffic, but the rains did give us a chance for a most welcome breather—and at least we can say that the situation has stabilized—for today at least.

5. Some Raven FACs requested permission to spend the night at Long Tieng, but because the enemy is probably still poised for an attack, permission was denied.

120

Note from Valerie Horowitz to Major Blake, on paper headed "From the Desk of A. Horowitz," dated "Sunday."

Bill:

I'm sitting in Daddy's office writing you this because things aren't very peaceful at home. When I left to go "shopping," Daddy was still stomping around the house, threatening to have me sent to a convent, or something. Honestly, what does he think I am, anyway? Just because his dumb pool party was rained out and just because I spent the night with you doesn't seem like reason enough to me. He must think I'm the Virgin Mary. Mother's locked herself in her room with a jug, and I'll send this over to you with one of the drivers, because Daddy has said, "You'll never see that man again," and I don't want to get you in any more trouble.

I'm sorry for the other night—honest I am—and I'm even sorrier that I blew up at Daddy when he nailed me about it. I should have told him the truth—or rather the real story—right off the bat, but when he asked me what happened, I told him I didn't know—that we were all bombed and that all I knew was that I woke up in your bed. And that's the truth, sort of. When I tried to tell him later that nothing "happened," he wouldn't listen to me. *I* know nothing happened (I should be able to tell by now when I've been laid, shouldn't I?), and you know that too—but I'm afraid Daddy's acting like the father of a violated sixteen-year-old. I'm rather glad he doesn't have a shotgun in that collection of silverplated Meo rifles people keep giving him.

Anyway, things are all in a mess and I'm afraid it's all my fault and I'm sorry. You're a great guy, Bill, really you are. I guess sometimes we just don't have any control over what happens to us.

Love,
Valerie

121

Teletype message, AOC 20A to OUSAIRA, Vientiane, 30 March.

SUBJECT: Daily Operations Report

1. With General Vang Pao's decision to return permanently to Long Tieng, operations here are being resumed normally as quickly as possible. Two Ravens, along with key maintenance personnel, will spend this and hopefully all following nights here. Please send up two dozen blankets on tomorrow's courier, as well as suitcases with clothing for Blake, Hamilton, and Harrison.

2. The reason for our decision to remain with Vang Pao is a multiple one: first, it looks good and inspires confidence in the troops to see us here; second, we can commence recce efforts an hour earlier in the morning; and third, VP reports that his patrols fanned out this morning and encountered absolutely no, repeat, no signs of the enemy within a two-kilometer radius of the valley. One Raven FAC did draw light groundfire about three and one half kilometers northeast, but two flights of F-4s which were called in effectively silenced the enemy, obtaining numerous secondary fires as they did so. Finally, the weather forecast for the next few days is good, and every-

one knows that with air support assured, the ground troops will hold their positions. And if today was any indication, there will be plenty of that. Thanks.

3. The visibility all day was unlimited, and we could see the strain on the little guys' faces relax more each time a flight of U.S. aircraft passed overhead. Tonight at dinner VP himself poured the scotch, and we toasted everyone we could think of, including the enemy General Giap, whom Vang Pao gives complete credit for planning such a nearly successful operation. When we asked Vang Pao what he meant by "nearly successful," all he said was, "That is all for this year. You will see."

4. A final request: please order a new heater for the Ice House. Someone left our present one on full bore while we were gone, and the main coil burned up. Blake.

122

Draft copy of DIA Summary, OUSAIRA, Vientiane, to DIA, Washington, 31 March. Attached is a memo, which follows as item 123.

1. All evidence points to the fact that Long Tieng has been held, but for reasons which are not, repeat, not entirely clear. Even though Sam Thong was reoccupied today without opposition and the enemy there has apparently abandoned his positions on the north ridge, even though Vang Pao's troops now occupy all territory around Long Tieng, there is an air of deepening mystery infusing the entire operation.

2. Some of the questions are: How many NVA were actually out there? How many friendly troops did *we* have? What were the enemy's real intentions? Why didn't they take Long Tieng any of the three days prior to the rains, when they apparently outnumbered a demoralized, tired handful of men? After the rains, what happened to them? Might there have been, in fact, only a few sapper companies, whose instructions were to harass us? Did they extend their supply lines too far and get caught by the rains? Does VP really believe there

were "thousands" of NVA out there? Did they actually bring in all that heavy equipment and did it get stuck in the mud? Was our interdiction campaign successful, so that the enemy really did not have all that big stuff in after all? Did our airstrikes chew them up so much that they could not continue? Were they afraid of determined resistance by the combined Meo-Lao forces? Did we win a battle, or did the rains save our ass? Or just what the hell went on up there, anyway? I'll be swacked if I know. All I know is that everyone I've had the pleasure of serving with here deserves the highest praise his country can give him.

123

Memo from OUSAIRA, Vientiane, to Major Blake, dated 31 March.

Bill:

Attached is a draft of the DIA Summary I wish I had the guts to send. But I don't. Furthermore, I doubt if it would do any good anyway. I think you can understand by now, however, why I have decided to submit my retirement papers immediately, even before the results of the promotion board are announced. I don't think I can take another Long Tieng, even if I'm not here to see it. And, quite frankly, I don't see why I should be expected to. If I had any answers to give you, I'd pass them on—but I don't.

So I'm going to leave the whole fucking thing in someone else's lap, my friend, and it's not my baby anymore. Incidentally, I suspect the feeling is somewhat mutual in Washington. I may have been fired. I've just been informed that my replacement is due in next week, three months earlier than I had expected him.

Call me at your convenience when you're down, and I'll buy you that drink I've been promising. From now on, color me FIGMO [slang acronym for "Fuck It, Got my Orders"].

JB

PS: Here's a copy of the DIA message I *did* send. Note the qualifiers.

124

DIA Summary (Xerox copy), OUSAIRA, Vientiane, to DIA, Washington, 31 March.

1. According to General Vang Pao, Commander of Military Region II, the siege of Long Tieng has been lifted. He has called upon all his people to return to their homes, and has announced that the enemy has suffered a disastrous defeat. Plans are already underway to assist refugees in returning to the valley.

2. In the face of what was reported to be a vastly superior enemy force, defenders consisting of allied soldiers from many contiguous regions successfully withstood an 11-day assault which included 122mm rockets, mortar and artillery fire, and direct attacks. Despite extremely poor weather and miserably dangerous flying conditions, U.S. air support assured the success of this major engagement. General Vang Pao himself has said, "If it were not for your (the U.S.) help, an NVA general would now be living in my house."

3. When the weather was below visual minimums, radar bombing continuously pounded the enemy, destroying unknown numbers of supplies and no doubt inflicting numerous casualties. Our small force of Raven FACs repeatedly distinguished themselves, even while living under conditions of privation and hardship when ordered to evacuate. Nearly constant air attacks disrupted the enemy's timetable, and when the weather finally cleared, massed airstrikes harassed a withdrawing, no doubt demoralized North Vietnamese division.

4. All praises should go where they are most deserved: to the valiant soldiers of General Vang Pao; to the intelligence community, who kept so well abreast of developments; to the USAF officers and men, both FAC and strike pilots, who relentlessly and efficiently did their jobs; and finally, to the combined determination of all joint forces in-

volved, whose courage and devotion to duty ensured that Long Tieng, this year, would not fall.

Holograph note in Col. Barnes' hand: "You see, Bill? It's all true—that's why it's all so tragic."

APRIL

125

Blake, *Journal*, p.147.

Wednesday, April Fools'—Long Tieng. Went down south for our weekly planning meeting—Barnes looked relaxed as hell—had a good chat—he handed me a copy of the newly published and declassified Senate Foreign Relations Committee Hearings and said I should be interested in its contents—will get to it soon. There's not too much time to read up here at Alternate—lots to do. With the return to "normalcy," I think there's a chance to get this show moving in the right direction. It's not that people haven't had the right answers—it's that they haven't known enough to ask the right questions. Maybe I can. Al and Hamilton agree (a good talk last night—then we all went down to VP's. Have his blessing. He introduced me to a couple of his "daughters"—wonder if he'll make me an offer I can't refuse?).

Got a couple of important letters off. I wonder if she'll answer. What the hell. Moved all my stuff up from Vientiane. Van was sorry to see me go. I told him there'd be someone else soon. Flew three hours. Thoughts whirling in my head now—*someone* has to win even a small part of this war, and if Al means what he says about ignoring Horowitz, we're on our way.

126
___

Letter from Major Blake to OUSAIRA, Vientiane, on official USAF stationery, dated 1 April.

SUBJECT: Request for Extension

1. Pursuant to AFReg 89-1, para. 4(d), I wish to request a six-month extension of my SEA tour. I wish also to remain in my present job.

2. It is my understanding that such extensions are almost automatically approved, providing the requestor has been doing a satisfactory job and is not in a critical skill area needed elsewhere. I will stand upon my record and accomplishments, and I do not believe there to be a USAF requirement other than in Southeast Asia for an experienced combat FAC.

[signed] William Blake, Major, USAF

127
___

DIA Summary (Xerox copy), OUSAIRA, Vientiane, to DIA, Washington, 1 April.

SUBJECT: Long Tieng Wrapup

1. We can now report with assurance that the threat to Long Tieng, thus to all northern Laos, has ended, and plans are already being formulated for a limited friendly offensive when the monsoons start in earnest. Although the word "euphoria" might seem too inclusive, nevertheless the mood in government circles here is decidedly optimistic. The Lao General Staff points with pride to the low casualty figures, and there is even talk of promoting Gen-

eral Vang Pao to three-star rank, a move which was opposed by General Ka and his supporters until a suggestion was made that everyone on the General Staff also be raised one grade, thus preserving the balance.

2. On the northern front, government patrols moving farther and farther out from Long Tieng are encountering only sporadic resistance. It appears that the enemy is withdrawing to his rainy season positions a full three weeks earlier than he did last year. There has been no sign of enemy presence in Muong Soui, and today Mr. Buell and the USAID team reestablished themselves in Sam Thong. The initial order of business was to conduct a tour for newsmen, the first such since the enemy offensive began.

3. To the south, the rains seem to have put a damper on enemy activity on and around the Bolovens Plateau as well. Very little to report there.

4. In short, with good flying weather being forecast for the remainder of this week, operations in Laos have returned to normal.

Note on 8×10½" bond, dated "Thursday morning." The attached white legal-sized envelope reads "Mr. William Blake/20A/Deliver Personally."

Bill:

Forgive me for this—especially right now, but I have to talk with you. Mr. H. asked me some questions today—about you—that I just can't answer until I talk with you.

Can you come down tonight and call me at home? Or maybe tomorrow?

Please,
Sheila

129

Article from the Bangkok *Star*, April 2, p. 1. The one-column headline reads: "North Vietnamese Defeated."

Leading the team of Lao officers who formally declared the battle for northern Laos to be won, Major General Staff said today, "We have dealt the Communists a mortal blow." The General, standing beside the Sam Thong hospital, which only a few days before had been occupied by North Vietnamese troops, added that never before had such national unity been achieved in the face of the enemy and that the end of the war might well be in sight. When asked if there might be just another wet-season lull in the offing, General Ka replied, "Not this time. This time it will be different." He noted that all those who had fled Sam Thong were now returning and that there would be more government soldiers stationed permanently in the town than ever before.

According to first-hand reports, the situation in Long Tieng, the real military headquarters of this war-torn region, is somewhat the same. Many Meo refugees were seen departing from Sam Thong to the east, presumably returning to their homes there. Even so, the United States Aid Coordinator for Laos, Edgar "Pop" Buell, refused to make a definite prediction of government success. "Let's just say we're still in business," was his only comment.

In Vientiane, a city busily cleaning up from the worst rains in more than a decade, the only outward sign of the abrupt change in mood could be seen at night when the city lights came back on brightly and residents were observed removing the black tape from their automobile headlights. xfrt—North Viet. Def—caps—city lights came back—King visits university and Angkor Wat—30—

130

Newspaper article (source unknown). Headline reads: "Peace Talks Meet."

Paris, April 1—Chief North Vietnamese representative Le Duc Tho opened today's plenary session with a restatement of the North Vietnamese-Viet Cong seven-point peace plan to end the war in Indochina. Attacking again what he called the "U.S. Imperialist Aggression" in Southeast Asia, he repeated the identical demands made in all previous sessions.

United States representatives, alert for any innuendoes which might signal a softening of the opposition's hardline stand, expressed regret after the session was concluded. "It's the usual propaganda," one delegate said. "Nothing has changed at all."

131

Letter, OUSAIRA, Vientiane, to Mr. Blake, AOC 20A, dated Thursday, 2 April.

Dear Bill:

Enclosed is a message (copy) which speaks for itself. Horowitz concurs, *strongly*. Let me know ASAP what you think. As I said earlier, something's brewing down there. I still don't know what—but you're the doctor—you decide.

Also—Colonel Fritz Henry, my replacement (class of '48—a real fast burner), is arriving next Tuesday. I'm going to hang on for a couple of weeks anyway and show him the ropes. I think you should be down here to meet him when he lands.

JB

PS: *Now* what's got Horowitz irked? He seemed quite terse when your name came up. Please be very careful how you handle him. He's a dedicated, sincere person who means very well indeed, but don't let him get down on you.

132

Teletype message (Xerox copy), Wellington to Horowitz, 1 April. Enclosure to item 131.

Ref our conversation yesterday, I want Blake and two additional experienced Ravens assigned TDY to southern Laos ASAP. The heat's off you for a while, and with the pending kickoff in my area, I'll need some additional hands. Phasouk concurs. Maybe it's my turn now. Wellington.

133

Blake, *Journal*, pp. 146–147.

Saturday, 4 April. Talked with Barnes today by phone. I will not go down south. He said I might not have any choice. What the hell does he mean? Says I'll know within a few days. Tried to get Horowitz but couldn't. Jesus Christ, anyway. I'm just getting going up here, and now "they" want me to go away. What for? I smell Horowitz behind this—just because he thinks I screwed his daughter. Hell, I'm the only guy who's been assigned here who *hasn't* screwed her. And what the fuck—Weird said he screwed the NVA Ambassador's daughter, anyway, and nothing came of that. What do they except when they send families to the "war zone"?

Barnes mentions "something big." That's a laugh. What are they going to do, invade Cambodia? Take some "decisive military action" to end the war once and for all? Or maybe they're going to send South Vietnamese across the Trail and block it for good. Hah. Anyone who's been there can tell you about the AAA in the caves. I'd hate to see what the '37s and '23s could do if they were depressed against choppers and ground troops.

What would Lunderberg say? I can hear him now: "There's only one thing that's going to end this war once and for all. Get out. Give them all the concessions they want—promise them anything—throw the SVN government out—agree to everything they ask—and then, when they've given every last one of our prisoners back—every last one of those wonderful guys who are the only real heroes of this war—when the whole list is accounted for and they're all safe—then send every airplane we've got in the world up north, nuke the shit out of them, make Hanoi a deep-water port, and turn what's left into a parking lot for all those Japanese cars." What was it Goldwater said, "I'd have turned North Vietnam into a mud puddle within two weeks." Hah!

How's that for a plan, conscience? How's that, Mr. Horowitz? Mr. President? That one's worth beating drums for, eh? (Triple roll and a double paradiddle, followed by a clash of cymbals and a mushroom cloud.) Program *that* one into your computer, Pentagon, and draft Gene Krupa and Buddy Rich to hammer out a tune which would really let the dragons loose. Enough nonsense. Meanwhile, back in the real (?) world, tomorrow is just another day, regardless of the calendar. Tomorrow Blake's Brigade begins battling bountifully, with the help, of course, of General Vang Pao and the United States Air Force. And for my own little game plan—aha, Blake, don't write ultraclassified information in your journal—Horowitz is everywhere and is no doubt watching. Now *there's* civilian control of the military for you.

134

Letter from Major Dante Hamilton to Colonel Barnes, with copy to Mr. Horowitz, on standard 8×10½" bond, dated 8 April.

SUBJECT: Events of 5 April

1. As per your request, my personal report concerning last Sunday's unfortunate incident follows. I have taken the liberty of attaching a tape recording given to me just this morning. It was routinely transcribed by Prince Control during the rescue effort. It reports much better than I could exactly what happened from the time we first made the decision to eject, recording as it does the radio transmissions of all aircraft involved.

2. I offer no excuses for my actions. I was ordered by Major Blake to accompany him in Eagle Blue Lead on a strike mission, perhaps because of my familiarity with the target area, the same cave complex near which I had been previously shot down. When I asked Major Blake why he wanted to hit this particular target, he merely said, "because it's there." He added, "Besides, nothing else remains." I do not know what he meant by that.

3. On Major Blake's instructions, we scheduled the mission, armed the aircraft with two Mk. 82s each, and took off from Alternate at 0913. Flight time to target was 45 minutes. After being airborne for 20 minutes, Eagle Blue #4 developed high oil pressure and RTB [Returned To Base]. Major Blake did not say very much on the way up, except to require standard flight and armament checks. We did not contact Brickbat. Target weather was clear, visibility was more than seven miles in very light haze.

4. This particular complex is one of the largest and most prominent in Southeast Asia. Unlike most caves, which occur on sheer karst hillsides, these exist in what appears to be a solid rock mass set off by itself. It resembles a gigantic, eroded pyramid. Some of the pilots call it "The

Ruins." It's about one kilometer to the west of Route 61, and there are well-worn truck tracks running between the caves and the road. (I might add here that this cave complex must be gigantic inside and is probably interconnected. Reports have implied that it is used not only for storage but probably houses at least a divisional headquarters. I personally have seen trucks entering and exiting, and because the trucks do not have to back out, there is obviously enough room to turn around inside. I would estimate that there are thirty or forty feet of solid rock protecting the interior, making it about as impregnable to our authorized weapons as NORAD [North American Air Defense] Headquarters in Colorado Springs is to nuclear bombs.)

5. Major Blake and I had discussed this particular target often, and he concluded that the only way to strike it effectively would be to skip delayed action bombs (we used a three-second fuse) directly through one of the cave entrances and hope that the ordnance would reach ammunition stores before detonating. I am certain you know (and there is no offense meant) how often USAF jets have struck this target, accomplishing many direct hits in the cave mouths. Unfortunately, the jets' angle of delivery with conventional weapons is such that their ordnance usually explodes prior to penetrating the cave more than a few feet. In every instance, the enemy has merely cleared away the rubble and no doubt thanked us for further excavating his access routes.

6. Major Blake briefed the mission well and selected Lt. Vongsaly, who volunteered as soon as he heard where we were going. He is always ready for a fight. He grew up in the immediate area and knows the caves intimately. "All the good Phi," he said, "went away when the North Vietnamese came." He is also the best and most daring pilot in the RLAF. We approached the target from the south, Major Blake signaled the two other aircraft into trail formation, and we began our attack from about 7500 feet indicated altitude in a much shallower dive than normal because of the delivery angle we hoped to achieve. Our pattern more resembled a napalm run than it did a dive bomb pass. We released our first bomb at an altitude of about 50 feet AGL [Above Ground Level] and pulled up sharply to

avoid the jagged rocks. Our first bomb impacted about 10 meters to the right of the main cave mouth, as did number Two's. Lt. Vongsaly placed his bomb squarely in the cave mouth, where it disappeared from sight. We could not tell if it exploded or not, because we were distracted by moderate groundfire from ZPU and small arms at this time. Our second pass was made on the same line, directly into intensified groundfire, and just before releasing our second bomb, I think I heard Major Blake say, "A caveat for the generals, babes. And for Billy Mitchell too." On this pass, both our bomb and number Two's entered the cave mouth. I think that Vongsaly's delivery angle was good, but his bomb hit a few meters short and must have skipped above the cave entrance.

7. It was right after the pulloff from our second pass, just after I heard Major Blake say, "S---, three f------ bombs in the f------ cave mouth and we don't even know if they went off, much less if they hurt anybody. Oh the b-------, the b-------," that we were hit. I remember seeing big and little white smoke puffs, indicating both 23 and 37mm AAA, and we must have taken hits simultaneously in the fuselage and wing root section, as well as in the engine bay area. Our oil pressure went to zero, the cockpit filled immediately with smoke, but the engine somehow continued to run. For some reason we had also lost our interphone, but our radio continued to function. Major Blake initiated a hard climbing turn to the south, jinking all the while, and I saw over my shoulder that Eagle Blue Two and Three had shifted their attack from the cave mouth to what were well-camouflaged gun emplacements, at least two of which appeared to have open metal doors and whose guns were firing from smaller caves near the top. I had seen the positions before, but thought they were merely shadows, not real caves. Attacking the guns was a foolhardy thing for Two and Three to do, but they should be decorated. Their action no doubt diverted the attention of the gunners long enough for us to get out of range and probably saved our lives.

8. We were just approaching Route 7, having alerted Prince and Brickbat, when Vongsaly called and said we were on fire and should get out. We had opened the canopy by hand, which had effectively cleared out the smoke, but

upon Vongsaly's statement Major Blake turned in his seat and motioned with his right thumb over his left shoulder for me to eject. I did so immediately, got a good chute, and then saw Major Blake's chute open a second or two later about two hundred yards above and to the right of me. A few seconds later our abandoned aircraft exploded. Eagle Blue Two and Three circled around us until increasing groundfire forced them to climb to a higher altitude. They had expended all their ammunition against the AAA on the caves. I hit in the trees just north of the dirt road, and because I had assumed the tree-landing position with my face buried in my arms, I did not see exactly where Major Blake came down. I do know, however, that he seemed to be heading for a large clearing (probably the one referred to in the tape) about three hundred yards south of the road.

9. The rest of the information relative to my day and night on the ground and the incredibly heroic actions of the Sandys and the Jolly Greens in picking me up are recorded on the tape and contained in my official debriefing, a copy of which you have. The attached tape, incidentally, does add quite a bit to what I heard from the ground relative to Major Blake's situation. I do not see how anyone could have lived through it. Frankly, all I knew (except for occasional radio contact with Sandy or Jolly) was that the whole war had moved into my area and that there were an awful lot of guys up there who were busting their tails to get us out.

10. I sincerely regret the outcome of this incident and am also sorry that you have decided to enforce the USAF two-combat-bailout rule in my case. I honestly feel as willing and capable as ever to perform my duties here, and respectfully ask that my request to remain here be favorably reconsidered, if not by you, at least by Colonel Henry when he arrives. If history is any indicator, I suspect that there will still be work to do in Laos for some time.

[signed] Dante Hamilton, Major, USAF

Note: unfortunately, the tape recording referred to in Major Hamilton's letter was not included with Major Blake's papers. I have been unable to obtain another copy. According to official Department of Defense records, Major William Blake is one of over a thou-

sand Americans listed as "Missing in Action." His name did not appear on any Prisoner of War lists released by Hanoi, and he is not, of course, among the returned POWs. I have talked briefly with Major Hamilton, locating him in Florida after quite a search, but he respectfully declined my request for an interview, stating that he did not feel he should discuss military actions in Southeast Asia. I have been unable to find Colonel Barnes, and my inquiries concerning a pilot named Weird have been understandably fruitless.

135

DD Form 95, memo, typewritten in pica type, addressed "To Whom It May Concern," no date. This memo was lying loose, affixed to no particular document, notebook, or folder. There was a paper clip attached.

Everyone here knew that Bill Blake was keeping some kind of a record of events. I add this material in the hopes that it will fill in some gaps.

[unsigned]

136

It was the following letter, dated 1 April, which once again involved me with Major Blake. I did not receive it until two weeks after his being shot down, due to the fact that he had addressed it to the university where we had first met. Because I had not been offered tenure there, I had left two years after Major Blake had taken his degree. I had been reading in the newspapers, of course, about Southeast Asia—reports and analyses concerning U.S. involvement, troop movements, battles, and governmental crises—but like so many Americans at the time, I was ignorant. Muong Soui, Dak To, Xieng Khouang, Quang Tri, the Plain of Jars—these names had blinked from Oriental darkness almost without meaning. Also, the politics of the Far East were not in my field, and I had then been deeply involved in my book on the French Revolution. It was this last letter, however, which kindled my interest and sparked the chain of events which resulted in my obtaining the documents.

Dear Professor Harding:

It seems somehow fitting that I write you on this day. I doubt if you'll even remember me, but I recall enjoying your classes, as well as your kindness when I took my orals [I still do not think I was on his board]. In particular, I will never forget a comment you made one day about the Renaissance—that for the first time in recorded history, the seat of true political power began to shift from the landed aristocracy, even if ever so slightly, to the people themselves. [True, I did say this, but in recent years I have modified my views somewhat. I now believe the power in politics remains where it always has been—with those who are in office at the time.]

I wish I could go into detail about where I am and what I'm doing, but for official reasons I cannot. Let it suffice to say that I'm fighting a war in the best way I know how, am flying airplanes, and that I look forward very much to my return home. I am considering studying for a Ph.D. and will be honored, if I may, to use your name as one of my references. I would like to begin school, if approved, sometime after the first of the year, when my tour here is complete.

As you might expect, I do plan to pursue the field I've been rather intimately associated with during this past year. There is so much that has to be done, but progress can be made only by people who thoroughly understand Southeast Asia from both a theoretical and practical point of view. Fortunately, my jobs over the past ten months have allowed me a wider range of experience than that afforded to the normal pilot, and I do think that I have obtained some insights denied the majority of Americans who have been sent here in an ordinary combat role. Eventually I would like to work in Washington, either in a military or a civilian capacity, or perhaps teach, although I fear my patience may not be extreme enough for that.

If you are willing to recommend me, I will have the forms sent to you from the pertinent universities. I have queried quite a few, but as yet have not heard from them about their initial assessment of my qualifications. I wouldn't be surprised if some of the universities take a rather dim view toward admitting a member of the war corps, but that's to be expected, I suppose. At least I won't be trying to burn down their administration buildings.

I wonder if I might ask another favor? Along with the self-addressed, stamped envelope, I have also included my wife's address. She's living not too far from our old alma mater, and should you be in the area, I'm certain that she would appreciate a phone call. Our communications have been a bit spotty of late, and I'd be most grateful if you would just give her a call and let her know that I'm still alive and well in Indochina.

Sincerely,
[signed] William Blake, Major, USAF

Epilogue

I did contact Mrs. Blake a week later. After informing me of her husband's loss, she invited me to visit her. I did not know what to expect, possessing as I did only one slim letter and an address in an unfamiliar town where there was, I discovered, an Air Force installation which coexisted on the city's airport. Our Boeing 727 made a perfect landing in a driving rain, and as we taxied in toward the terminal, I could faintly make out row upon row of large gray airplanes parked on the military side of the field. I do not know what kind they were. At the end of the runway I saw four fighter planes with triangular wings and tails, housed snugly in individual aluminum hangars, their black needle noses protruding into the swirling fog and rain and pointing, so it seemed for an instant, directly at me.

It was with no little trepidation that I had decided to visit Mrs. Blake, not remembering really who she was or knowing, then, anything at all about Major Blake. If I had seen the *Fragments* at that time—I wonder. I had no clear perception of what it was that I really wanted. Perhaps it was an impulse of unconscious loyalty, or the fulfilment of one of those ironic necessities that lurk in the facts of human existence. I don't know. I can't tell. But I went.

Perhaps, too, it was an academician's vain desire to conquer ignorance. A human being, a man to whom I had been of some importance, was lost. His voice had spoken to me after a silence of many years, but nowhere had he given me the slightest hint of the dangers he had experienced or the horrors he would only too shortly undergo. I did not know that then, but it was something I learned later, something I can never forget.

It was growing dark when I arrived at her house, a well-kept split-level in a typical suburb. After huddling for a moment at the door, I was ushered into the living room by a boy of about ten years, who called upstairs that "the man" was here, then disappeared into another room where I could hear a television set in operation. I did not see him again. There was one lamp burning and a fire glowed from the red brick hearth. Otherwise I cannot remember anything significant about the room.

She came forward, dressed in what she later told me was an *au dzai*, the long national dress of Vietnam. Her husband had sent it to her. It was blue silk and the slits up the side revealed her most attractive legs. She was a truly beautiful woman—I mean that her expression was one of benign, beautiful calm. "Welcome," she said, taking both my hands in hers. "Do you like this gown? I hate to wear the pants with it." She had long blonde hair, tied, as was the fashion, in back. She was not very young—I mean, not girlish—and at first she seemed to be in remarkable control. "Please sit down," she said. "I'm so very glad you came. Bill spoke of you so often when we were in school."

I had not dared imagine what to expect. Now, knowing her husband as she never did, I think I know even less. I cannot visualize them together—laughing, eating, loving, quarreling. At the time, and even more so now, I wondered what I was doing there, as if I had blundered into a situation where I, a mere observer, did not belong. "I think," she said, "that you probably knew him as well as anyone," then repeated, "I'm very glad you came."

She stood up then and looked out through the streaked picture window. "I admired him so," she said, "and I loved him very much. He thought so well of you." Throughout our conversation she used only the past tense, as if her husband, despite his official status, were indeed dead.

"I have something for you," I said. I placed the letter on the table beside the couch.

She looked at it, covering the envelope with her hand. "I don't want to read it," she said. "It's addressed to you. Did he say anything about me?"

"No," I lied. "I'm sorry." I replaced the letter in my inside jacket pocket.

"Ironic," she said. "The last thing he wrote was your name on the envelope."

"I was flattered," I said, "after all the years—"

"All the years," she interrupted sharply. "What about all *my* years—*our* years? I don't even know where he was or how he died or what he felt or even"—she buried her face in her hands—"who he really was." She shook her head sharply, her hair tossing.

"You know him best," I repeated. And perhaps she did, after all. But with every word the rain seemed to be beating harder on the roof, on the windows.

"He must really have admired you to write," she said. "I did not hear from him after Christmas. He never answered any of my letters or my lawyer's . . ." She stopped. "But that doesn't matter now." She rose, offering her hand. "Come downstairs with me. I have something for you.

We walked down five steps into a lower level, where there were three or four large old portraits hung on the walls and a baby grand piano in the corner. "Bill's family," she said. "He always thought a lot of his ancestors." We turned right, through a blue door, into a small room which was lined, I could see even before she switched on the light, with bookshelves. "Look," she said, "here's Bill Blake." Two walls were covered with books, a third held a window over a dark oak desk, and the fourth wall was almost solid with photographs and certificates in thin black frames. "There's my husband," she said, "from his highschool days to the last picture he sent the boys from Vietnam. And all his books, those damned books. *I* put them up for him here so he would have them when he got back, even though we would probably have had to move right away." She was crying now, leaning on the side of the desk, her shoulders shaking and her hair just touching the shining surface. "I did this . . . and he never even answered me when I wrote him that I'd changed my mind . . . that I had been stupid and childish and dumb."

I could say nothing. Should I have consoled her? Said that I too was sorry, that perhaps the letters she mentioned were never received—or perhaps, as I think now, never opened and thrown away? Or did she really write at all? No—I could not have said anything then. I looked closely at the photographs showing a boy playing a set of drums, a young man in a second lieutenant's uniform standing beside a smiling girl (the younger Mary), a captain sitting in the cockpit of a jet aircraft, and a major leaning against what looked like a tiny private plane. I found out later that it was his O-1 FAC aircraft. Interspersed among these and other pictures were plaques from the organizations with which he had served. I made out words such as "in appreciation," "with thanks," and other similar tributes. Piled neatly upon the desk were four or five blue plastic folders and an equal number of smaller blue boxes. "His medals," she said. "Yesterday. In the mail. For the boys. A colonel wanted to present them formally, but I said no—that I couldn't go through with it. He sounded miffed." She raised her hand in a sweeping gesture toward the wall of photographs. "Here's Bill Blake. Now do you remember him?"

"Yes," I said, with something like despair in my heart.

"What a shame," she said. "What a damned shame it all is."

"He may not be dead," I said. "There's still some hope."

"No there isn't," she said frantically. "You don't see it at all. Even if he's alive, how long will that be? Where is he? And even if he does come back—sometime—then what? What would we do—take up where we left off?" She then cried out, "And in the meantime, what about me?"

She reached under the desk and pulled out a battered overnight case, one clasp missing, on which was a faded, torn decal, a block "Y." It was his old overnight bag from college, she said, into which she had put all the papers, tapes, books, and other items which she had just received by mail from Vientiane—the fragments which make up this book. There had been no return address. If she had read or removed anything, I did not and do not know.

It was almost totally dark when I left her house and it was still raining very hard. I thought of walking down to the airport, but the small suitcase was quite heavy, so I called a taxicab instead. Despite the weather, my plane departed on time.

Since then, my coming to know the *Fragments* has caused what has subsequently been revealed about the war in Indochina to have, if not more meaning for me, at least more clarity. Not that I can ever feel truly involved, but then again, neither could Mary Blake. But while preparing this book for publication, while deciding which mode of presentation to use, I began almost to wish that there were someone to whom I could apologize. I might have ended up doing just that if I had interpreted the meaning of events for the reader, or if I had added additional views from sources which were external to the experiences of Major Blake. Such approaches, I came to believe, might make me less an editor than an actual character in the drama, so I chose my third alternative: that of keeping the *Fragments* just as they were and letting the reader provide his own context.

This method is, after all, the only objective way, even though any selection and arrangement of facts, whether in a newspaper article, a tape recording, or a private document, inevitably mirrors someone's point of view or state of mind. If in doing so I may have submerged the personalities of the participants into what some might call the laws of space, time, and causation, thus failing to show the independence of each individual's personality, I am sorry. For it is only, I am beginning to suspect, by admitting our inescapable dependence on all known elements of the external world that we are led finally to what we think we know as truth.